LOS

A NOVEL weepers

D1198804

NICOLE WILLIAMS

Cover Design by Sarah Hansen of Okay Creations
Editing by Cassie Cox
Formatting by JT Formatting

CHAPTER one

I'D BEEN ON the losing side of life for so long it had become my marching beat. I'd become so good at losing it was all I believed I was capable of. Things like winning, coming out on top, and success were concepts that had floated to the horizon, becoming so distant I'd almost lost sight of them.

When you've been told for most of your life that you're nothing, you start to believe it. When you're reminded you've got an impressive record of screwing up and told that record's only going to continue, you fulfill that expectation. When you're told you'll never amount to anything, that's exactly what you do.

When your mom bails when you're a kid and the only thing your dad coddles is a bottle of whiskey, you question things like love and loyalty. You realize that the same blood that ran in their veins runs in yours and every piece of your make-up came from them. Not a scrap of your DNA isn't tied to theirs, and questions like "Will I become just like him one day?" or "Will I ditch my family one day too?" or "Will I wind up a pile of ashes inside the charred shell of a trailer after drinking myself into such a stupor that the fire ripping through all that was left of my life wouldn't even rouse me?" play on repeat through your head.

Those are the questions that have haunted me my entire life. The answers have haunted me even more.

What took me decades to realize was that instead of trying to convince myself that I could never be just like them, I could all too easily become like them. That was the big eye-opener. Getting there was just one more choice made because it was the easy one instead of the right one. Once more turning to the bottle instead of confronting the real problem. Once more pushing away the few people who cared about me instead of reciprocating the sentiment.

Freedom came the day I accepted that being a better person was a daily battle, fought one moment at a time, choice by painstaking choice. Forgiveness came when I realized both of them had probably started out like me, wanting to do right, but they had lost the battle, one easy choice after another. I was more in danger of becoming like them than I wasn't, and that knowledge kept me sharp. That daily reminder molded and shaped me into the man I was today.

Don't get me wrong. I wasn't some perfect chump who smiled too goddamned much and wore his heart on his sleeve like Walker, but I was a different man from the one I'd been before. At least in the places that counted. I still cussed like I was competing for some kind of award and I still preferred my fists over more diplomatic measures and I might have taken being hotheaded to new heights, but I'd changed where it counted. That was what mattered. At least, that was what I'd been told by the person who counted most.

Joze—or Josie when we were tangled between the sheets or in the heat of an argument. The woman who'd brought me to my knees or cut me off at the knees or taken a sledge hammer and shattered my knees. Something having to do with knees malfunctioning.

She'd been my salvation in my darkest hour, when I was nearly past saving. I'd loved her in secret for so long I'd given up hope of that love being returned. Of course that was the moment it came . . . and when it did . . . shit, there was nothing like it in the whole entire world. I had nothing to compare to the way she loved me, and that's what made it so special. No one but her had ever come close to loving me like that. No one had ever believed in me the way she did. Her love was so big and overwhelming that each day with her erased another day of pain and failure from my past. Her love was magic, healing me as it lifted me up, and though she tried convincing me otherwise, I knew I could spend ten lifetimes trying and failing to give her what she'd given me in a year's time.

If tonight went as planned though, I might tip the scale in my favor this once. For something that only weighed a few grams, it shouldn't have felt like a damn bull had crawled into my back pocket and was jabbing its horns into my ass.

The guy at the jewelry store had assured me I'd made a solid pick—that if I'd been proposing to a starlet, even she would have been wowed—but I still wasn't sure. Josie wasn't some vain, shallow starlet who gave a shit about size or status or labels—that wasn't why I'd purchased the rock I had. I'd picked it out because I'd tried words and actions, but nothing had seemed to explain how I felt about her. I wasn't stupid enough to believe a fancy ring would either, but it was something, and if any woman deserved to have some giant-ass diamond on her finger, it was Joze.

I wanted every last guy who looked at her in a way that would make me want to shove my boot up his ass to take a good look at her ring and realize I wasn't just any other husband but one who wanted the best for his wife and wouldn't stop at anything to give it to her. I wanted Joze to be reminded of that every time she looked at it. I wanted the world to know that I'd spent a large fraction of a year's worth of winnings, of getting bucked, bruised, and beaten, to get her the ring currently burning a hole in my back pocket.

I wanted the world to know that a man loved Josie more than any human had ever loved another in the history of the world. That was all. Not much, right?

If I spent the rest of my life trying to prove to Joze how much I loved her, and if she finally came to some understanding of it the exact moment before I died, then I'd won. Score.

Yeah, I might have given Jess a hard time for going and getting all whipped before I'd fallen victim to the same fate, but I rode bulls. I could dress in drag every Saturday night and sing Cher on a stage and still be more of a man than any other whipped sap out there.

Josie was my salvation—she always had been—and bull riding was my penitence. It kept me sharp. Focused. Connected to that wild part of me that could never be tamed, or should never be tamed, because like it or not, I needed to look danger and death in the face from time to time or risk losing myself.

I didn't need to have asked them to know my parents had lost themselves years ago. The trouble with losing yourself was that you never knew where you might try to find yourself after. For Clay, it was at the bottom of a bottle. For my mom, I guess it was on the open road and traveling light. For me . . . I didn't want to imagine. So I kept bull riding close and the people I cared about closer.

Thankfully, Joze was an understanding woman who wasn't concerned with "taming" me or turning me into a carbon copy of every other man no longer in possession of his balls. So life was good. No, that wasn't right . . . life was fucking amazing.

"Hey, Black! Your fan club's waiting, bras on display and Sharpies in hand."

I shoved back from the rail lining the arena and lifted a brow. "Why don't you go instead? You've got my permission to 'be' me and sign bras until your eyes go crossed. Besides, you've got plenty of experience posing as me, don't you?"

Justin adjusted his belt buckle—since it might have been a whole two millimeters off center—glancing over his shoulder down the hallway where I guessed the Sharpie-wielding bra-flashers were waiting. "I don't know what all the fuss is about you, Black. I'm taller, better looking, and a way better dresser. You'd think the girls in every city would be lining up for me instead of you."

I patted my back pocket again—still there. "You might be taller thanks to those high heels you like to call boots and you might be better looking to a female orangutan and you might be a better dresser to someone who believes rhinestones and purple belong on a man, but the reason I have the fan clubs in every town is because I'm the best damn bull rider on this circuit." I hitched my thumbs under my belt, framing my belt buckle, which had "champion" stamped onto it. "I'm better where it counts, and I win. If you want to earn the right to sign girls' bras, why

5

don't you try staying on the bull's back longer instead of focusing on what you're going to wear?"

Justin shook his head, giving me a look. "I hate you."

Half of a smile worked its way onto my mouth. Justin was a show pony and probably would have preferred a career modeling men's underwear, but he was a solid guy. He was a decent enough rider, and he did it because his dad had died a few years back. He was just trying his best to take care of his mom and younger sisters. As human beings went, he was one of the good ones . . . but that didn't mean I wouldn't give him a hard time for dressing like a tool.

"You might hate me, but you're still going to go impersonate me for a few vicarious moments, aren't you?" I called after him.

He was already heading down the tunnel toward the girls. "Damn straight I am. One of us has to reap the benefits of your fame." He adjusted his hat as he continued down the hall, those boots of his making a sharp, look-at-me sound.

"Happy reaping!" I shouted.

He replied with not one but two raised middle fingers.

It was getting close to being my turn to ride, but I liked to wait until the last possible moment to make my way to the chute and the bull. I liked taking my time and running the dirt through my fingers before I got sucked into the adrenaline vortex that resided within a fifty-foot radius of the chutes.

Crouching, I cupped a handful of dirt from the arena and felt the weight of it. This past year, I'd spent more time riding indoors than outdoors, which meant I'd "arrived" in the bull riding world. It seemed kind of backward to me that when a rider made it big, he started spending more of his time indoors than out, but that was the way it worked. The soil in the indoor arenas had taken some getting used to. Don't get me wrong, it was still dirt, but it had a different feel. It was heavier, grittier almost. Like every grain of dirt was vying to get its own attention. It was darker too.

After spending long summers riding outdoors, where the dirt got dry and hard in August, and spending plenty of time in the red soil of eastern Montana, the dark, thick indoor soil had been as foreign as the bright lights and giant crowds. After a few months, I'd gotten used to it. The bright lights and giant crowds at least. The soil still felt wrong, but I couldn't let rituals die just because the dirt felt strange.

I was sifting the last of it through my fingers when I heard someone come up behind me. I knew who it was without looking. Before I knew it, I was smiling . . . and I wasn't supposed to be the goddamned smiling idiot.

"There's a rumor going around that Garth Black is signing women's bras at the end of the rider's hallway."

The last of the soil slipped through my fingers. "You know what a rumor is, right?"

"A half truth."

I lifted myself up, fighting every instinct to whirl around and wrestle her into my arms. The other thing I hadn't known about "realizing" my dreams in the arena was that it meant spending plenty of nights in roadside hotels and waking up to a cold bed. Being away from Joze so much was the worst part of it, but a bull rider's career only lasted a few years. My plan was to win as many competitions and cash as many checks as I could before I was

7

either forced or broken enough to retire. Then I'd spend the rest of my life crawling into bed beside the woman I loved. If I made the same kind of money for the next couple years that I had this past year, we'd be all set to remodel the old farmhouse we'd purchased last summer and purchase the thousand acres around the house to raise cattle on. That was our goal. The guy who'd wanted nothing better than riding bulls and winning buckles wanted to retire as a cattle rancher. Go figure.

"Are you asking me or accusing me?" I tilted my head back just enough to see her silhouette behind me.

Josie's hand flew to her hip, making my smile stretch. She was about as jealous a girlfriend as she was a prim and proper one, but she was up to something.

"Neither," she answered, moving closer. "I came to get my own Garth Black autograph . . . right here."

The coy act was over. Whipping around, I found Josie unbuttoning the top couple buttons of her shirt and pulling it down to reveal the top of her bra.

"Joze," I warned, looking around and ready to prod any wandering, gaping, or otherwise inappropriate-looking eyes.

"Come on. I want an autograph." She fingered the top ridge of her bra, playing with it. My throat went dry. "With the way he's been riding this past year, an official Garth Black autographed bra should fetch me at least a few hundred bucks on eBay."

I feigned a look of insult. "A few hundred? Try a few thousand."

She smiled, continuing to play with the cup of her bra. "That's nice . . . but sign my bra already. Before I'm forced to get physical with you." She wet her lips, slowly and deliberately, as she moved closer.

Shit. I was supposed to be focusing on my ride and doing the whole visualization thing, but the only thing I was visualizing was Josie's bra and the rest of her clothing winding up in a pile at her feet.

"Now why would I give you your autograph with that threat on the table?" My boots couldn't stay where they were any longer. I found myself moving toward her without making a conscious decision.

When my arms were about to ring around her waist, she pulled a pen from her pocket and lifted it in front of my face. "My autograph," she said in a firm voice, tapping the lace of her bra with her finger. "Now."

I took the pen and pulled the cap off with my teeth. "I can't say no to my biggest fan, now can I?"

Josie's eyes held mine as she raised an eyebrow. "Saying no isn't exactly your strong suit when it comes to me."

A crooked smile slid into place as I dropped the tip of the pen to her chest. "No, it isn't."

Signing a girl's bra was harder than a guy might like to believe. The unevenness of the lace matched with the knowledge of what that material is covering or, depending on the style, just *barely* covering, made focusing on signing one's name legibly and correctly next to impossible.

"Oops," I said as I finished signing my last name on her skin. It may or may not have been done intentionally.

Josie gave me a look, knowing every bit how intentional it had been. "So? How did it compare?"

I capped the pen and handed it back to her, admiring my autograph . . . or admiring the spot where it was. My handwriting was sloppy as hell and looked more like a middle schooler's graffiti than a grown man's signature. "How did what compare?"

"Signing your girlfriend's bra next to signing the rest of those"—Josie cleared her throat to substitute the word, or string of words, she'd been considering—"bras?"

My brows were nearly hidden beneath the brim of my hat, so she couldn't see them pull together. "There is no comparison."

She smiled at where I'd signed my name, tracing the letters of my last name with her finger. I realized just how perfect this moment was for pulling out the ring in my back pocket. I had planned on waiting until after the competition, when I'd had a shower and was in fresh clothes, and doing it over a fancy dinner with a fancy bottle of champagne, but this was the moment. I knew it. She was with me for the first time in three weeks, and she was smiling at my last name scribbled on her body—the same last name I was hoping with everything I had left to hope with that she'd want to make her own one day.

I might have had a plan for how I'd wanted to propose, but life was meant to be spontaneous. The same went for engagements.

"Have you been working on that 'there is no comparison' answer for a while, Black?" She finished tracing the K before lifting her eyes to mine. "Because it was a good one. I guess since I've hardly seen you for a solid twenty-four hours this past month, you've had plenty of time to work on it."

I patted my back pocket for the hundredth time. It was still there. I didn't know where I'd thought it would go—it wasn't like an inanimate object could just hop out of my pocket and bounce out of the arena. "Joze, when I said there was no comparison, I meant that in both the literal and figurative way."

She lifted an impressed brow. She liked it when I talked as though I used my brain for more than just a cushion when I landed headfirst after being thrown from the back of a two-thousand-pound animal.

"Your bra-slash-chest"—my eyes lowered to my name and everything around it—"correction, your *perfect* chest, is the first one I've ever autographed, so there is, literally, no comparison." When her forehead started to crease, I continued. "But even if I had signed all of those bras you've heard from the rumors I have—even if I'd signed millions—there would be, figuratively, no comparison whatsoever. None."

She was fighting to keep that stern expression, but it was close to slipping. Joze was a champ at giving me a hard time and making me walk a fine line, but she could never stay upset at me, for real or pretend, when I was layering on the good lines.

"Let's get a bit more figurative with this whole thing then." Her gaze dropped to her chest, her finger hooking under the clasp at the center of her bra.

My gaze followed hers.

"Let's fast forward thirty years or copious amounts of tanning without sunscreen and bouncing up and down stairs without a bra . . . can you still say there'd be no comparison?" I was opening my mouth to reply when she added, "And look me in the eye while you answer?"

I tipped my hat back just enough so she could get a good look at my eyes. Since we were kids, Josie had been able to call out my lies just by taking one good look into my eyes—that was why I'd avoided letting them drift her way for a good portion of our lives—but I didn't divert them anymore. Not even when she was asking a hard question, and with a history like mine, there was no shortage of difficult questions to ask and answer.

I had to work to keep my face straight before I let myself say one word. "That's what lots of money and a skilled surgeon are for, so yeah, I can answer that even thirty years from now, with all of that sun . . . bouncing . . . *stuff*, there will still be no comparison." I worked my tongue into my cheek when she crossed her arms. "Post operative, of course."

Her arms crossed tighter. "You drew VooDoo, right? I'm going to go have a little chat with him and request that he drive one or both of his horns into your ass after you give the eight-second ride of your life."

Josie started toward where the bulls were being sorted into the chutes before I grabbed her hand. I couldn't let her go one more step without asking my question. I couldn't let myself go one more step without knowing her answer.

Sure, we'd purchased the old farmhouse together and talked as though we would live and die together, but the actual topic of marriage hadn't been discussed. I guessed she wasn't against the concept, but my palms were still breaking out in a sweat, and my heart was thudding so powerfully I could practically feel it vibrating against my chest armor.

"Joze, wait." I tugged on her hand to bring her back. "I've got to ask you something before you go ask VooDoo to pierce my backside." I peaked a brow at her as I slipped my hand into my back pocket.

The ring was curled around my pinkie finger and my right knee just starting to bend when I heard my name boom through the loudspeaker. It took me a moment to process why my name was being announced because somewhere in the midst of signing Joze's bra and preparing to ask her to spend the rest of her life with me, I'd forgotten all about the reason I was there.

To ride. To ride *well*. The ride that would qualify me for nationals if I stayed on long enough and scored high enough.

"Garth." Josie's hand wrapped around my arm and gave it a little shake. "Garth," she said a bit more firmly as everything finished registering.

I muttered a curse before my gaze flickered to the chute I was supposed to be climbing into right that very moment. VooDoo was there and ready. I had maybe thirty seconds before I got myself DQ'ed.

"Whatever it is you need to ask me, it can wait until after." She spun behind me and pushed my back in the right direction. "I'll be right here waiting when you're done. You can ask me then."

I didn't need much of a push before I started sprinting. Glancing back, I winked at her.

"Hey, Black?" she called. She waited for me to look back again. "See you in eight seconds."

I grinned at her. "See you in eight seconds, Joze." I watched her for another moment. Then I hauled ass to where I should have been two minutes ago—if I hadn't gotten all distracted by my girlfriend's bra and the ring that would hopefully upgrade her girlfriend status to fiancée.

"Nice of you to show up, Black!" one of the support guys hollered as I flew up to my chute. "Looks like someone's getting a little too big for his paycheck if he thinks he doesn't have to show up until after his name has been blared around the arena."

I wiped my hands off on my jeans and smirked at him as I crawled up the rail to get into position. VooDoo's nostrils were flaring, and he was already stomping his giant hooves. "Sorry I'm late. I was trying to propose to my girl."

"Did she say yes?" he asked as I straddled the chute, preparing to lower down onto VooDoo.

"I was about five seconds too late to ask." Slowly, I lowered myself onto the giant bull's back.

When my weight settled over him, I felt him tremble. We both had our fair share of adrenaline firing into our systems. This would be one hell of a ride. From the bull's energy alone, I knew earning the points wouldn't be a problem—VooDoo was going to try to snap my back in every place it could crack out there—so the ride just depended on me being able to hang on for eight seconds.

I was going to nationals, the big show, if I could keep my ass on that bull's back for eight tiny seconds. So much rode on those seconds that I'd have been lying if I'd said the pressure wasn't getting to me.

"Do you think she'll say yes when you have a few seconds after your ride to ask her?" Thomas inspected my grip on the leather strap, making sure it wasn't too tight or too loose, just like I was double-checking.

"Pretty sure, but I'll feel a hell of a lot better when I know for sure." I adjusted one thing on my grip, rolled my fingers a few times over the braid, and then shifted my position on the bull in anticipation of VooDoo spinning to the left out of the gate.

"Why don't you get out there, give the ride of your

life, and qualify for nationals? I can guarantee you your confidence of being pretty sure she'll say yes will increase to positively certain." Thomas's investigation ended with a nod before he crawled down the side of the chute. "Go raise hell, Black."

"Planning on it," I said to myself.

Now it was just me and the bull. Everyone else had cleared out and was waiting for the nod. As soon as I gave it, eight seconds was all that separated me from shuffling around the regional scene and making a name for myself at the national level. Eight seconds. Twenty years of life felt as if they had led up to that very moment, the instant where I'd prove myself to the country before I asked the woman I loved to marry me. This night felt heavy with fate, and maybe that's why I felt a bit distracted.

Normally when I climbed onto the back of a bull, my mind went empty and instinct took over. Not tonight though. Tonight, so many things were winding through my thoughts that they were forming a giant knot. When I tried clearing my head for the third time and was unsuccessful, I gave the nod. The longer I waited, the worse it would get.

The moment the gate flew open, VooDoo exploded out of the chute. For the shortest moment, I heard the roar of the crowd. I imagined being able to distinguish the hoots and hollers of Josie and my other friends who were in the stands, but then I muted them all out. My hearing, along with my vision and attention, tunneled in on Voo-Doo's every move and my every counter-move a millisecond after.

The sound of his hooves pounding the ground echoed in my ears. The sound of my breathing became my world. No other sounds registered. Just VooDoo and me. For

15

those eight seconds, that bull was my world, and I was his.

He went left out of the gate like I'd been prepared for, and after that, he went from spinning in one direction to spinning the other. In between, he liked throwing up his back legs in an effort to get me to topple over his horns. When that didn't work, he got back to spinning. I met everything VooDoo threw at me. Every shift of my body followed the bull's lead as if it were a carefully orchestrated dance.

Eight seconds wasn't a long stretch of time. Ask anyone, and they'd tell you the same thing, but eight seconds on top of two thousand pounds of muscle and rage that was doing everything it could to fling you off while you did everything you could to stay in place felt infinitely longer. Those eight seconds moved like molasses through the hourglass, seeming like they'd never pass.

Right when I felt like the buzzer would never sound, I heard it. I'd done it. I'd stayed on one of the toughest, most notorious bulls in the circuit. From the few times I'd been close to flying off, I knew the bull had given me a good ride. I knew I'd qualified. I was on my way to nationals. I'd earned some serious cash tonight, and if luck was on my side, I'd place high enough in nationals to earn some serious *serious* cash there too.

Against every odd and foretelling, my dreams were becoming reality. Twenty years of shit luck was shifting. The ring in my back pocket and the girl at the other end of the fence caught my attention and held it when my attention should have stayed on the monster still bucking beneath me.

My gaze was locked on Josie, a smile slipping onto my face, when I felt it. My balance on the bull shifted from solid to slight. Half a second might have passed between that moment of recognition and when my body fired off the back of that bull, flying like an arrow before arching to the ground. Head first. I had one second to lift my arms in an effort to protect my head and neck from the impact, but when I hit, all I felt was the overwhelming impact before a cracking sound echoed in my ears.

After that, there was nothing."

CHAPTER two

I WASN'T GOING to open my eyes. No way. If I didn't open them, then I could keep on pretending that the bright light I didn't want to open my eyes to see wasn't the light people talked about when shit hit the fan. If I didn't open my eyes, I didn't have to wonder why I couldn't feel my body. Bright lights and senseless bodies . . . oh dear God, what was happening?

My last memory played on repeat. Hearing the buzzer go off while still on VooDoo's back. Exhilaration siphoning into my veins. Finding Josie in the crowd and sharing a fleeting look right before I went shooting into the air . . . right before I went crashing headfirst into the same soil I'd run through my fingers minutes before. I felt my face pull together as I remembered the impact. It drew in even tighter when I recalled the snap. I wondered if the reason I couldn't feel my body was because . . .

"Fuck," I muttered, my voice barely registering and sounding all ragged and wrong. I heard something else—footsteps getting closer.

"See? I told you he'd be okay, Josie. He's his usual charming self."

If Rowen Sterling-Walker was there, then I sure wasn't in heaven or anywhere close to it. I forced my eyes open, but they instantly snapped closed again, thanks to that god-awful bright light. It wasn't *that* kind of light but instead harsh fluorescent light flooding from ceiling panels. Other than school and jail, only one other place I was familiar with used that kind of institutional-type light.

I was in the hospital.

"What the hell's going on?" I asked.

"Happy to see you too, peaches. Nice to see this new leaf you've turned over that Josie has been gushing about for the past year." It was still Rowen talking, although I knew Josie was close by.

I could feel her presence . . . along with hear her sniffles . . . which meant she was or had been crying . . . which meant . . . "Fuck." My throat felt so dry a tunnel made of sandpaper would have been a welcome replacement. "What happened?"

My eyes were still squeezed closed from the overwhelming light, but I wanted to open my eyes. I needed to see where I was, who was around me, and gauge what was happening based on their expressions. I needed to know what I was dealing with before I could figure out how to solve it.

"There. Is that better?" Jesse's voice filled the room as the lights dimmed enough for me to chance opening my eyes again.

After several blinks, I could keep them open, and a few more blinks after that, I could make out the objects and people around me. The first thing I noticed was the television hanging in a corner just below the ceiling. It was turned off. Below that was an industrial-looking chair stacked high with a couple of duffel bags. Beside the chair was a long window. From the traces of light coming in from outside, it was either dawn or dusk; I couldn't tell. On the shelf below the window were a couple dozen flower arrangements complete with those tiny cards jutting out of them. Seeing so many of those earned another muttered cuss from me. I knew I didn't have that many "real" friends who'd take the time and money to send me flowers unless something was really bad.

"Well, your ability to be vulgar sure isn't broken."

My gaze skidded to the other corner, where the window was, to find Rowen draped across a chair, looking tired and worse for wear. From the look plastered on her face, she was trying to make this seem like any old day, but I could see in her eyes that she was worried. Or sad. Or some combination of the two.

"Where's Joze?" I asked before swallowing. My throat was killing me.

Rowen's forehead creased, and her gaze drifted off to the side of me. "Right beside you."

Taking ten times the amount of effort it should have, I managed to rotate my head to the other side of my pillow. Josie was there, and where Rowen was trying to hide her worry, Josie had taken it the other direction. Her eyes were bloodshot, the rims red and puffy. Either fresh or stale tears still streaked her cheeks, and one corner of her mouth had been chewed close to raw. Her hair was a mess—half of it still in her braid, half of it fallen out—and her clothes looked so wrinkled she could have been living in them for weeks.

She was the most beautiful, welcome sight I'd ever seen.

"What happened?" I asked her as Jesse came into view at the foot of the bed. His expression fell right in between the two girls', although when I took a closer look at his red-rimmed eyes and noticed his inability to look me in the eye, I realized he was more in line with Josie.

Josie sniffed and tried straightening her shoulders before answering. They fell a few moments later. "You were thrown from the bull." She looked to Jesse and Rowen as if she were looking for guidance.

Jesse turned to face the wall, his arms winding around his head. Rowen slid out of her chair and approached her husband. She wound an arm around his back and whispered something to him that I couldn't make out.

After a few more moments of watching them, Josie cleared her throat. "Do you remember where you were last night? What you were doing? Do you remember anything?" Her voice grew smaller with each question. "The doctors said you might not . . ."

I was getting more and more impatient, waiting for the explanation as to why I was racked out in a hospital bed with the three people I cared about most looking as though they were attending my funeral instead of waiting for me to recover. Whatever had happened, the people in the room seemed to view it as being on par with being at my funeral. "Joze, I remember the night of the competition. I remember everything right up to being catapulted by that piece-of-shit bull whose hide I'm going to turn into a piece of wall art as soon as I'm out of here." Even my attempts at humor were doing nothing to lighten Josie's mood. "I just don't remember a single thing after that. Can you catch me up? Before I arrive at the worst possible conclusion for why the woman I love and two of my best friends are looking at me like my life is over?"

I'd barely finished my sentence before Josie started

crying. Again. Actually, it was more like sobbing. Violent, shaking, loud sobs that sounded as though they were choking her. Rowen moved from Jesse to Josie, threw her arms around her, and rubbed circles into her back, making soft shushing noises. Rowen wasn't the hugging type. That she was running point on the hug situation meant the more sensitive two of the bunch were in bad shape.

"Hey, it's okay, Joze. It's okay." I wanted to crawl out of bed and comfort her the way Rowen was, but my body didn't seem capable of much, let alone climbing out of bed and holding myself up. "Take my hand, baby. It'll be okay. Hold my hand."

Josie's sobs dimmed enough to where her whole back wasn't quaking anymore, but when she looked at me with that anxious expression, I almost wished for her sobbing face back. This—the wide eyes that didn't seem to blink—was far worse. At the same time, Rowen's and her eyes dropped to a spot on my bed. Josie swallowed, moving away from Rowen and closer to the bed.

"I *am* holding your hand," she whispered, staring at the same spot with tears filling her eyes again. "I am holding it."

My eyes dropped to the place she was focused on. Sure enough, Josie's hand was wrapped around mine, her fingers braided between each of mine. I noticed her hand tighten. It wasn't the way my fingers seemed to look limp woven through hers that unsettled me so badly that I broke out in a sweat—it was that I couldn't feel her squeeze. In fact, I couldn't even feel her hand. I couldn't feel the warmth of it or the softness of her palm, and I couldn't feel the cool metal of the sterling silver ring she wore on her right thumb. I couldn't . . . feel.

"What the fuck's wrong with me?" I managed to get out, not sure I wanted to know.

Josie's answer was another round of sobs. Jesse's response was turning back to the wall, sliding his hat off his head, and dropping it into the chair. It was Rowen—*of course* it was Rowen—who stepped up, looked me straight in the eye, and inhaled. Had I been anyone else, I probably would have raised my hand and cut her off. Shit, that was *if* I actually could have lifted my hand, which I couldn't. I couldn't even feel my girlfriend's hand in it.

If I wasn't made of piss and grit, I would have told Rowen not to say anything. I would have begged her not to say what I knew she was going to. I would have preferred to stay ignorant rather than be told what I knew no one in the room could work up the guts to tell me.

Wrapping one arm around Josie and pulling her close, Rowen didn't blink as she held my stare. "When you got thrown from the bull, you landed on your head. Hard." When Josie's sobs picked up, Rowen patted her back, almost as if she were comforting a child. "So hard you went unconscious. The paramedics brought you here, to Casper Mercy, and you've been unconscious for over twenty-four hours." Rowen worked up a half-smile. "Long enough we were about to tell them to pull the plug."

I lifted my brows, not amused. "Gee, thanks. Glad you guys were willing to stick with me through the long haul. Nice to know I've got friends who have my back instead of wanting to break it when I'm down."

Josie's whole face froze, and then it creased into deep lines before the waterworks flooded on all over again.

"Nice analogy," Rowen muttered at me, patting Josie's back more furiously to match her sobs. "Asshole," she tacked on when Josie started shaking.

"Hey, I'm the one on my back in a hospital bed trying to figure out what happened, and I'm the asshole?" I went to throw my hands in the air, but they stayed plastered to the bed. That was when everything came together. Like, all the way came together. "My back." I concentrated on Rowen because I couldn't keep looking at Josie in her current state and feeling totally helpless. "It's broken, isn't it?"

Rowen took one long breath before she replied. "They're not sure." She diverted her eyes long enough to make panic settle into my stomach.

If even the iron fortress Rowen Sterling-Walker couldn't look me in the eye, it had to be bad. I'd witnessed her barely blink when I had to put a calf out of its misery last spring when she and Jesse had been in town visiting. A baby fucking calf had been crying in pain one moment and dead the next, and the girl hadn't even flinched. That she was flinching and avoiding eye contact with me now was one of the least welcome signs I'd ever seen.

"They wanted to do X-rays when you arrived, but the doctor was afraid to move you too much. He said that he'd try if you woke up." Rowen caught herself and gave a single shake of her head. "*When* you woke up."

"Rowen . . ." I swallowed, my throat no longer feeling dry. It felt as if it had been stuffed with wet cement and I couldn't choke it down. "Give it to me straight. Please."

Jesse was still facing the wall, but now his forehead was leaning into it. Josie had stopped sobbing, and she looked as though she was frozen in some shell of shock. Rowen and I were the only ones in the room still in possession of our wits, although they were both fraying. I wasn't sure if hers or mine would run out first.

"Am I paralyzed?"

God bless that girl for not blinking or looking away or sucking in a heavy breath. God bless Josie for giving a final sniffle, rolling her shoulders back, and crouching beside the bed so her face was level with mine. I had to check because I couldn't feel it, but her hand was still securely fastened in mine. God bless Jess for shoving off that favorite wall of his, turning to face me, bracing his hands around the foot rail of my bed, and looking at me so straight on. I knew the big city hadn't worked its way too far into him yet.

"They don't know, baby," Josie whispered, her voice as hoarse as mine. "The doctor said there was no way of knowing for sure until they did the X-rays."

I nodded and tried working up a smile for her. I knew she needed one. I could tell she was desperate to be comforted and told everything would be okay. That smile took more effort than it should have. "Did the doctor say anything about what it would mean if I woke up feeling . . ." I moved my head—it felt stiff and tender, but I could move it. When I tried moving my arm, my leg, or even my toes, I came up empty. "If I woke up feeling nothing from my neck down?" I filled my lungs, searching for a scrap of courage I could hang on to while I talked with my girlfriend about the possibility of being paralyzed from the neck down. "What it might mean if I woke up not being able to move anything at all?"

Josie glanced back at Rowen, her forehead creasing as if she wasn't sure how to answer.

Rowen dropped her hand onto Josie's shoulder and

stepped closer. "The doctor said we wouldn't know any-thing for sure until he got the X-rays. That's the only way of knowing for sure if you broke . . . something."

"If I broke my back, you mean?"

After a moment, Rowen nodded. "That's a possibility, but he also said you could have just suffered some trauma to your spine that might take some time and therapy to heal—"

"Cut the sugarcoating, Sterling-Walker. Give it to me straight. The way you always do. I can take it." When my eyes closed, I forced them to reopen. I wouldn't skulk away from this. I would grab it by the horns and wrestle it to the ground until I'd forced it into submission. "What *else* did the doctor say that you're too chicken to tell me?"

That comment got the reaction I was hoping for. The skin between Rowen's brows pinched together as she glowered at me for a whole two seconds . . . then that glower morphed into something that too closely resembled pity. That hole in my stomach expanded.

"The doctor said that if you woke up not being able to move anything . . . or feel anything . . . that it might very well mean you'd severed your spine." Rowen's chest was rising and falling harder than normal, and Josie's head dropped to the bed. Actually, it dropped so that her fore-head was resting on our combined hands, but the only way I knew that was by sight, not by feel. "But he also said if your spinal cord had suffered a big enough trauma, it might take days or even weeks for the swelling to go down enough for you to move again. Just because you can't move anything now doesn't mean you never will again."

I didn't realize how short my breaths had become un-til I started to feel light-headed. I forced myself to breathe more slowly, but it only worked fractionally. Being a bull rider as long as I had, I knew more than any one person should about spinal injuries and what they meant. I'd seen more than my fair share of riders leave an arena on a stretcher only to spend the rest of their lives in an electric wheelchair. In our world, spinal injuries, along with just about any other injury, weren't only a hazard of the job but a likelihood. However, up until I'd woken up five minutes ago, I'd been under the impression that it would never happen to me. I'd believed I was too damn tough and mean to get injured like this, but I guessed the truth had been more along the lines of me just being foolish and letting my ego overinflate my confidence.

"Percentages," I snapped, grinding my teeth. "I know he gave them to you, so let's have them. What was the likelihood he gave you—the percentage—that I'd walk again if I woke up having no feeling from my neck down?"

"Ten percent," Josie said in the littlest voice I'd ever heard her use. She lifted her head and looked me in the eye. "He said you'd have a ten percent chance of walking if you woke up"—her gaze skimmed my body, her eyelids dropping—"the way you did."

My breathing got away from me again. "He said this even without the X-rays?"

Josie nodded, one lone tear cutting down her cheek. "He said we wouldn't know for sure if you'd broken your back until you woke up and got an X-ray, but given the way you hit the ground and how hard . . . he said that it was likely."

"But they won't know anything until—"

"Thanks, Jess, but I think I've heard enough." I tried

to lift my hand again, but it stayed frozen at my side. "If you guys don't mind, I'm tired. Would you mind giving me a little space? I'm going to need my energy to face whatever it is I have to confront, I'm guessing. You know, it takes a ton of energy and stamina to curl into a wheelchair twenty-four-seven. I better save up my reserves now since I'll be spending the rest of my life as a cripple." I heard that edge working back into my voice. I felt that instinct to push people away and hurt them before they could hurt me clawing to the surface. I knew those were vices I shouldn't let back into my life, but I couldn't seem to hold them back. The reality I'd just been confronted with was proving too much for me to handle as the new, less surly and jaded Garth Black. The only way to face this was as the darker version of myself that I'd been sure I'd left behind forever.

Rowen crossed her arms and leaned over me so I had no choice but to look at her. "Just because you might have severed your spine doesn't give you a right to treat all of us like shit, Black."

"Thanks for your understanding. Now would you get out and leave me to my bright future?"

Her eyes narrowed as she leaned closer. "You want to push someone away? Fine, push me. You want to be a son of a bitch all over again to someone? Here I am." She tapped her chest, her eyes boring holes into me. "You want to take out your frustration and anger and blame on someone? Give it to me. But don't you dare, for one moment, for one fraction of a moment, push her away." I didn't need to see the direction Rowen's finger pointed. "Because if you try, so help me God, I will finish the job of breaking your back if it isn't done already."

I huffed, turning my head away from Rowen. Turning my head away from Josie. Turning my head away from the life I'd had because it would never be the same again. "And here I thought marriage was supposed to tame a woman, not make her even more belligerent."

Josie was crying again, but instead of loud, racking sobs, she was crying quietly to herself. That was by far much worse.

"Black, that's my wife you're talking to. Watch it." Jesse's grip tightened around the foot of my bed as he lifted a brow at me, challenging me.

"What, Jess? Are you going to kick my ass if I keep at it? You might actually be able to beat me now that I'm paralyzed. Let me have it. What are you waiting for?"

Jesse's forehead creased as if I'd just stabbed a knife into his gut and given it a twist. Looking around the room, I saw that I'd successfully hurt or pissed off everyone I cared about most in the whole world. I felt on the inside what I felt outside—like shit.

"You want to see belligerent, you just keep it up, bub." Rowen peaked a brow in challenge before grabbing Josie's shoulders. "I think you're right about something though. You do need some privacy to get your shit worked out again."

Rowen had to help Josie up, but she wouldn't let go of my hand. Even though one part of me wanted Josie to let go, another part hoped she never would.

"It's okay, Joze. Go get some food." I swallowed, not sure how I was supposed to look at her as though I could be her husband and provide for her when I couldn't even take a piss without assistance. "And some rest too. You know where to find me. I'm not exactly going anywhere."

Jesse moved up beside Rowen, took her hand, and led her out of the room. Him reaching for her and leading her out of a room was natural, effortless. It was something I'd taken for granted with Joze and something I'd never do again if the percentages didn't lie. Rowen threw me one last look of warning before she disappeared into the hall. I pretended not to see it, but I didn't need her looks or threats to know that Rowen Sterling-Walker wouldn't hesitate to kick my ass if I hurt Joze as I was capable of. Unlike her husband, Rowen wouldn't let any disability, like my inability to move, stop her or even temper her punches.

When I chanced looking at Josie, I saw a conflicted look on her face. I knew she wanted to stay. I knew she'd crawl in bed beside me and wouldn't leave if I asked her to stay. She wasn't the type to bail when life got hard or, specifically, her boyfriend's body stopped working. But I wouldn't wish that kind of life on my worst enemy. How could I let the person I loved most in the world live the life of a caregiver whose days and nights were burdened with responsibility and duty?

I might not have known with absolute certainty that I'd never walk again, but I didn't need X-rays or a doctor to confirm my prognosis. I might have let myself believe that my life didn't have to end as it had started, but I should have known better. Fate sometimes gave a person a temporary furlough, but it never gave them a pass. I'd been foolish to believe differently.

"Go on, Joze. Really. I'll be good. Go take care of yourself, okay?" I nodded at the door, where I could just make out Jesse and Rowen waiting for her. Even they knew what I did—she couldn't stay with me. "We'll talk more later. I promise."

She studied my face for a moment, a smile working into place on hers. Lifting my hand, she kissed it. I didn't feel a damn thing. Not the feel of her lips or the heat from them or the softness of them. In addition to the rest of my body, my heart broke right then too.

"I love you, Black," she whispered before resting my hand back at my side. She tucked the blanket around my arm, gave me one last smile, and then backed up toward the door. "I'll be back in the morning, and we'll figure this all out together, okay? It'll be fine. I know it. *We'll* be fine." She waited for me to nod, but I couldn't. A minute later, she left with her head bowed and the smile gone from her face.

"I love you too, Joze," I whispered to the dark room long after she'd left.

CHAPTER three

I WATCHED THE sun rise through my window, not having slept a minute through the night. I'd been tired enough that I could have passed out with no problem, but I knew I had better ways to use my time alone. Josie might have been willing to leave last night to grab a bite to eat and a night of sleep, but I knew her too well—she'd be back first thing this morning, and she wouldn't leave my side until I had to beg her while Rowen tugged her away.

Josie was persistent, and she didn't waver. I admired those qualities in her, but I'd have to figure out a way around those qualities. The whole reason I'd spent the night as an insomniac was so I could come up with a plan to let her go. In the event I never recovered, I would not allow her to waste the rest of her life waiting on me and wiping my ass. She'd argue around every point I could bring up as to why she shouldn't have a lifetime of taking care of me, but I had to get her to see that I didn't want that kind of life for her. I wanted the best for her.

I knew enough to accept that if this was how I was stuck until the day I died, staying at my side would be the opposite of the best for her. I could try pushing her away, but something told me if I tried that, she'd only hold on tighter. I could play the hopeless and helpless card, which wasn't a stretch from reality, and hope it sent her running. Maybe I could give denial a try to attempt to frustrate her until she couldn't wait to be rid of me. I'd spent the night sorting through dozens of different things I could try, but nothing I came up with was likely to scare her away. Josie wasn't the type of person who abandoned ship when life got hard. She was the one who battened down the hatches and held on for dear life until the storm had passed.

A part of me didn't want to let her go. The self-serving part. I wanted to spend every day with Josie, just as I'd been planning, but with the way I was now, I couldn't keep her in my life without shifting her into more of a mother role.

I'd had one mother, and that was more than enough. I wouldn't sentence Josie to that kind of future.

Of course, I knew mapping out my future as a paralyzed man might have been a bit premature, but I also knew the way I felt and the impact I'd taken. Karma had finally found me and was paying me back for twenty years of being a piece of shit to most everyone and everything. As far as people who deserved to walk again following this kind of an injury, I was at the tail end of that line.

I wasn't going to walk again. I didn't need a doctor to tell me that.

But when an older man wearing blue scrubs slipped into my room a few minutes after the sun had risen, I guessed one was going to try. I thought I'd had a rough job, riding pissed off animals that were trying to kill the person hanging on to their backs, but this guy had to look a person in the face and tell them life as they knew it, and the one they had planned however many years down the road, was over. Cancer doctors had to tell patients they only had months to live, and ER docs had to tell families their loved ones hadn't made it, but this doctor had to look patients in the eye and tell them that they were going to live but the lives they'd lead would make them wish they'd died.

I almost felt a moment of pity for the doctor grabbing the chair from across the room and pushing it toward me . . . then I noticed he was looking at me with the same expression. I saw pity and something in his eyes that led me to believe he was counting his blessings that he could still move. Pity and relief. That was the way people would look at me from now on, I guessed. Pity for me, relief for themselves.

That realization made me glare holes into the ceiling tiles.

"I'm Doctor Payton, the spinal trauma specialist here," he said as he settled into the chair pushed up next to me. "How are you doing this morning, Mr. Black?"

I huffed, continuing to glare at the ceiling. "I'm feeling fucking on top of the world."

Doc Payton sniffed, leaning back in his chair. "Happy to know you're in good spirits. Most patients in your situation find themselves depressed and pissed off at the world, so your outlook is a nice change of pace."

I gave him a sideways look. "I was shittin' you, Doc."

He scrolled around on the tablet in his lap. "I was too."

Great, I had a smartass for a doctor.

"So when can I bust out of here?" I asked, though I continued to focus on the ceiling. During the course of the night, as a handful of nurses had come in to check on me, I'd found it hard to look at people who could still use their legs and bodies, as if they were to blame for what had happened to me. The bitterness and resentment theory was already holding up.

The doctor looked up from his tablet. "You've sustained a serious injury to your spinal column. You won't be released for a few more days. We've still got to run tests, schedule an MRI, some more X-rays—"

"Hold up." My eyes cut in his direction. "Did you just say *more* X-rays? As in I've already had some done?"

"We did X-rays immediately after you were admitted. It's standard when we're dealing with anyone in your kind of situation."

"My kind of situation?" My brows lifted—at least they could still move. I'd have to get really good at using them.

"Your kind of situation being the potential to have injured or severed something in your spinal column." The doctor's voice was calm, as though he was used to having this kind of a conversation every day. I felt as though my life was ending, as if I was waving good-bye as it floated away, and he was talking to me like he was discussing the weather over a cup of coffee.

I felt the blood in my veins heat. At least the veins from my neck up. "Why did my friends tell me no X-rays had been done yet then?" I didn't say "girlfriend and friends" because the sooner I stopped thinking of Joze like that, the sooner I could embrace my bright future of being paralyzed.

"Maybe because the results were inconclusive and they guessed I'd be better at explaining that to you than they would." Doc Payton was back to messing with his tablet. If I could have used my arms, I might have grabbed it and tossed it against the wall.

"Is my back broken or isn't it, Doc?" I asked a bit more sharply than I'd intended.

"In the way you're asking, no, it isn't." I was just thinking about exhaling a hell of a lot of relief when he continued. "But there is some serious trauma, or swelling, to the middle part of your spine, meaning there could be some serious nerve damage."

I should have been relieved I hadn't broken my back, but something about the nerve damage part and the uncertain note in the doctor's voice gave me pause. "Well, does that mean I'll walk again? Does it mean I'll recover from this?"

He typed a few more things into his tablet before looking at me again. "It's too early to say."

I shook my head, wanting to shoot up in bed and punch something. Putting my fist through that beige wall I'd been staring at all night would have been a good start. "Will I walk again?"

The doctor was looking at me as though he was waiting for me to return the favor, but I couldn't do it. Hearing him tell me my life might be over would be bad enough without seeing the same message in his eyes.

"Maybe," he said at last. "Maybe not. Like I said, it's too early to tell. After some more tests and your body has some time to heal, we'll be able to answer that question, but for now, I don't want to offer false hope. At the same time, I don't want to offer no hope."

"Aren't you just a regular ray of sunshine," I muttered.

"I've been accused of worse."

The sun had risen high enough to stream through the

window, bathing the whole room in light. I wished the curtains were drawn. I wished there wasn't a window there to begin with. I didn't want the light, because it reminded me of the dark . . . the place I was retreating into.

"When's the soonest I can be discharged?" I asked. "It's not like I packed anything and got comfortable, so it shouldn't take long, right? Think you can find someone to wheel me down to the curb? I'll hitch a ride home from there."

The doc let out a sigh as long as it was loud. "If you want to guarantee you'll never walk again, that sounds like the way to do it."

I finally made myself look at the doctor. He wasn't as old as I'd originally thought from just seeing his eyes. I guessed being in his line of work, seeing lives ruined, must have had a way of aging him in other ways. He stuck his hand in the air and waved when he noticed me looking at him.

"You and I both know I'm not going to walk again, don't we, Doc?" I said, steeling my face. "You know the likelihood, probably down to the exact percentage, of a person ever walking again if they wake up paralyzed from the neck down. So why don't we cut the 'therapy and tests' shit and get me out of this hellhole?"

To the doc's credit, he didn't flinch. He didn't even blink. "I also know that percentage decreases every single day you stay paralyzed. Would you like me to give you those numbers as well?"

I blew out a sharp breath. "I don't need to know the numbers to realize I'm fucked."

Doctor Payton scooted closer to the bed and set his tablet in his lap. "You want to know how many people

I've treated like you?"

"There's only one 'people' like me," I said under my breath.

"That's the answer I get from everyone. You all think you're invincible right up until you're not. Then when you're forced to confront your mortality, you throw in the towel and give up completely." The doc's voice filled the room in the same way the sunshine did—way too damn much. "You cross your arms, wave the white flag, and settle into the mentality of being 'fucked.'" The doc huffed, shaking his head. "If you think your approach is unique, you're deluding yourself."

I shook my head when I wanted to rip the room apart, piece by piece. "Okay then, doc. If you can look me in the eye and tell me I've got a good chance of walking again, I'll stay and do whatever tests and therapy you've got up your sleeve. You tell me that, then I'll stay. But if you can't, then I'm not going to lie to myself and the people I care about while I suffer through tests that tell me what I already know and therapy that won't do anything but keep my muscles from atrophying."

Knowing what back injuries did to people was a blessing and a curse. I'd been around the bull riding circuit long enough to hear the stories and watch former competitors turn into vegetables, breathing into wheelchairs to get them to move. Like the doc had said, I'd never thought it would happen to me. I waited for the doctor to look me in the eye, and when he finally did, I knew what he was going to say.

"My job isn't to lie to you, Garth. My job is to be straightforward with you and work on a treatment plan to help. You're right—it's more likely you'll never walk again than you will, but that doesn't mean you won't walk again. It isn't a guarantee."

My gaze drifted back to the ceiling before my eyes closed. Reality? Fuck off. "Then if you don't mind showing me the door, I'll be on my merry quadriplegic way."

The doc stood, shaking his head the entire way to the door. "Sure, I'll get right on it. Let me see if I can find a taxi to drive you all the way home to Montana."

The doctor had barely left the room before a couple other people surged through it.

"Where's Joze?" I asked before I caught myself.

"Nice to see you too, cupcake. Thanks for the warm welcome." Rowen clomped into the room looking like she was prepared to wrestle a bear. She plopped into the same chair the doc had just been in, and Jesse came in behind her, waving at me as he came around the side of my bed.

"Shit, Jess, and I thought I was in bad shape." I looked at my friend, trying not to resent him for being able to stand and rest his hands on the shoulders of the woman he loved. It wasn't him I was mad it—it was my spine and the bull who should have known when he was beat and the circumstance I was neck-deep in. Literally.

Jesse rubbed his face, where the stubble was long enough to be noticeable. But it wasn't just his lack of shaving that stood out. He had dark rings below his bloodshot eyes and rumpled clothing. From the look of it, he'd slept in those clothes. During the whole ten minutes it looked like he'd slept.

"I didn't sleep well last night," he said with a shrug, looking away. "Hotel beds suck."

I knew the real reason he hadn't slept, and it wasn't because the bed at whatever hotel they'd stayed in had been a little too soft or hard. Jess was like me—we could sleep anywhere, anytime, even on a slab of granite if it was the only flat surface around. Cowboys slept when they could, where they could, and they sure as hell didn't whine about some plush hotel bed.

"Yeah, hospital beds suck too," I replied, not be-grudging my friend for lying to me. Had our roles been reversed, I wouldn't have been able to sleep either. "So where's Joze?" Apparently I couldn't catch myself the second time either.

Rowen was in the middle of chugging a monster-sized cup of coffee, but she stopped mid-gulp to answer my question. "Josie is talking with someone about wheel-chairs—"

My head whipping her direction paired with the look in my eyes was somehow enough to get someone I'd thought un-shut-up-able to shut up. Mid-sentence. At least I hadn't underestimated my ability to be intimidating.

"And moving on . . ." She glanced at Jesse with a raised brow before looking back at me. "How's the food? Five-star-worthy?"

I blinked. "Gee, I don't know. Since I can't lift a fork or a spoon or a damn French fry, unless they position a trough two inches in front of my face, I won't be eating." Rowen's face fell, and I felt like a prick for making her feel bad, but I couldn't shut my mouth. All of my anger and frustration was boiling out in the form of cruel words. "Ought to be a great way to lose weight, don't you think? I think I'll patent it and market it as the 'Paralyzed from the Neck Down' diet."

"Garth," Jesse interjected, warning in his voice, "we're not your enemies. We're your friends. I know

40

you're pissed off at the world and what happened and what it might mean, but don't take it out on us." He moved closer so he was looking down at me. He'd always been a couple inches taller than me, but he'd never towered over me the way he did now. "At least don't take it *all* out on us."

I was searching for either a comeback or an apology when I heard hurried steps thundering down the hall, each one growing louder than the last. Someone was coming to my room . . . and not in a good mood.

"Garth Black, you and I have to talk." Josie's voice streamed into the room before she'd rounded into it. "Now."

When she did show up in the doorway, her expression was more harrowing than her footsteps had sounded. Like Jesse and Rowen, she was in the same clothes she'd been in last night, but her sleeves were rolled up to her elbows, and her hair was pulled into a couple of side braids. She knew that was my favorite way for her to wear her hair because the bad guy in me couldn't help but think dirty thoughts when I saw those braids bobbing down her shoulders. I liked to grab one in each hand and give them a tug . . .

I'd *liked* to do that. I wasn't sure I'd ever be able to tug those braids or comb my knuckles through her hair or rinse the conditioner out of her hair when we took a shower together after . . .

Fuck me. Forget about tugging her braids. If the doc's percentages didn't lie, I wouldn't be doing *anything* to her again. I had to squeeze my eyes closed to keep what felt like tears from forming. I couldn't let her see me cry. If she saw me cry, she'd never let me push her away for good. Instead, she'd go all martyr on me, and I couldn't let her do that.

"I'm right here. Not going anywhere." I kept my eyes shut, trying to shove the images of her and me in my bed . . . or her bed . . . or the bed of my truck . . . or wherever the opportunity arose from my head. "So talk." I heard her footsteps move closer.

"Why did Doctor Payton just tell me you're checking yourself out of the hospital today? As soon as possible today?" she added in a voice that implied I'd committed the worst kind of crime against humanity.

"Because I *am* checking myself out of here ASAP."

My reply was immediately followed by three sighs from three people—one quiet, one annoyed, and one outraged.

"And just where do you think you're going once you check yourself out?" Josie's voice boomed loudly enough that she'd probably woken anyone who had been trying to sleep in the nearby rooms.

"Home." I kept my eyes on the ceiling so I wouldn't have to witness three pairs of eyes gaping at me like I'd busted something in my brain now too.

"Home?" Josie practically spit the word. "How exactly are you planning on getting there? And once you're there, how are you going to get around, heal yourself, and receive the medical care you need, Garth? Mind telling me what your big plan is? Because I'm not seeing it." From the corner of my eye, I saw her head shake, sending her pigtails whipping around. "You're hurt. Badly. This isn't one of those times you can fix yourself with a bag of frozen peas and gritting your jaw. I know that's your favorite way of dealing with injuries, but this isn't a cracked rib.

This is you not being able to move from your neck down."

She wasn't crying, yet, but I knew she was close. Josie cried when she got angry as often as she did when she was sad.

"Yeah, I'm really aware of the fact that I can't move. Thanks for the recap."

"Are you?"

Josie's head lowered so it was above mine, but I continued to focus on the ceiling. She was right, to a degree, but I also knew I couldn't stay in the hospital another day without losing my mind. I'd already likely lost my body— I couldn't lose my mind too. It was all I had left.

"Because how is checking yourself out going to help this situation at all?" she asked.

I smelled her favorite cherry lip balm on her lips. I wanted to kiss her, like I always did when I caught the scent of it, but I couldn't. Sure, I might have been able to lift my head off the pillow a few inches, but I couldn't kiss her and expect her to walk away. Kissing her while I wanted her to go live her life kind of sent a mixed message.

"There's nothing that's going to help, Joze. Staying in this hospital sure as shit won't. I need to get home." My voice stayed strong, but it seemed to be the last part of me that possessed strength.

"You *need* to get better," she argued. She looked across the bed at Jesse and Rowen, probably searching for one or both of them to back her up.

Rowen opened her mouth first, Jess still seeming at a loss, but I cut them all off. I had to force my jaw to untighten before I could say the words all of them were in denial over. "I'm not going to get better." Each word came out louder than the last until the final word seemed to echo around us. "There isn't a medicine that can be prescribed that will cure me, no amount of rest and rehab can heal me, and there sure as shit aren't any tests they can run that will tell us something different from what we all already know." I'd spent so long glaring at the ceiling tile above me I wondered if by the time I was out of there, it would crumble apart. "I'm not moving again. I'm . . ." I had to swallow and roll the word around in my mouth a few times before I could get it out. "Paralyzed. The sooner we all accept it, the better off we'll be."

The room got quiet. Real quiet. Other than the sound of the second hand moving on the wall clock across from my bed, silence filled the room. It didn't last though. It couldn't with what I'd said and who I'd said it to.

Leaning over me even farther, Josie lowered her face so close to mine I could see each and every fleck of bronze in her eyes. I would have been content to spend the rest of my life counting each of them too.

"Fine. You want to give up and roll over after a day and a half? That's your choice. Be beaten. Give up. Accept you're doomed. That's your prerogative." Her voice wasn't quaking as it had been earlier—it was so strong and seamless it was like she'd been rehearsing this speech for weeks. "You go right on ahead and play the victim and tell yourself you're never going to walk again. But don't you dare, Garth Black, for one fricking minute, try to order me or any of us"—she jabbed her pointer finger toward Rowen and Jesse—"that we have to accept the same thing. You don't want to hold on to hope, big surprise, but don't try to take a shit on all of ours."

After that, she waited. For me to say something or argue or for what she'd said to settle in, I didn't know, but I knew the way I felt. Nothing she could say and no amount of time she could wait would get me to change my mind.

Jesse was just clearing his throat and stepping closer, probably to say something that would solve all our problems along with world hunger, when I heard another set of footsteps enter the room. They didn't travel far before the newcomer stopped and cleared his throat . . . saved by the doc.

"The ambulance will be here in a half hour to escort you home if that's still want you want." I heard the edge in his voice—he wasn't quite, but almost, as pissed as Josie that all I wanted to do was get the hell out of there. "As your doctor, it is my duty to strongly advise you not to leave until we've had some time to more accurately diagnose you and give you a chance to recover—"

"But this isn't a jail, and you can't hold me against my will, now can you?" I said, trying not to laugh at the word recover. Last I'd heard, "recover" meant someone would get better.

"No, it isn't a jail. Though in your case, I wish it were."

Josie's mouth dropped as she gaped at the doctor as if he were as batshit crazy as I was.

"Well, thanks for everything, doc. I feel like a new man," I said dryly. I didn't miss Rowen leaning into Jesse and hissing something into his ear that I couldn't quite make out, though I picked up enough to decipher she thought I should be declared insane or have my ass kicked.

"I'm going to send you off with discharge orders, some prescriptions, and a couple of referrals for doctors in your area who specialize in back injuries. I know you seem to hate taking it, but I strongly suggest you take my advice of making an appointment to go to see one of them immediately."

Josie approached the doc and took the handful of paperwork from him. She clutched it against her chest as if she were afraid someone would rip it away from her. "You can't just let him check out, Doctor Payton," she whispered in a tone that suggested she was begging. "Can't you talk to him again? Try to make him stay?"

I'd only heard Josie come close to begging a few times in my life—she was too prideful a person to beg—and hearing her do it because of me made me feel about as low as I'd ever felt, and I'd been in so many low places so many times I was a contender for the record.

"I can't force him to stay. I'm a doctor—I help the people I can who want to be helped." The doctor's gaze drifted to where I was laid out, immobile and stubborn. He was a good man. I could tell that from the few words we'd shared, but he knew no amount of talk or debate would get me to see his point of view. "Even if I could force him to stay, it doesn't take a psychiatric evaluation to see that he doesn't want to be helped. Good luck to you, Miss Gibson." The good doc exited the room, moving on to whom I guessed was the next patient on his list, one who actually wanted his help.

Josie stood frozen for a minute, clutching the paperwork close to her. Every breath she took seemed to get longer and louder until it sounded as though she was gasping for air. "I need to get some fresh air." She rushed for the door like she couldn't get outside quickly enough.

"I'll go with you." Rowen followed her, but not before firing a potent glare at me.

I pretended I hadn't noticed.

About two seconds after the girls had gone, Jesse's boot-steps echoed through the room. He got so close to me he bumped into the bedrails. "What are you doing, Black?" His voice hinted at exhaustion. "I thought you kicked your self-destruction habit months ago."

A sigh escaped past my lips before I knew it was coming. Oh well. If I could sigh in front of anyone without them judging me or reading some deeper meaning into it, it was Jess. "You can never kick a habit like that," I said, staring at the place Josie had just been standing. "You can only wrestle it into submission. After this though, I'm afraid it's wrestled me into submission."

Jesse's hand wound around the bedrail. "Then fight back."

Another sigh—this one a bit more final sounding. "You need both a literal and theoretical backbone to fight back. And I've got neither."

CHAPTER four

YOU WANT TO know what the longest, most uncomfortable ambulance ride in the world feels like? After what I'd just gone through, I could have explained it in precise detail, recapping every last awkward moment.

After she'd argued against me discharging myself from the hospital, I would have guessed Josie would want nothing to do with my escape plan, but she hopped up beside me after the paramedics had loaded and locked my stretcher into place in the ambulance. She gave the two paramedics a seriously impressive look when they suggested she ride with Jesse and Rowen, who were heading back in their truck. I knew they'd been planning on heading back to Seattle after the rodeo, but after their friend had gone and broken his back, they probably felt obligated to come get me settled in. Or maybe the obligation rested more with supporting Josie while, as Rowen had made a point of noting, I was behaving like a selfish, defeated asshole.

I was thankful they were coming back for a few days, for Joze's sake. She'd need someone to lean on as she navigated this new chapter in life, and that person couldn't and shouldn't have been me. I wanted to make my removal from her life slow and gradual . . . but that was only for my benefit. The best thing for her would have been a sharp and sudden break because even though it would hurt like hell, that wound would eventually leave no trace of a scar. If I drew it out, I'd only cause a deeper scar to form. I'd already left Josie with enough of those.

When we'd crossed the Montana state line, the driver asked for more specific directions about where we were heading. After I gave him some, I got another earful and a half from Josie, and thanks to the confined space and volume she employed, so did the paramedics. One of them rolled earplugs into his ears at about the five-minute mark of her outburst.

I'd given them directions to Joze's and my old farmhouse instead of directions to her family's ranch, and you'd have thought I'd signed the execution order for a litter of puppies. She reminded me that the only bathroom that worked (well) in the farmhouse we were remodeling was the one on the second floor, and since we didn't have an elevator, I'd have no way to get up there without the aid of fairy dust. I'd been too choked up to reply because she obviously hadn't wrapped her mind around how a quadriplegic's "call of nature" routine was drastically different from hers.

After that, she went on to argue that the floors were in such bad shape that I could tumble right through them in my wheelchair, not to mention there wasn't a ramp to get me inside in the first place. I tried to remind her that her parents' place didn't have a ramp either, but she wouldn't let me get a word in. She went on and on about the farmhouse being too far away from everyone and how I couldn't be all alone when she had to go do something, and she warned me if I didn't stop acting like a lunatic, she would start the paperwork to have me declared incompetent so she could take the wheel at the helm of my healthcare needs.

That was more than enough of a threat to get me to shut up and not say a word of protest when she gave the driver different directions. I knew she didn't understand it, but I wanted to be alone. I didn't want a stream of people filtering through the Gibsons' kitchen, dropping off casseroles and sympathy cards while taking a quick peek at the immobile freak show. I didn't want people's sympathy or their morbid curiosity or their compassion. I wanted to be left alone, and the farmhouse was the perfect place to do just that. I wasn't sure how I'd take care of myself or what direction my life would take, but I did know I'd have plenty of time to think about that during my isolation.

By the time the ambulance crunched up the Gibsons' driveway, I'd had way too much time to ponder my future and contrast it to what I thought I'd have. So I was feeling particularly pissed at the world when the ambulance doors swung open and the paramedics unloaded me.

Josie jumped out behind me, looking almost worse than I knew I did, and she shot a wave toward the house. I didn't look, mainly because I felt like me showing up at their front door in a stretcher while their daughter followed with red-rimmed eyes was like fulfilling every last premonition and hang-up Mr. Gibson had had when Josie and I had gotten together. He'd seen me for the piece of shit I was and been willing to overlook it when he saw how much I cared for his daughter and she for me. But months later, there I was—a piece of shit being carried into their house on a stretcher, sentencing their twenty-two-year-old daughter to a life as a caretaker.

It wasn't just Mr. and Mrs. Gibson waiting on the front porch though. Jesse and Rowen were there too, looking not quite but almost as tired as I knew Josie and I did.

"Nice trip?" Rowen asked Josie when she crawled up the porch stairs.

"Don't ask," she replied, sounding exhausted.

As the paramedics carried me up the stairs, everyone went into action, though no one seemed quite sure where to go or what to do. Mr. Gibson and Jess opened the screen door. Mrs. Gibson reached out for my stretcher as though she wanted to help the paramedics carry me in. Joze and Rowen swept through the door at the same time, managing to bottleneck in the doorway before Josie wiggled free and led the way into the kitchen.

Rowen hung back, slowing her pace to match the paramedics'. As they guided me through the kitchen, she glanced down at me. An all-too-familiar expression was plastered on her face. It said she was debating whether to rip off my balls and shove them down my throat or kick them so hard they wound up in the same place. Unlike most people, I didn't doubt Rowen would follow through on whatever choice she arrived at.

"You and I are going to talk," she said, just barely lifting a brow. "And by talk, I mean I'm going to talk and you're going to listen, and when we're done with our little 'talk,' you're going to pull your head out of your ass."

"You know how much I look forward to our talks, Mrs. Sterling-Walker," I replied, putting on an overdone smile. "I'll pencil you into my calendar."

I could just make out Josie flagging the paramedics down the hall as she opened the door to the guest room I'd camped out in for a few months last year. I had some great memories from that room—more of my good memories had originated from that room than from any other facet of my life—and I wanted to keep it that way. I didn't want to be swept into it as a cripple to spend my waking and sleeping hours trapped in the same bed I'd made love to the woman I cared about. Putting me in there the way I was now, doomed to watch the world and weather pass me by day after day, felt like desecrating a sacred place.

But before I could request I be put up in the barn instead of this room with all of its memories, the stretcher was maneuvered through the door and guided toward the bed. I closed my eyes and swallowed. When I hadn't been floating from motel to motel working the rodeo circuit, I'd been camped out at Willow Springs in the hand house, occasionally spending a night or two at Josie's and my farmhouse. I almost felt like a lifetime had passed since I'd last laid my head on this bed.

Once they had the stretcher out from beneath me, the paramedics glanced toward the door. They wanted out of there as badly as I did. After the long trip they'd just had, and having had to play third party to Josie's and my arguing, I couldn't blame them.

"Thanks for the lift, guys. Just put the bill in the mail, and I'll sell a kidney or something to pay it off." I tried to wave, but my hand stayed limp on the bed. Sure, Life, why don't you just keep taking swings at me while I'm down?

They muttered a couple of good-byes before escaping, their footsteps hurrying down the hallway and out the front door. What I wouldn't have given to be able to do the same.

"Is there anything we can get you, Garth?" Mrs. Gibson bustled about the room, pulling open curtains and switching on lamps. She hadn't been able to look at me yet.

"You wouldn't happen to have a new spine in that apron of yours, would you?" I asked, trying to sound like my usual self . . . my old self . . . the self that never could be again.

She paused in the middle of refolding the blanket hanging over the back of the rocking chair. Patting the pockets of the apron she was rarely seen without when she was in the house, she worked up a smile before finally looking at me. "I've found a little of everything hiding out in these pockets, but no spines yet. You'll be the first I inform if that changes though."

Since she'd worked so hard to form hers, I returned the smiling favor. "Thanks for letting me crash here for a few days, Mrs. Gibson. I don't want to be an inconvenience . . ." Though how could I not be when I couldn't move and had to depend on people for everything besides blinking?

"You're no inconvenience," she said, almost sounding like her daughter did when I'd said something that ticked her off. "And you can stay as long as you like. No need to rush out before you're on your feet again . . ." Her whole face fell as she realized what she'd just said.

I wasn't sure exactly what Josie had told her parents about what had happened to me, but even if she'd told them nothing, it didn't take a genius to see me and figure out what was wrong.

"I'm going to get dinner started, I think." Mrs. Gibson powered toward the doorway, pausing to rest her hand on her daughter's arm. "Let me know if you need anything, okay? I'm just a shout away."

From the look of it, she'd been talking more to Josie than to me, but I answered when it looked like Josie was too choked up to. "Thanks again. I appreciate it."

Mr. Gibson was hovering in the doorway, his head bowed and his hands stuffed into the pockets of his denim coveralls. From what I knew of him, he was probably warring with feelings of wanting to do the right thing for his daughter and the right thing for me, knowing those two agendas could never align now. I didn't envy Mr. Gibson, not even though he still had the use of his body.

"Sorry I won't be able to help you replace the cattle gate this week, Mr. Gibson. I had to go and bust my back," I said, lifting my chin at Jesse. "But this guy here's a strapping young lad and always eager to prove he's a saint."

Jesse didn't scowl down at me as I would have done if he'd just volunteered me for a few hours of gate removal and installation. Instead, he looked at Mr. Gibson and nodded. "Rowen and I will be in town this next week, so I can swing by and help you with it. No problem. Just let me know when."

A rush of air filtered from my mouth. "I thought you guys had a busy week coming up? You said you could only spare a few days before Rowen had to get back to finish a piece for her art show next month."

Rowen stepped up to the plate next, crossing one arm over the other as she approached the bed. When everyone else was looking at me with varying degrees of uncertainty or pity, at least she still looked at me as she had pre-broken back—with pure and utter disdain when I pissed her off. "Yeah, and something more important came up, like being there for a good friend when he needs it. So if you could stop acting like an asshole sooner rather than later, that would be spectacular."

I didn't make my eye-roll subtle. "Listen, this homecoming reunion has been a blast, but I just travelled across a couple state lines in a confined space with a guy who was under the impression flatulence is something that should be shared with others, along with his opinions on the whole wolf control issue. That boils down to me getting a whole two and a half minutes of sleep in the past twenty-four hours. I'm bushed. So if there isn't anything else that requires my immediate attention, think you all could move this powwow into another room? I need my beauty rest."

I shut my eyes, as if what I'd said was less of a question and more of an order, and one by one, I heard them filter out of the bedroom. A minute later, only one still remained in the room. I didn't need to open my eyes to know who that one was.

"Joze, you look in as rough of shape as I do. Get some rest, okay? There's nothing you can do by hovering beside my bedside day in and day out that's going to help me get better or make me more comfortable, so get some rest. Go out and live your life for a few hours. Only one of us broke our backs, so there's no need to act like we both did."

For a moment, she was silent, so silent I almost cracked open my eyes to see if I'd been wrong about her lingering behind. She finally spoke. "It's comments like those that make me wonder if you even know the person you're in love with."

My brows pulled together, but I kept my eyes closed. "What does that mean?"

I heard her take a step closer. "It means you rise, I rise; you fall, I fall. You hurt, I hurt; you succeed, I succeed. You break your back—" Her voice caught in her throat for the shortest second. "I break my back. Please stop acting like you're the only person in the world who's affected by this. Because you're not. You're not alone, so stop acting like you are."

Her words, along with the tone she'd said them in, were enough to make a ball the size of my fist form in my throat. At exactly the right time, she'd said exactly the right words. In a few short sentences, she'd comforted me more than a person in my condition should have been able to be comforted. The problem wasn't her—it was me. She knew the right words, did the right things, believed in the right ideals . . . but she was hovering beside the wrong man. I wanted to let her camp out at my side and never leave, but I also knew of no surer or quicker way to crush her spirit than to allow her to stay at my side.

"I *am* alone, Joze. So why don't you stop acting like I'm not?"

She replied in the way I'd both hoped and dreaded she would: by walking out of the room and closing the door.

CHAPTER five

MY DOOR STAY closed for I didn't know how long. Might have been half an hour, might have been a decade. I couldn't tell. When I finally fell asleep, I slept hard and long. I slept the sleep of the dead, but when I woke up to the sound of my door opening, I wished I would have stayed with the dead. What was left for me with the living wasn't worth living for.

Jesse strode in and shifted a few things in the corner to make room for what was coming through the door. What was *wheeling* through the door. A middle-aged guy sat in one of those huge electric wheelchairs and puttered into the room, heading for the spot Jesse had just cleared. The rooms in the Gibsons' old farmhouse were small to start with, but having that giant machine inside it made the guest room seem like a coat closet. It became tough to breathe, as if either the oxygen had been stripped from the room by that wheelchair or it had brought in too much. I couldn't tell, but I knew I needed it out of there.

"Who are you?" I asked the man in the wheelchair. I guessed Jess knew better than to invite some other crippled person to come over and commiserate with me like some kind of mini support group, but I couldn't figure out another reason why the hell a guy in his wheelchair would be rolling into my room right after I'd been deemed paralyzed.

The guy didn't glance up as he finished maneuvering the chair into the corner. From the look of it, he needed to take a few more driving courses with that thing before he ran it through a wall or ran over a person. "I'm Steve."

I waited for something else, but nothing else was offered. I was just about to ask Steve why "Steve" was in my room when he shoved himself out of the wheelchair onto two strong legs and approached me with an outstretched hand.

"I'm the manager of the medical supply company in town," he said, letting his hand hang in the air for another moment before he realized that unless he picked my hand up and put it there, I couldn't shake his hand. His arm dropped back at his side as he cleared his throat. "I don't usually do the home deliveries, but when I heard who this chair was going to, I had to see to it personally." A smile spread across his face as he looked at me. "I used to follow you in the local circuit when you were just starting out, so I was a fan before you hit it big. You're a talented rider, Mr. Black." Steve nodded at me in what I guessed was approval.

While I'd been complimented and praised by hundreds this past year, instead of the flattery making me feel awkward yet grateful, Steve's made me feel like each word was a knife slashing at my throat.

"I think what you mean is that I *used* to be a talented rider," I replied, my tone so bitter I could actually taste it on the back of my tongue. "Kind of hard to be any kind of a rider, good or bad, when I can't even wipe away the drool rolling down my chin."

I noticed Jesse shift on the other side of the room. He wasn't used to not knowing what to say or how to fix something. I'd never seen him at such an utter and total loss in all of the years I'd known him.

Steve shifted a couple times too. "I'm having one of my best employees—he's the most familiar with this type of chair—come over later this afternoon to go over how it works with you and get you all set up. This baby's got too many bells and whistles for me, and with my luck, I'd wind up running you over."

My throat did that running dry thing it had been doing a lot lately. I wasn't sure if that was due to the paralysis or due to the rough topics being discussed, but it seemed like shit luck that one of the few pieces of my anatomy I could still feel would be uncomfortable. "Well, the nice thing about running me over, Steve, is that you wouldn't have to worry about injuring me any more than I already am." I winked at him, but it had the opposite effect of what I'd intended.

His face ironed out before he glanced at Jesse like he was flagging him down for a lifeboat.

"Thanks for swinging by personally, Mr. Winters. We appreciate it." Jesse came forward to shake the guy's hand.

"You might as well take it back with you though," I piped up, trying not to glare at the towering piece of machinery stuffed into the corner of my room.

From Jesse, a sigh followed a few moments later. From Steve, his brows drew together as if he'd misunderstood me or wasn't following.

"You'll need a chair, Garth," Jesse said. "No matter what happens or what changes, you'll need a chair for a while to get around."

I snorted. "That's not a 'chair,' Jess. That's an upright spaceship with wheels and a joy stick." I shook my head and looked away from where it sat, taking up a chunk of my room. "Take it back."

"We're not sending it back," Jesse said in a gentle enough tone that I knew he was addressing Steve and not me.

"Maybe *we're* not, but *I* am." My eyes flashed to find Jesse hovering above me while Steve hovered over me from the other side. Everyone hovered over me now. Even if I was sitting upright, they'd still be hovering. I hated it. I wanted to be able to look a person straight in the eye when we spoke, but I couldn't. "I mean, did you see how he drove it in here? With his hand. I don't happen to have the use of my hands, so even if I wanted to be strapped into that thing, I couldn't go anywhere once I was."

Jesse looked at Steve, who cleared his throat. "The chair is designed for both paraplegics and quadriplegics. You can operate it with your hand or with your mouth."

I shouldn't have been able to feel my heart thundering in my chest and about to break through my ribcage, but right then, I felt like I could. Maybe it was beating so hard it was pounding in my ears and vibrating my brain, but I could feel my heart. "Take it back." I sounded out-of-breath. "I won't be operating it with my hand, my mouth, or anything else."

"Garth—"

"I'm not trying to deny what's happened to me or playing ignorant to the shape I'm in, Jess," I said, shaking my head. "However, I'm not ready to exchange two legs for four wheels. Give reality some time to settle in before you roll a machine like that into a person's room, okay?"

He was opening his mouth to say something else, but I cut him off again. "Besides, I don't need to have shopped for something like that to know it costs way more than my pay grade."

"Garth—"

"Especially since I don't have a pay grade anymore, probably never will again, and am fortunate enough to not have health insurance, thanks to a lack of forward thinking and the professional bull riding circuit being under the impression that health benefits are for sissies." The silver lining to the night of my accident was that I'd stayed on long enough and earned a high enough score to score a nice chunk of prize money. However, since it was highly likely that would be the last ride I'd ever make, I needed to make my bull riding winnings stretch as long as I could. I wasn't going to drop thousands of dollars on something I wanted no part of.

When I was finally finished, Jesse didn't jump right back in. He stood beside my bed silently, looking at me expectantly. He let another minute pass.

"Are you done now?" he said, arching a brow. "Can I get a few words in before you cut me off again?"

I would have made a smartass proceed motion if I'd had the use of my hand, so instead I answered by staying quiet.

"I wasn't the one who ordered it. I was just the one who was the one closest to the door and answered it, so stop blaming me for the chair." Even though I could tell Jesse was irritated, he wasn't raising his voice. He was like the Zen master of keeping his cool. "And no matter what happens, you're going to need a chair to get around in for a while. You don't want to spend day in and day out in that bed, do you?" He paused, waiting for me to answer, but I wouldn't answer his rhetorical question with a rhetorical answer. "Being able to move around the house and get outside for some fresh air seems only about a thousand times better than being trapped inside this ten-by-ten-foot room."

"Speak for yourself," I muttered. "You won't have to put up with people gawking at you while you breathe into a tube to make some wheels turn. There hasn't been anything this gossip-worthy since crazy old Pete Whittaker held a nail gun to his temple and pulled the trigger."

I exhaled sharply, picturing what I'd look like scooting along in that spaceship of a wheelchair. I'd never seen anyone use a chair like that in person, but I'd caught glimpses of some documentary about a scientist who used one when I'd been in the waiting room at the mechanic's. That kind of chair might work for genius scientists, but how was a bull-rider-slash-rancher supposed to carry on working in something like that?

"But on the bright side, I could rent out a space at the county fair every year and charge to give rides and spins in the freak-show chair. The kids ought to love that, right?"

Jesse had long ago gotten used to my smartass approach to life and how when I was presented with two ways to address a problem, I usually went with the more controversial, but even his patience with me looked to be waning. It was either that or the dark shadows under his eyes were due to lack of sleep. "You obviously want to fight the chair topic, so I'm going to send in the person who took the time and energy to get it for you."

He didn't say anything else before marching out the door and down the hall. Beside me, Steve shifted again. If he'd been a fan before he'd arrived, he wouldn't be after leaving. That was the way it would happen though, I guessed. One by one, each of my fans would fall away, either forgetting my name when it wasn't on their screens or in their papers anymore or being repelled by my current state and the extra-surly attitude that accompanied it.

Reality after reality kept assaulting me. As if waking up paralyzed weren't enough, I was figuring out just what that meant, one harsh realization at a time.

Steve let out a relieved sigh when we heard sharp, rushed steps growing closer. How those steps were a relief to him was beyond me because whenever I heard them, I knew I was in trouble. Those steps and the way the heel of her boot echoed down the hall meant she was barreling for me.

When she tore through the doorway, I knew she'd probably been helping her dad with the ever-malfunctioning tractor. Grease was streaked down her cheeks and plaid shirt. Where some girls shied away from anything that might put dirt under their nails, Josie dove right in. It was one of the many traits I found so damn attractive in her.

"What seems to be the problem?" Her voice cut through the room as her arms folded over her chest.

"Um . . . I'm not really sure, ma'am," Steve said with an apologetic look.

"Thank you, Mr. Winters, but I wasn't directing that question toward you. I was asking him." Josie's eyes cut in my direction as she lifted a brow and waited for me to say something. When I stayed quiet, mostly because she could still take my breath away just by walking into a room all riled up and stained by tractor oil, she lifted her other brow too. "What seems to be the problem, Garth?"

I saw through her tough act though. I could tell she was closer to tears than she was to throwing a fit. It broke my heart seeing her like that. It broke it again when I couldn't go to her, pull her close, and whisper in her ear that everything would be okay.

"That thing, Joze. That's the problem." I lifted my chin in the general direction of the chair, but I wouldn't look at it again. I couldn't.

"How is having a way of moving around a problem?" She moved closer.

I could tell she wanted to grab my hand or give me a hug, but she held back, probably because our last few conversations hadn't been all that kind. My plan was working—she was slowly pulling away—so why did I feel as though I was dying inside instead of flipping internal cartwheels . . . the only kind of cartwheels I'd be capable of from here on out?

"Because a person shouldn't have to breathe into a tube to move, Joze. Because I can't afford that thing, and I don't want to take out a thirty-year loan to do so. Because I don't want to be stared at and pointed at and laughed at when I roll by. I don't want to be a joke. I don't want to be like my . . ." The word rose up my throat and froze in my mouth. I hadn't consciously thought about Clay since I'd woken up in the hospital, but based on that near-slip, I guessed my subconscious had been plenty focused on him. Probably because I was crippled, laid up, and in even worse shape than he'd been after getting the short end of the bull riding stick.

Josie's face softened instantly before she rushed the rest of the way to me. "You're not a joke, baby. You never have been, and no matter what, you never will be." Her head shook feverishly as she sat on the edge of my bed and slipped her hand into mind. "And if anybody even thinks about laughing at you, it will be promptly and sharply followed by my fist driving into their jaw."

For the first time, a natural smile pulled at my lips. I didn't have to force or fake it, and it felt so damn good I sighed without meaning to. "It would almost be worth making someone laugh just to witness that."

She smiled at me and slid a bit closer until her back was propped up against my side. I couldn't feel her, but knowing that I could still support her in some way, small though it might have been, was a comfort. "Then I better start practicing my right hook."

"From what I recall, it's never gotten out of practice."

She laughed with me, being transported back to a time in our lives when life hadn't been so complicated. "Yeah, you were the whole reason why that right hook never got out of practice, weren't you?"

"That's a crime I don't mind being guilty of." I felt a crooked smile slide into place, and instantly, that little glint in her eyes fired to life. One was tied to the other, and when combined, my crooked smile and her glint led to the same thing . . . except they couldn't now. Or, if my dick stayed as uncooperative as the rest of my body, ever.

That smile fell from my face as suddenly as it had appeared.

"What's the matter with the wheelchair, baby?" she asked softly, brushing my hair off my forehead. That was a touch I could feel, and it was so gentle and warm and comforting that my eyelids dropped closed. "It's a tool to make your life easier, not a life sentence."

My eyes stayed closed as I replied, "It *is* a life sentence."

I heard her exhale, but she kept stroking my hair. "We don't know that yet. It's only been a few days. Maybe if I took you in for another X-ray or an MRI, we could get a more definitive answer—"

I shook my head. "I can't move. It doesn't get any more definitive than that."

Another exhale, this one longer. "Mind telling me where the Garth Black who didn't know how or when or even the meaning of the word 'quit' went? Where did he go? Because I need him to get through this with me. I don't need this substitute who's already waving the white flag before we've even gotten started."

She waited for my answer. She waited for me to reassure her that I was still there and that I was just waiting for her to call me out on it before I put up a fight, but I couldn't answer her honest question with a guaranteed lie. I couldn't promise her the guy she'd grown up with and fallen in love with was the same one sprawled out beside her. I wasn't that guy anymore, as much as I might have wanted him to come back.

After letting another minute pass, she cleared her throat. "Thank you, Mr. Winters. I believe I already signed all of the paperwork?"

"It's all taken care of, Miss Gibson, and Tom will be over later this afternoon to demonstrate how it works." Steve shuffled through a few papers and handed Josie a few copies before backing out of the room. "It was a pleasure meeting you both. If you need anything, just give me a ring. I wrote my personal number on the paperwork there." He was passing through the doorway when he stopped. His gaze drifted to me, and a smile I was all too familiar with crept onto his mouth—the apologetic version. "Good luck, Garth."

I nodded. "I think it's going to take a hell of a lot more than luck to get me through this, but thank you for the sentiments."

His eyes drifted to Josie and lingered on her a moment before moving back to mine. "It looks like you've got a lot more than just luck on your side." He let that hang in the air for a moment before he waved and disappeared down the hall.

I didn't want to think too long about what he meant, because I already knew I had the best woman in the world at my side, along with more good friends than I deserved. But even before I'd broken my back, I'd struggled with the guilt of accepting that I could never give them what they'd given me, though I'd die trying.

Now though, I couldn't even change the oil in Mr. Gibson's truck or fix the leaky kitchen faucet for Mrs. Gibson. I couldn't help Jesse toil a long day away over at Willow Springs, and I sure as shit couldn't crawl onto the back of another bull to put more money into creating Josie's and my dream ranch. I couldn't do anything to be worthy of their friendship, nor could I do anything worthwhile to earn it.

I was a charity case. That was just as paralyzing a realization as the condition my body was in.

"Please tell me you didn't sell a kidney or sign up to have your eggs harvested or anything like that to pay for that thing, Joze. Please tell me you didn't pay for it at all and this is all some big mistake and once Steve realizes that, he's going to come marching back without so many smiles and nice words and repo that baby right out of my room." I paused to inhale. I didn't know why, but talking seemed to have become a rigorous activity. "Please don't tell me you blew a load of cash so I could drool upright too."

She gave me a pity chuckle, but I could tell she didn't find any humor in my words. "Then we just won't discuss it, okay? If you don't want to know the truth, I won't give it to you. I'll let you just imagine whatever you want."

"Joze . . ." My jaw ground together as I accepted what she was saying. I didn't need to check the price tag to guess that that thing had cost more than my new truck.

"You needed a wheelchair, you've got one. We can check that off the list," she said. "The next thing on the docket I need to discuss with you is making an appointment with the local doctor Dr. Payton referred us to. He said this doctor was like some spinal cord miracle worker or something. I called to set up an appointment, and they said they couldn't get you in until next week. When I said that wasn't good enough, they changed next week to tomorrow at two o'clock. Now I'm not sure how we're going to get you there—*yet*—but I'll have something worked out by then. I just wanted you to know so you could prepare yourself since I know you're such a non-fan of doctors and them actually trying to help you." She didn't sound as if she planned on coming up for air, probably because she knew I was just waiting to pop in and argue with her. She was right.

"Might as well cancel it, Joze." I rushed to get my words out just as quickly as she had. "Because I won't be going. Let someone else see the 'miracle worker.' Someone who actually believes in miracles."

She flinched. Just barely, but enough for me to notice. She recovered quickly though. "Be serious. You have to see a doctor. Sticking your head in the sand and pretending like nothing's happened won't help you get better."

"I'm not going to get better." My voice was rising, filling the room.

She shoved off the bed. "Don't you think I know that? Don't you think I've realized and agonized over that and accepted that you might not get better in the way you're so fixated on right now?" She was talking with her hands and arms, flailing them like she was tossing dozens of invisible Frisbees. "But there is more than one way you can get better, and until you meet with a doctor or doctors, that's never going to happen."

I couldn't look her in the eye any longer, so my gaze drifted to the ceiling. "There's no doctor or doctors who can make me better, short of figuring out a way to fix my back so I can walk again. Sorry, Joze. I know that's not what you or anyone else pacing around your living room wants to hear, but I'm not going to smile and lie through my teeth that with some occupational therapy and a support group, I'll be able to 'get better.'" My voice was even louder. Was I shouting at her? Was she backing away from me because of the shouting? Or because of what I was saying? Or because of both? Oh God, what was I doing? "I'm not getting better so accept it already! I have!"

She charged forward, her mouth opening as if she was ready to shout back at me just as loudly and with just as much conviction, but a second later, her mouth closed and that determined gleam in her eyes faded. I watched it fade completely until all that was left was a glazed-over smolder of finality. Then she backed away.

"Accept this," she said in a voice so low I had to strain to hear it. "You can push me away all you want, but I'm not going anywhere."

CHAPTER six

THE WHEELCHAIR TRAINING guy came that afternoon. He left about five minutes later. Along with him, the electric wheelchair left too. I told him to make sure Josie got a full refund, and he promised he'd take care of it.

After he'd left with the wheelchair, I'd expected to hear the same rushed boot-steps bursting into my room, but instead I was met with an eerie quiet. It was as if the house were empty, though I knew someone was lingering close by. I'd caught a glimpse earlier of a folded up piece of paper hanging out of the back of Jesse's pocket. It was a schedule of who was on "Garth" duty when.

I was like a child who needed both a babysitter and a caretaker. As someone who'd been so uncomfortable being dependent on other people that I used to break out in hives, I didn't know what to do with having to be babysat around the clock.

From the light streaming into the room, I knew it was getting close to dinnertime, but the endless hammering that had commenced a few hours ago continued on, making me wish I had a pair of earplugs. I didn't need to ask what was being built outside. Even though I'd sent back the wheelchair, I knew what they were working on. Poor Mrs. Gibson. She'd probably figured she'd one day have to accept a ramp being built up to her front door since her husband's body would have to give out eventually after ranching for sixty-plus years, but I doubted she'd anticipated her daughter's boyfriend who'd become paralyzed after getting thrown from a bull named VooDoo being responsible for the ramp.

To drown out the sound of the hammering, I squeezed my eyes closed and tried to fall asleep. Somehow, that only exacerbated the noise, so I just kept my eyes open and hoped that when night fell, they'd put away their hammers and give it up for a few hours.

But when night finally did come, those hammers were still pounding. I was getting close to throwing my head back and hollering for someone when a figure magically appeared in the doorway. I thought I'd seen Rowen pissed before, and I had—only about a few hundred times—but this was different. Based upon her expression, this was pissed to the tenth power.

Stepping inside the room, she shoved the door closed. It slammed, rattling the window across the room. Her hair was pulled back into some messy bun, and she was wearing a mix of her country clothes and what I guessed was her Seattle wardrobe, making her look as though someone with split personalities had dressed her. Rowen's skin was so white I'd always teased her that sunlight actually bounced off her skin instead of absorbing into it, but tonight, at least in her face, she was so flushed she looked more red than white.

She stayed by the door, butting her shoulder into it and shifting her eyes in my direction. "We're going to have our talk now," she stated in a relatively calm voice.

"Been looking forward to it."

Her eyebrows peaked. "You remember how this is going to work? Maybe I should recap . . . by having a talk, I mean I'm going to talk and you're going to listen." She pointed at me before zipping her fingers across the seam of her lips. "Is that understood?"

My eyes rolled. Rowen and I didn't do one-sided conversations too well. "No promises."

Shoving off the door, she reached into her back pocket and removed a roll of duct tape. From the look of it, the roll was brand new. From the look of her, she was planning on using every last scrap of it on me.

When she took her first step my direction, I would have made a zipping motion across my lips if I could have. Instead, I clamped my lips tight and gave her a "Happy now?" look. She paused, probably waiting to see if I really could keep my mouth shut, before moving closer and sliding the duct tape roll over her wrist like it was a bracelet. I didn't doubt that she wore duct tape rolls as bracelets any old time, which meant Jesse got off cheap and easy when it came time to go jewelry shopping.

"You're behaving like an asshole. A really big one," she said, situating a hand on each hip as she glowered at me. "But instead of concentrating your assholery on yourself, as you typically have in the past, you're focusing it on everyone who cares about you or wants to help you. That's not okay." Her voice was mostly calm, although that was probably because I was keeping up with my whole lips-zipped thing. "I know why you're doing it. I get why you're pushing us away when, really, you need us most."

Of course another eye roll was in order, but she didn't threaten me with the duct tape again, so I guessed eye rolls were acceptable.

"I understand what you're thinking because, God, it actually pains me to say this—no joke, I feel like I'm about to shove a samurai sword through my stomach right now"—Rowen's face pulled into a pronounced wince before continuing—"but I understand what you're thinking because you and I are more alike than we're different. And shit, I just said that, didn't I?" She shook her head, looking as if that might have been the most sobering reality she'd had to wrap her mind around to date. "But my point is that I get you, Garth. You go and bust your back, and instead of relying on people to help you because that's what people do when someone they care about gets hurt, you'd rather push them away because that, Garth Black, is how we think we're proving our love for those people. We love them, therefore we can't allow them to spend their time taking care of us or attending to our needs or staying at our side, even when life throws us a cruel curve ball. I get that kind of thinking so much it's scary." She looked around like she was searching for a chair to settle into, but since none were close by, she just sat on the edge of my bed and curled her leg beneath her. "We love them so much we don't want to bury them with burdens. Right?"

When she seemed to be waiting for some kind of response from me, I offered a nod, eyeing the duct tape roll still swinging from her wrist.

"There was a time when I would have rather let Jesse go than have him stay and feel obligated to dole out my medication or wipe my butt."

My brows hit my hairline in warning. All things of a toileting nature were a sensitive topic, for obvious reasons.

"I thought that mindset was like the purest form of love there was—cutting someone loose when my life became a clusterfuck to spare them from the same thing happening to theirs—but that's a seriously messed up view of love, and it sure as hell isn't pure." She shook her head, pulling at a thread dangling from the hem of her dark jeans. "That's conditional love. The kind we might justify as being okay because it's not us saying we'll only love them if they do this or don't do this, but instead we'll only let *them* love *us* if we do this or don't do this. But how is that real love, Black? How can we feel the way we do about the people we do and justify letting them go?"

When she paused again, I could tell from her eyes that she wanted me to answer—in words instead of facial expressions. "We justify it because we want the best for them, and we realize we're not that." My voice sounded tight. I wrote it off as being from the prolonged silence instead of the real reason I knew it was off.

"But would letting them go be what's best for them really?" she asked in what was quite possibly the quietest voice Rowen Sterling-Walker possessed. "Would you like it if Josie did the same thing to you if she was in this bed instead of you? Would you believe her pushing you away and letting you go was what was 'best for you'?"

She let those questions hang in the air for so long I doubted I'd ever be able to forget them. In some way, I knew those questions would always haunt me.

I felt my brows pinch together as I worked to put my thoughts together—they didn't seem to want to stick. "Just because I know what I'd do if Josie's and my situations were reversed doesn't mean I can assume that's the same choice she'd make for herself. Just because she'd have to wrestle me into an iron box, padlock it, and ship me off to Tel Aviv to push me away doesn't mean I'll have to do the same to her."

Rowen graced me with a look that made it seem like she was having a conversation with a kindergartener. "Have you tried asking Josie for *her* opinion?" She lifted a brow and gave my arm what looked like a hard shove. I didn't have to feel it to realize that was Rowen's way of trying to shove, cram, or force some sense into me. "Have you tried talking to the woman you love, the one who loves you in return, to see what she has to say about what happens next? You know, hear her input on what she'd like for her future instead of choosing for her?"

I narrowed my eyes at her. "I'm picking up on your sarcasm, and after putting up with it for so long now, it no longer has an effect on me."

"Come on, Black." Another arm shove. "Ask her. That's all I'm asking of you. Could you imagine if Josie started acting the way you've been lately because she was trying to do what was best for you without even asking you for your opinion on what was best for you?" Rowen's nose wrinkled. "Damn, that was a mouthful, but did you get what I said?"

"Yeah, I got it. You've never had much of an issue at getting your point across, Sterling-Walker."

She lifted her eyes toward the ceiling before getting back to boring through mine. "Yeah, but does you getting it mean you're actually going to ask her about what she thinks and wants? Or are you going to keep on playing the martyr who's convinced himself that maybe he tricked life for a while but deep down he's never deserved anything good because there's nothing inside of him that's good?"

When I looked away, she leaned over me until she was in my field of vision again. When I looked away again, she did the same thing. Finally, I gave in and met her pointed stare with one of my own. "Don't project your warped views on me."

"I'm not," she said in that still-calm voice. "I'm identifying."

My heartbeat was starting to pick up, not really from what Rowen was saying but from how what she was saying was hitting me. "Stop identifying then."

She tilted her head, a partial smile crawling into place. "I will. When you stop trying to force my best friend into a life she doesn't want."

I huffed sharply. "That life she doesn't want meaning taking care of a cripple for the next fifty years?"

Rowen leaned in closer and arched an eyebrow. "Spending the rest of her life without the person she loves."

CHAPTER seven

YESTERDAY I'D BEEN hell-bent on skipping the doctor appointment Josie had made for me. How I'd wound up in the medical transport service van today, propped up in one of their loaner wheelchairs—which looked identical to the one I'd sent back—was beyond me, but I supposed it had something to do with what Rowen had said to me. Or more accurately, what she'd pounded into me.

I wasn't sold on what she'd said or converted to the way she viewed love versus the way I did, but she'd given me enough to chew on through the night and into the morning. So when Josie had peeked her head in earlier, asking me if I still wanted her to cancel the appointment, I told her I'd go, doing my best to keep my doubt and skepticism to myself. If she wanted to believe there was a chance for me to make a recovery, I wouldn't rob her of that. I would have given my useless left nut to still feel any margin of hope.

She'd been so out-of-her-mind happy I'd agreed to go that she'd rushed over, thrown herself over my lap, and kissed me so hard and so long I almost forgot I couldn't feel anything from the neck down because everything north of that area was feeling pretty damn amazing. Only when I went to fold my arm around her back to pull her closer was I abruptly reminded of my predicament . . . if you can consider being a quadriplegic a "predicament."

That kiss had been an escape, a vessel capable of transporting me to another world, and that realization led me to wonder if I could just spend the rest of my life kissing Joze. Then being paralyzed wouldn't be so damn hard to face. If I could always feel her lips formed around mine, her soft breath warming my neck, her hands tangled in my hair . . . if I could just freeze that moment of perfection for the next however many more years I had left, I could do it. I could live as a paralyzed man and leave this world with a smile on my face. If only I could just keep Josie this close . . . if only . . .

I'd had so many "if only"s in my past I'd let them suck the life out of my present. But "if only" didn't just apply to a person's past—it could also direct one's future. If only I'd gotten into that top-notch college. If only I'd gotten that promotion. If only I'd gotten that girl to fall in love with me. If only I'd achieved, earned, or succeeded at such and such, my life would be perfect. But that was a falsehood. A lie wrapped up in the veneer of what appeared to be the truth. If only I'd saved the world ten times over, earned the fame, glory, money, and the girl . . . and got to eat prime rib every day for breakfast, lunch, and dinner . . . my life wouldn't be perfect. If only I could just keep kissing Josie for the rest of my life . . . my life wouldn't be perfect. Because hers wouldn't be.

I might have been, and still was to a certain extent, a selfish, single-minded son of a bitch, but even I couldn't be okay with allowing my quest for a perfect life take away hers. Josie couldn't spend the rest of her life kissing me. She had so much more to give and to experience and to see. She had more worlds to light on fire as she'd lit mine. She had more people to make laugh and smile and leave her impression on. She had a whole life to live, and just because my life had been so scaled down that kissing her for the next fifty years was all I wanted didn't mean that was all she wanted. Or deserved.

My life had grown small. Microscopically small. Hers was still immense, spilling over into the realm of infinite almost. I wouldn't allow her to shrink her world in order to stay in mine. I couldn't. It would have been the cruelest, most despicable thing I'd ever done . . . and I'd done plenty of things that fell into those categories.

That didn't mean I was resolved to keep pushing her away as quickly as I could—Rowen's mini-sermon was still sitting heavily on my mind, and I couldn't seem to shake it off quite yet—but it also didn't mean I would let her spend her days and nights at my bedside. If there was a way to stay in each other's lives while she still lived hers as fully as I knew she could and deserved, then I'd consider—*consider*—abandoning my pushing-away agenda. But I recognized that was more of a baseless hope than a founded reality.

Josie could tell my head was heavy with something, and by the time we rolled to a stop in front of the doctor's building adjoined to the hospital, she'd already asked me three times what I was thinking. I didn't tell her what was really on my mind, but I answered with a partial truth about thinking of the future. From the way she'd looked away from me after I answered her the same way for the third time, I knew she could tell I was hiding something. She was right of course, but I couldn't very well tell her I was contemplating the best possible future for her and if that involved me in some fraction of a capacity.

The guy driving the medical van came around to open the large back doors. I didn't know how much this little trip had cost—probably not nearly as much as the fifteen-hour ambulance ride—but I couldn't keep racking up these kinds of bills. I felt the hospital bill from down in Casper coming, and from what I knew of the tests they'd run on me, paired with people's complaints about the astronomical costs associated with hospitals stays and procedures, I knew I'd probably require a fifth of Jack before I could open that envelope. Too bad I'd given up drinking the hard stuff months ago. I'd probably never needed a drink more, so of course this was the point in my life I'd grown a conscience.

"Have a nice ride?" the driver, whose nametag identified him as Lou, asked. He lent Josie a hand to guide her out of the van.

I tried not to glare at his hand curling around hers. But it was a gesture I would have sold my soul to be able to do, and I couldn't keep my glare contained. I think it became more of a scowl even.

"It was fucking fantastic," I answered as he messed with some dials and buttons to lower the platform I was on. "But since I didn't see any comment cards floating around back there—not that I could fill them out in my current state—here's a few suggestions: Get an air freshener because it smells like nothing short of a hundred people have shit themselves in the back of this thing in the past month, screw down whatever the hell is rattling around in the front of the van before you become responsible for driving a physically disabled person mentally disabled to match, and please, this is the most important part

. . ." My gaze lifted to the bumper stickers plastered around the interior of the van as the ramp lowered me closer to the ground. "Get rid of the slew of positive affirmations you have glued to every inch of bare wall inside there. 'Believe you can, and you're halfway there'? 'Every day is a second chance'? 'Don't be afraid to fail, be afraid not to try'?" A sharp laugh slipped past my lips as I shook my head. "You do realize that with the business you're in—transporting people so handicapped they can't move themselves—concepts like every day being a second chance and just giving it your best are *not* realistic or even viable solutions to our problems, right? Just thinking myself happy or inhaling love and exhaling hate won't make me whole. So why don't you rip down those damn things and save the rest of your transports from being reminded of how small their lives are and how they've lost most, if not all, control of them?"

I hadn't meant to end my spiel shouting and red-faced. I hadn't even meant to go off like that, but from the looks on Lou's and Joze's faces, I might as well have been spilling my internal organs on the pavement. Lou's smile fell as he focused on lowering the platform the rest of the way to the ground, and Josie's eyes shifted from narrowing to looking close to spilling over with tears. I regretted saying what I had. Thinking it was one thing, but spewing all of my anger and frustration when people were around—especially the person I cared about most—was not acceptable. Even if I did decide I needed to push her away.

"Sorry," I said around a sigh. "Just ignore the bitter, raving madman in the wheelchair. The world pissed on him, so he's trying to piss on it right back. I'll try harder not to take it out on innocent bystanders."

When I looked at Josie, she was clearly avoiding making eye contact with me. Lou seemed to be of the same mindset. Josie stepped up on the curb and waited while Lou moved my wheelchair from the platform and headed for the sidewalk.

"Just give me a ring when your appointment's over, and I'll pick you back up here," he said in a formal voice to Josie.

She nodded, working up a small smile as she stood beside me once Lou had me on the sidewalk.

"Do you want me to show you again how this operates?" he asked her.

"Nah, I'm pretty sure I've got it," she said. "If I need some help, I can play a pretty convincing damsel in distress."

That got a chuckle out of Lou and a bristle out of me. I didn't like the idea of someone besides me rushing in to save the day or the moment or whatever needed saving in Josie's life. I didn't like scanning the people moving in and out of the hospital and wondering which one or ones would rush in to help a girl like Joze.

"I'll see you later then," Lou said. He closed up the back of his van before crawling behind the wheel.

Behind me, I heard Josie exhale. It was a slight sound, and the emotion in it might have been imagined, but it almost sounded like she was standing at the base of a mountain and staring up at it after being told she had an hour to summit it. It was the kind of exhale a person gave when they were tasked with an impossible challenge.

"Hey, Joze?" I tried glancing at her over my shoulder, but the chair made it difficult. "I'm sorry about all that. I really am—"

"Shit," she said under her breath.

"Yeah, I know I've been acting like a piece of shit," I said. "That's an understatement, but—"

"Not shit you." Her voice was hinging on hysterical. "Shit I just left my purse in the van that's currently driving away." She flew around the side of my wheelchair, raising her arm to try to flag it down.

"Joze, wait!" I knew her purse would be okay for a couple hours, and the upside to leaving it in the back of Lou's van was that when she was reunited with it, her purse would be the most enlightened and insightful purse in existence, brimming over with positive affirmations and shit.

Josie didn't hear me though. She was one-track minded. She was about to step out into the road when something came into view from the corner of my eye: a big truck with big tires and big sounds. How Josie was oblivious to its size and sound was beyond me, but I guessed whatever was in her purse seemed more important.

"Josie, stop!" I shouted as she took a step into the road, the truck barreling closer.

Still she heard nothing, neither my voice nor the thunderous growl of a diesel engine powering closer. The road leading up to the hospital was rounded and at an incline, so while I could see the truck coming, the driver couldn't see us yet. Even if he could have seen us, he wouldn't have, because the driver was flailing one arm, looking frantically at the buildings instead of the road. Beside him, a young woman was breathing heavily and seemed to be holding her stomach.

Shit.

The driver didn't see Josie. Josie didn't see the truck. A catastrophe was moments away, and other than my raised voice, I had no way to stop it.

"Josie!" I cried, my voice more of a plea than a warning.

Right as she was about to take another bound into the road, someone snagged Josie's hand and whipped her back onto the sidewalk seconds before the truck came speeding by. Something I couldn't understand slipped from her mouth when she finally noticed the truck and how close it had come to hitting her. I was in the middle of exhaling the most relieved sigh I could recall when I twisted my head back to thank whoever it was who'd swooped in to save Josie. Only when I found the space behind us empty did I look over to find a hand still firmly clutched around Josie's. Like me, she was staring at that hand. Well, she was more like gaping at it.

"Oh my god, Garth," she whispered, her voice shaky from either what had almost happened or what was currently happening. Her hand twisted, her fingers tangling through the ones secured around hers. "Your hand . . . it moved . . . it's *moving* . . ." She smiled at our conjoined hands, returning the squeeze my hand had just given hers. "What just happened?"

I recognized my hand was in hers. To have gotten there, it had to have moved, which had to mean something good, but that wasn't what I was most concerned with right then. "You just ran out in front of a truck whose driver looked like he was minutes away from becoming a father and wasn't exactly paying attention to the road or pedestrians."

The truck was long gone, hopefully finding the ER

entrance before his wife or girlfriend delivered their baby in the cab, but I still lifted my middle finger toward where the truck had disappeared. Just thinking about it got me all riled up. When my other hand started flying about, Josie's gaze drifted toward it, her eyes widening.

"I mean, shit, Joze, do you *want* to end up like me? Stuck in a wheelchair for the rest of your life? Do you want to spend the rest of your life dead?"

She bit her lip to subdue her grin, but it didn't work.

"Please, Joze, work with me here. I can't move. A little help preserving your life would be much appreciated."

I could have gone on and on—I was so worked up about what had just happened and just *could* have happened—but when she crouched beside me, her lips pressing softly then not so softly into my knuckles, my mind shifted gears. What else had just happened started to settle in.

"I can feel your hand," I said, sounding out of breath.

Josie smiled as she continued to slide her mouth along the ridges and valleys of my knuckles.

"I can feel your lips." My eyes closed from the pure, unparalleled pleasure of her lips moving against my hand. Even at our most intimate, I wasn't sure I'd ever felt something so intense. "I *moved*."

That made her laugh. With her mouth still pressed to my hand, her laugh vibrated up my arm and seemed to work its way deep inside. "I'll say you moved," she said as her laugh rolled to an end.

"Someone had to," I grumbled. Even though I was pissed like nothing else about what had almost happened, thanks to two people focusing on everything *but* the road, my anger couldn't dampen the hope trickling into my veins. I'd moved. Without willing my arm to lift or telling my hand to grab hers, something had fired to life inside me, and a minute later, it didn't seem in a hurry to extinguish itself.

"Just when I'm sure you couldn't possibly get any more wonderful . . ." She lifted her mouth from my hand long enough to smile at me.

I brushed her cheek with my thumb. I'd never realized until right then how Josie's skin was the smoothest thing I'd ever felt. "I go and lift my arm?" I peaked a brow at her.

Her smile stretched as she watched my other arm lift into the air. Then her eyes shifted back to mine. "You go and save me when I was supposed to be saving you."

CHAPTER eight

I WAS LATE for my appointment. I blamed it on Josie. If she hadn't gone and stepped into traffic without looking, then I wouldn't have had to save her. Then we wouldn't have spent a good half hour in a state of shock and surprise, trying to figure out what had just happened.

When we did finally make it to Dr. Miracle Worker's office, no one seemed to mind we were late. Probably because the patient they'd expected to see paralyzed from the neck down was only paralyzed from the waist down.

"Can you feel this?" Dr. Miracle Worker, whose actual name was Dr. Murphy, asked as he tapped above my knee with a tool that looked like it belonged in a torture room instead of an exam room.

I shook my head. "No."

Josie was standing beside my wheelchair and hadn't once let go of the hand that had grabbed her. Even when we'd had to fill out some paperwork, she hadn't let it go. I thought that, like me, she was afraid the spell would wear off if she let go, so she kept hanging on.

"Can you feel any sensation at all?" Dr. Murphy tapped at the same spot with what looked like a bit more force.

"Nothing," I answered.

Dr. Murphy nodded, squinting as if he were lost in some internal dialogue. "And up until just outside, you were unable to move or feel anything from your waist to your neck, correct?"

I nodded.

More internal dialogue. From my estimate, Dr. Murphy had said five times more to himself than he had to Josie and me.

"What do you think that means?" Josie asked, sliding closer to me. "Does it mean he's getting better?"

Dr. Murphy put away the torture device and shoved backward on his stool. He rolled halfway across the room, toward the phone hanging on the wall. "The spine doesn't 'get better' in the traditional way we think of some parts of our body healing. If a vertebra is broken, it doesn't just 'fix' itself, or if there's extensive nerve damage, those nerves won't heal on their own. Generally, if a person is paralyzed from a back injury, they stay that way. There are very few instances of a patient starting out paralyzed then regaining motion."

"Gee, don't soften the truth, Doc. Make us bend over before you slam it up there."

Josie threw me a mild look of disapproval, but her hand didn't loosen around mine.

The doctor lifted a salt-and-pepper brow at me. "I didn't take you for the kind of patient who preferred the truth in a softened version. Shall I tailor my approach? I've got plenty of methods of explaining this."

I'd barely spoken a handful of words to him, and I already knew he was the best doctor I'd ever had. "Nah, you got me profiled correctly. I don't like it sweet and slow. I much prefer it rough and hard."

Any other girl would have been a blushing red mess, but instead of shifting and hiding behind a sheet of hair, Josie flashed me a wink and settled the edge of her backside on the arm of my wheelchair.

"Then I guess it's time to take a look at those X-rays and see what the future has in store for you." Lifting the phone off its hook, he pressed a button. "Jody, would you bring in Mr. Black's X-rays please?" He paused for a moment, nodding before replying, "Yes, I understand. Thank you for taking a look at them for me." After that, he hung up.

Before I had a moment to prepare myself for whatever was coming, in walked a woman I assumed was Jody, carrying a file containing my X-rays—more like a file containing my fate. Josie's hand tightened around mine. Mine did the same, and just feeling that seemingly small measure of comfort, though there was nothing small about it, reminded me that no matter what those X-rays told us, I was holding Joze's hand, something I'd never thought I'd be able to do it again. Whatever came next, I could take it in stride.

Jody opened the file and slid a few X-rays onto the dark screen, acknowledged us with a nod, and slipped out the door. I swallowed. She hadn't smiled or offered a greeting; she'd graced me with the slightest of glances before ducking out that door. If those X-rays told the story of a man whose back would be just fine, I doubted she would have just hightailed it out of the room like she wanted to be at the far end of the building before Dr. Murphy took a look at them.

"Let's see what's going on here," Dr. Murphy said to himself as he headed over to the X-rays.

From the time he stood to the time he flipped on the screen lights and illuminated the slides of my spinal column from varying angles, I didn't think Josie or I took a single breath. By the time the good doctor lifted his hand to his chin, rubbing at it as if he were searching for what to say, I felt like I was close to passing out from lack of oxygen.

"This is . . ." Dr. Murphy shifted his weight, still rubbing at his chin. "Interesting." He leaned in closer to the slides, narrowing his eyes.

I stretched my neck, cracking it. Josie practically flinched when she heard the small pop.

"That's a diagnosis I'm not sure what to do with, Doc," I said, making sure to strip the anxiety from my voice because Josie was swimming in so much of it that it was spilling out of her ears. "What does that mean in cow-boy-with-a-GED terms? Will I keep the movement from my waist up? Will I regain the feeling from my waist down?"

Dr. Murphy stayed quiet, leaning forward before leaning back and repeating the cycle. When I studied the X-rays, all I saw were a bunch of grayish-white shapes surrounded by darkness, but he apparently saw something else entirely. I saw a word where he saw a thousand-page novel.

"Doc?"

"Well, now I see why the doctor in Casper was so confused when I spoke to him about you." He tilted his head to one side then the other.

"You've been staring at those things for what feels like an hour, and I still don't know what my X-rays mean, in layman's terms, about what I can expect in the future."

Josie slid a bit closer when my voice rose. "Rough and hard, Doc, remember? I can take it." I waited for him to tear his eyes away from the X-rays long enough to meet mine. When he did, I leaned forward in my wheelchair. "What's going to happen to me?"

"You want my professional opinion?" he asked, shoving his hands into the pockets of his big white lab coat.

I shrugged. "That's why we're here."

He took another look at the X-rays before sighing. "I don't know."

I stayed quiet, waiting for him to expand on that. Surely a doctor wouldn't just say *I don't know* without adding some clarifying comments, right? No doctor would look a man in the eye and tell him he wasn't sure if everything south of his belt would ever move again and not give some additional commentary.

"With all due respect, we didn't come here for 'I don't know,' Dr. Murphy." Josie's voice sounded far more controlled than mine would have been. "Would you mind telling us what you *do* know?"

Mr. Murphy's gaze left mine to land on Josie. The wrinkles lining his face flattened. "I can tell you that none of Garth's vertebrae are fractured."

Josie and I exhaled at the same time.

"But his spinal column has gone through a serious amount of trauma, and my guess is that extensive nerve damage and swelling are causing his paralysis."

"So that means that eventually he'll recover, right? He'll walk again one day?"

I hadn't realized how hope-deprived Josie was until I heard her voice right then. It was bursting with hope, but it only took one lined forehead from Dr. Murphy for her hope to peel away in layers. At the moment a doctor was about to tell me I'd never make a full recovery, I was infinitely more concerned about how the news would affect Josie than how it would affect me.

"If it's only swelling, then yes, maybe Garth will walk again," he said before clearing his throat. "But if nerve damage is also playing a part in his paralysis, that's impossible to say. Sometimes nerves can repair themselves, and sometimes they cannot. It just depends on the level of damage."

Josie was wringing my hand so hard it started to go numb. When I felt the sensation leaving my hand, I panicked and slipped it free of hers. Blood drained back into it, and the prickles started, but it took my heart a while longer to recover.

"If it is nerve damage, will he keep the motion from his waist up?" Josie sounded afraid of the question, but I knew she was more likely afraid of the answer.

Dr. Murphy turned off the light box, hooked his foot around his stool to bring it closer, and dropped onto it. "If you're looking for odds and probabilities, I can give you those." He clasped his hands and leaned forward. He looked both of us in the eye. "But until I can get Garth in an MRI and run some more tests, I won't be able to give you hard facts."

"MRI?" I said. "That's one of those machines they slide you into that's about the size of a mouse hole and tell you not to move for the whole hour you're in there, right?"

A smile tugged at the corners of Dr. Murphy's mouth. "That's about it, right. Are you claustrophobic? Because I can order a couple of sedatives to be administered before you're shoved into the mouse hole."

I nudged Josie when I saw her thinking about smiling. I shook my head. "Claustrophobic? No. The day my blood pressure starts to rise from the thought of climbing into small spaces is the day I'm going to have someone send me out to pasture and put me out of my misery. But it does sound expensive." When Dr. Murphy crossed his arms and nodded but didn't offer the actual price tag, I asked, "*How* expensive?"

"You're uninsured, correct?"

I made a face. "Lucky for me, I sure am."

Dr. Murphy came close to wincing with me. "I'd estimate that out-of-pocket, it'll run you upwards of four, maybe five thousand dollars. Tack on another thousand for the dye injection we'll do first, and that'll put you in the ballpark."

My eyes came close to bursting out of their sockets. "Are you telling me that this MRI thing is going to cost me a grand total of five to six thousand dollars?"

I couldn't comprehend it. An hour in a big machine would cost me more than I'd made riding bulls four years ago. All of the sweat and blood and bruises I'd endured that year to make that kind of money, and I'd have to wave bye-bye to it after spending one hour in a glorified mouse hole? If Josie hadn't been gaping at Dr. Murphy as well, I would have asked him to repeat himself to see if I'd heard wrong.

"That's why it's recommended that people carry some kind of health insurance. These kinds of tests don't come with coin slots you can just drop a few quarters in and hop in and out a minute later."

I rubbed my forehead, wondering how I could have just regained feeling from my waist up yet still feel my dreams slipping away. All I could envision was a huge stack of hospital bills eating all my winnings from the past year and, along with it, Josie's and my plan to start our own ranch. "What would happen if I didn't get the MRI?"

"The world would come to a screeching halt," Dr. Murphy answered promptly. Before my head could whip in his direction, he rolled closer and continued, "The MRI will show us what's going on with your spine. There's damage there somewhere, and we can guess what it is until we're blue in the face, but we won't know for sure until we get the MRI results."

Josie kept nodding her head while I wanted to shake mine. "Can it change anything if I do it? Or will it just change what we know?"

Dr. Murphy gave me a curious look, as if he didn't understand where I was coming from. That was ironic since I didn't know where he was coming from either.

"When we know what we're dealing with, we can figure out how best to move forward," he said. "I can't diagnose you blindly, nor can I create a rehab plan for you until we know what we're dealing with so we know how best to attack it."

Josie was still nodding along with Dr. Murphy's every word, making me wonder if I were insane for wanting to give some pause before dropping thousands of dollars or if they were. Like the ever-profound Clay Black used to tell me when I asked for a few dollars when we were out of milk, money didn't grow on trees. Shit, if it did, Clay Black would have drunk nicer whiskey.

"But how can you 'attack it' if we do find out extensive nerve damage is responsible for my paralysis? How can you 'fix it' if I'll always be paralyzed to some degree?" My hand wrapped around the arm of my chair and squeezed. In the few days since the accident, my strength seemed to have diminished. "Is surgery an option? Could you lay me on my stomach, open me up, and untangle all of those nerves before sewing me shut again? Is that an option?"

Dr. Murphy slid his hands back into his lab coat pockets and sighed. "No, it's not a very viable option, but that doesn't mean it's totally out. An MRI might show us something that would require surgery. We won't know for sure though until we get it done."

Surgery. He hadn't said it, but I guessed for a person in my condition, it could even mean *surgeries*. Not even I was brave enough to ask how much those surgeries would cost, with all the staff and equipment and time they would take, if an MRI cost five plus grand. "And what is the like-lihood I'd make a full recovery if you did surgery? What-ever it might be based on, whatever you might see from this MRI?" Could I speak in any more hypotheticals before I started to sound like a politician?

One of his shoulders rose. "Not promising. In terms of numbers, approximately two to five percent of patients make a full recovery, in terms of how you've defined it, after a severe spinal trauma like yours."

My eyes widened. Even the ardent pessimist inside me had guessed a number higher than that. "Then why perform surgery if the odds are that bad? Why not save a patient the pain, expense, and misplaced hope if only a few in every hundred actually get better?"

Josie was staying quiet beside me, no longer bobbing her head in agreement. Instead, she was twisting her hands in her lap and biting her lip as though she was nervous. I wasn't used to seeing her nervous, and witnessing it made a pit open up in my stomach.

Dr. Murphy rolled closer, not seeming to blink as he stared at me. "Just because the likelihood of failing is high doesn't mean you don't try." He lifted a brow, watching me carefully. "I thought that was a concept you bull riders would be quite familiar with."

CHAPTER nine

FIVE DAYS HAD passed since my appointment with Dr. Murphy, but I felt as if twice that number of days had passed. Being confined to a wheelchair, unable to go where I wanted to go or do the things I wanted to do, made life slow to an agonizing pace. I was used to spending my days working hard in some capacity, and even though I might have complained about it on those days I'd had to search for a stray calf in a blizzard and felt like my fingers and toes were so cold I could've snapped them right off, the work had made the time go by quickly. I'd been useful, filling my days with hard labor and earning a night of hard sleep. But now? I did next to nothing during the days, so the same followed me into the night. I'd never had such a hard time sleeping.

Joze suggested I call Dr. Murphy to get a prescription for sleeping pills, but I hadn't. I knew what my problem was, and it didn't seem like one I could fix. How could a person who'd spent a lifetime working hard instantly change to working hardly at all and expect to sleep at night? If I hadn't done anything during the day to make me tired, I didn't deserve to sleep. That was the whole reason humans slept in the first place: to recover.

But I hadn't done anything to recover from, so that

translated into me not sleeping, which translated into me spending wide-eyed nights thinking of nothing but what had happened and what should happen going forward.

I could move from my waist up, which was a miracle I was still thanking my lucky stars for. But after I'd gotten used to having the strength back in my upper half, I found myself getting impatient for the same to happen to my lower half. I was a greedy son of a bitch, I recognized that, but how could I not be? I'd gotten my arms back—I wanted my legs back too. I wanted *everything* that resided south of my waist back.

Wondering if Josie and I would ever be able to be close like we had been before also kept me up at night. I could wrap my arms around her and hold her hand now, but that wasn't where I wanted our physical relationship to start and end. Especially after having experienced just how fucking amazing the rest had been and could be again if

. . .

If . . .

"If" haunted me every hour of every day. It plagued me every minute of every night. It had become a poison to me, choking off one piece of me at a time.

As ungrateful as I might have seemed, I was grateful for the increased mobility that came with moving my upper half. Instead of that spaceship of a wheelchair that cost more than my truck, I could get around in a regular old wheelchair, using my own two arms to propel me. Rose Walker had had knee surgery last year and purchased a wheelchair to get around for the first few weeks afterward. When she and Neil heard I'd regained the movement in my arms, they'd dropped off the wheelchair and said I could use it if I wanted. One of the best things about it?

Totally free of charge. It didn't come with a price tag that would further dip into my diminishing savings account.

Although I supposed the wheelchair wasn't totally free, because when I could, I'd find some way to pay the Walkers back for their generosity. I could get around pretty well in the chair, although the Gibsons' farmhouse wasn't exactly wheelchair-friendly. Those old houses had been built with small rooms, small doorways, and small spaces. I'd gotten stuck more times than I could count, and I'd left more scuffmarks on Mrs. Gibson's walls than I guessed she wanted to count too. However, with the ramp at the front door, I could get outside whenever I wanted, and with summer in full swing, there couldn't have been a better time to be outside.

So I spent a lot of time outside. I spent some time inside. I repeated. I tried focusing on being thankful to be alive and able to move some of my body, but I couldn't appease myself with that. I couldn't tell myself I was lucky to be alive when I felt useless.

Tonight though, something eventful was happening. At least something more eventful than Joze creeping into my bed and burrowing close for an hour before she snuck back out so her parents wouldn't find us in bed together— because Lord forbid something like that happen. In my current state, I couldn't dodge Mr. Gibson's shotgun spray quite so nimbly as I could have before.

I lived for that hour though, that hour when we could lie beside each other and, if I tried really hard, pretend everything was just as it used to be, as though when her soft kisses at the base of my neck turned more urgent, I could gently roll over her and return the urgency until we'd met its demands. I could pretend when we woke up the next morning, I'd crawl out of bed to pull on some clothes and my boots before downing a few cups of coffee and hitting work early. During that sacred hour every night, it was easier to pretend life was how it had been, and I knew that was what was mainly what got me through the other twenty-three.

Tonight I'd get a few more hours of pretending life was back to normal. Jesse and Rowen were back in town for the weekend and had asked Josie if we could all go on a double date. Of course Josie had leapt at the invitation, because other than working the ranch and helping me, I didn't think she'd left the Gibsons' property since the doctor's appointment. She looked tired, weary. Almost as bad as I guessed I looked. She could put on the brave face and act the brave act with the best of them, but I knew my accident had affected her more than she told me it did. How could it not?

"What time are we meeting them again, Joze?" I hollered down the hall before rounding into the bathroom. Showers weren't a quick wash-and-go anymore. I needed almost an hour to do what had once taken me under two minutes.

"Eight o'clock!" she hollered back.

I heard pots bubbling and glass clinking from where she was in the kitchen. She and her mom had stripped their cherry trees dry earlier and spent the rest of the day canning cherry jam. I'd stayed out of the kitchen because the hot day had only been exacerbated by the lack of air conditioning and the stovetop that hadn't stopped boiling water for the past six hours.

"I'm going to hop in the shower and get ready." The last part of my sentence was cut off by the sound of something falling. It hadn't shattered, so at least it wasn't one of the glass preserving jars. From the tinny sound, I guessed it had been a metal pot. "Do you need some help in there?" I stopped outside the bathroom and started to wheel back down the hall.

"No!" Josie shouted. She stuck her head out of the kitchen and fired a wink at me. Her eyes drifted toward the bathroom, and her voice lowered so *hopefully* Mrs. Gibson wouldn't hear her. "You need some help in there?"

My heart pounded and my stomach tightened when what she was suggesting registered, but it didn't last long. She could suggest all she wanted, but I couldn't follow through. She could wink and give me looks and suck on her bottom lip the way she did now until the world had turned itself upside down, but that couldn't change what worked on my body and what didn't.

I conjured up a smile for her before rolling into the bathroom. "I think I can manage."

Closing a door while in a wheelchair was difficult, so it took me a while to get the bathroom door closed behind me. Once I was sealed inside, it took me far longer to regain my composure. If that was even what I could call it.

That hadn't been the first time I'd seen the *dot, dot, dot* in Josie's expression or the glimmer of mischief in her eyes, but instead of it getting easier to deal with, each time became more difficult. How could looking the woman I loved in the face and basically admitting I couldn't and might never again meet her needs in that way get easier? How could I get used to implying I wasn't capable of fulfilling that primal desire inside every single human being? Instead, each time I basically had to shoot her down tore off another piece of my heart, each piece larger than the last.

After giving myself a moment to regain whatever I'd lost and coming up empty, I began the tedious process of peeling off my clothes. Before I'd been injured, I was pretty sure I'd broken some clothes-shedding world records when leaping into bed with Joze, but now? I was breaking a different kind of record.

I'd wrangled a large herd of cattle together faster than the time it took me to get out of my shirt . . . and save for my hat, my shirt was the easiest part of the stripping down process. The pants were the worst because I was a stubborn SOB and hadn't surrendered to the elastic-band sweatpants that had been strongly suggested to me. I might not have been able to stay in a saddle or help heave a tractor out of a foot of mud, but I was still a cowboy at heart. That was the only part of me that could still lay claim to the title though.

My belt buckle was easy enough to get undone and the fly just as easy, but the actual sliding and shimmying out of a pair of jeans when I couldn't move anything south of my navel was damn hard. I was just bracing myself on one elbow to lift my backside up enough to begin the lengthy process of peeling my jeans off my ass when a soft knock sounded at the door before someone slipped inside.

"Sure you don't need any help?" Josie pressed her back into the door to shut it, grinning at me when she saw what I was in the process of losing.

I let my elbow go slack and fell back into the wheelchair, but I withheld my sigh. I wasn't sure why Josie was acting as though nothing had changed between us in that part of our relationship, but I didn't have to understand it. If that was what she needed to believe or wanted to hold onto, or if she just preferred to keep her head in the sand about the whole thing, if that helped her cope with all this, I didn't have to understand.

"What are you doing, Joze?" I readjusted my pants so they weren't about to fall off my hips. "Your mom's a room away, and you know how they feel about us being in the same room behind a closed door."

Josie turned the lock on the door, something I should have done the instant I'd wheeled in there so I wouldn't have to tell her I was incapable of giving her what she wanted. "My mom just went upstairs to take a nap. After the ten hours we spent picking, cleaning, and canning cherries today, her nap is going to turn into an all-night sleep-a-thon."

She pushed off the door and pulled her hair free of its messy bun. Rivers of long auburn hair spilled across her shoulders and back. Her skin was dewy with sweat, her clothes stained with cherry juice, and the beds of her fingernails were stained with the same. She'd worked hard, and she looked the part. I'd never found Josie more attractive than I did after a hard day's work when she hadn't let trivial things like manicures or callouses or sweat stop her from giving it her all. She was the type of woman who had a hundred times more grit than the woman next to her, and that, along with the way she could make me feel with even the briefest of looks from across a roomful of people, was what had always made Josie Gibson irresistible to me.

"My dad, if you're wondering, is at the monthly ranchers' dinner at the community center in town and won't be back until the ribs and cornbread run out, which, if it's like the dinners in months past, won't be until about ten o'clock." Her smile tipped higher on one side as she tugged her shirt free of her cut-offs. "That gives us all the time in the world to do whatever we want . . . however we want . . ." In one smooth motion, her shirt was up and over her head and falling to the floor. "As often as we want."

She had on her pretty white lace bra—the one that had so little actual lace more of her chest popped out of it than was actually concealed behind it. I should have looked away or closed my eyes or something, but the only way I would have been capable of not looking at Josie was if someone carved my eyeballs straight out of my sockets.

"Jesse and Rowen. We're meeting them at eight." My voice was shallow, my breathing rushed. "I've got to get showered."

"I've got to get showered too." Josie lifted her arms and spun. "Obviously."

"Would you like to go first? I can wait."

Josie moved so close her legs bumped into the edge of my wheelchair seat. She nudged my legs apart to fit hers between them and dropped her hands to the armrests. Her face lowered to mine. "I thought we could go green and shower together."

Her gaze dipped to my chest then lower, lingering on the place I should have felt was about to burst if I didn't bury myself inside Josie, which I already would have been busy doing if my back wasn't busted . . . or if I hadn't let my focus shift from VooDoo for half a second . . . or if I'd drawn another bull . . . or if I'd never climbed on top of a bull for the very first time as a kid. I could have been on top of Josie on the bathroom floor, making love to her the way she liked best—the way that required me covering her mouth when she came so we didn't scare the neighbors a mile down the road. I could have felt her legs tightening

105

around me as I moved inside her. I could have felt her pulsing around me as she came, pushing me the last little bit over the ledge of my own release if only . . .

If only nothing. Things were the way they were. I was what I was. No amount of wishing or dreaming or if only-ing could change that.

My hands lowered to the wheels, and I rolled myself back a few feet. "I don't think that's a good idea."

When she'd tried flirting while curled up beside me in bed, my rejection had hurt her. It had been instant and unmistakable on her face. But now, instead of punching her pursuit into reverse, she shifted into a higher gear and sped forward. "Fine. You don't have to shower with me if you don't want to." Winding her arms around her back, she unhooked her bra and slid the straps off her shoulders, one at a time, before letting it fall to the floor at her feet.

"Shit, Joze," I breathed, rolling back a few more feet. The increased physical distance between us didn't do anything to keep me from staring at her chest. Images of the way they'd felt in my hands or the way they moved when she was on top of me or how they tasted fired to life.

"My thoughts exactly." Her fingers worked at the top button of her cut-offs. "Other way around though."

"What do you mean?" I kept backing up until the wheelchair bumped into the wall.

"What I mean is, 'Shit, Garth.' I'm naked in front of you, practically begging you to jump in the shower with me and soap me up good and clean after you finish doing filthy things to me, and your response is to back yourself into a corner and break out in a cold sweat." She flailed her arms at me before tearing her cut-offs and panties down over her hips. When they landed at her feet, she slung them around her foot in my direction. The cut-offs fell on one of my feet, but the panties landed smack in my lap. They were silky and white, familiar from that time . . . "You remember those ones? God knows you've been acquainted with every pair of panties in my top drawer, but those ones you didn't just slide off or rip off or push aside like the rest."

I went from staring at the panties in my lap to her. She was naked and angry and ready and the most beautiful thing I'd ever seen. I wanted to draw her close and give her what she wanted, but it was impossible. How could I get her to see that? And then to accept that?

"I remember," I said slowly, trying not to let my mind drift too far or too long to that memory because it was a damn good one. To a point, memories were a man's greatest comfort, but past that point, they became a man's greatest torment.

"So what happened to the guy who sat beside me and just smiled when I slid out of those panties, gripped him with them the moment after I'd gotten his fly down, and rubbed one out under the table at that cowboy bar in Jackson last winter after he'd earned the highest score of his career? What happened to the guy who took me out to his truck five minutes later, laid me down, and flashed me another smile before putting his head between my legs so he could return the favor? What happened to him?" Her arms were flailing again, her voice echoing off the tile walls of the bathroom.

Instead of waiting for my answer, she charged to the shower, cranked the nozzle on, and leapt inside before it had had a chance to warm up. Thankfully the shower down here was a walk-in, so after adding a shower chair and a handheld shower head, it had worked out ideally for me. But right then, I wished it wasn't so accessible. I wished I didn't know I could just roll inside that shower and slide my hands all over Josie's wet body. Because I wanted to. I fought with everything I had not to, but I wanted to so badly I could taste blood thanks to how hard I was biting my tongue.

"I can't give you that, Joze," I said, wishing she'd close the shower curtain and put me out of my misery . . . every other moment wishing she wouldn't. "I'm sorry. I'd do a lifetime stint in hell to get another six inches below my waist to operate as well, but until the devil shows up at my door with a pen and a contract, I can't do anything about it." I swallowed against the ball trying to block every word I was saying. "I'm so fucking sorry."

She turned to face me. A moment later, I found myself wheeling closer. As soon as I realized what I was doing, I stopped. She made a point of noticing my nearer proximity to the shower and lifted an eyebrow. "There are more ways to be intimate than using what resides south of your belt buckle, you know. Lots of ways."

I felt my forehead wrinkle.

She shook her head at my apparent confusion. "Ways I know you're familiar with based on experience." Her tone sounded as if it was meant to be a nudge or a hint. "You've had no problem getting creative before, so what's stinting your creativity now? Did your imagination get paralyzed too?"

My body flinched like she'd just shoved me. "Josie —"

"What? I don't get it. I need to be close to you. I always have and always will."

I couldn't tell if she was crying or if the rivulets of water trailing down her cheeks were from the shower, but either way it *looked* as if she was crying. I pushed my chair closer until I could feel the steam across my face.

"Don't you need to feel close to me too?" Her voice sounded small as her eyes dropped to the shower floor.

The tightness in my throat came back in full force. "Of course I do, Joze."

Her eyes slowly lifted but not quite high enough to look at me. "Then what's the problem?"

Sighing, I motioned between her and my lap. Josie was naked, water streaming down her, and inviting me closer, but I had absolutely nothing going on down there. Nothing. If I wasn't so pissed off and frustrated, I might have cried. "Other than my malfunctioning dick?"

I hadn't meant it to be funny, but I noticed a smile tug at the corners of her mouth as she reached for a bottle of body wash and squeezed some into her palm. "Other than that."

When she turned away from me as she started to soap her skin, I found being vulnerable with her easier. For some reason, when her eyes were practically drilling holes through me, I found it more natural to tell her what I guessed she wanted to hear instead of the entire truth. "Isn't it obvious?"

"No," she almost snapped. "Whatever you're doing all the way over there while I'm lathering my chest here, there is nothing obvious about it."

Based on her experience with me before the accident, I understood her confusion. If she expected me to be the Garth from before instead of the Garth of right now, there was nothing obvious about what I was doing so far away from her. Part of me loved that she still saw me as that same man she'd fallen in love with, but the other part of me knew that would make everything so much harder . . . because I wasn't that man. Realizing that brought on a surge of anger.

"I'm in a wheelchair, for Christ's sake, Josie." I motioned at my chair—which I very likely would spend the rest of my life in. More anger coursed through me. "I'm handicapped. I can't move my legs. I can't get it up. I can't do anything a man my age should be able to do." Mrs. Gibson was only a few rooms away, and I should have kept my voice down, but there was no possible way to keep my voice down while saying the things I was saying. "Like stand up to a man who's disrespecting a woman. Or climb onto the back of a horse. Or drive a truck. Or take a piss on a fucking tree without having to cath myself first and wheel up to it. I'm half of a man, Joze." My voice broke, so I got myself back together before saying the rest. "You should be repulsed by me, not curling your finger and inviting me closer. So no, I don't understand why you'd want to be close to me after this."

For a long minute, nothing but silence and shifting stares passed between us. In that minute, I must have witnessed a dozen different emotions filter through her eyes, her expression keeping pace. Watching her was nearing the point of becoming too painful to bear when she stepped out of the shower. Water streamed down her body, collecting in puddles at her feet. Drops of water were fanned into her lashes and fell down her face when she blinked.

"You really can't understand why I'd still want to make love to you in whatever way we can figure out just because you got hurt?" Her eyes narrowed as they searched me for an answer. "Please tell me you're kidding."

I circled my finger around my face. "Not my kidding face."

Her hands curled into fists before she crossed her arms. I couldn't tell which she felt more, hurt or anger, but I guessed she felt some of both.

"I wanted to be with you before, I want to be with you now, and I'll want to be with you forever because *I love you*." She said each word so slowly, so purposefully, it was as if there was nothing she believed in more, as if there was nothing she was more passionate about. She didn't seem to blink as she continued. "I. Love. You. Do you really think that came with the condition that so long as you were still walking, I'd love you? Or with the condition that if you turned into a prudish lunatic who hid in corners while I pretty much handed you a play-by-play of how I wanted you to do me, I'd stop loving you? Do you really think that anything could happen to you or change you or that I could find out about you that could just make all the love I have for you disappear? Is that really what you think?"

I was quiet, not knowing how to reply. Before she'd, in so many words, reminded me that her love came without conditions, yes, I really had doubted why she'd want to be with me if I was going to spend the next fifty years as a mostly helpless invalid, but now . . . now I didn't know what to think.

I was still trying to sort through it all when she spoke again. "Then fuck you, Garth Black. Fuck you for confusing my love with the cheap, shallow kind you could find with just about any tramp begging you to sign her bra."

Now I knew with certainty the moisture running down her cheeks wasn't caused by the shower. How could I make it such a priority to make Josie happy yet be responsible for so many of her tears?

"You might as well have just chosen one of them because then you would be right—they would have bailed at the first mention of paralysis. They would have ditched you before finding out your dick might never work again, as you're so obsessed with, or before having to bathe, feed, and diaper the man they loved for the rest of his life even came up. They would have fled so quickly you wouldn't have known what happened. Yet here I've stayed beside you, *with* you, every step of the way. So maybe I really am a fool, if I'm the only one of us who expected me to be made of something better and stronger. Maybe I should have run, especially if that's as much credit as you've given me this whole time. But I didn't run. I didn't run because I *couldn't.*" She was almost sobbing, every third or fourth word breaking as tears streamed down her face. "I couldn't run from you, because I love you so goddamn much it's buried so far inside me I could never dig deep enough to pull it out. I love you so much that when I look at you, I don't see a man in a wheelchair." She shook her head, biting her lip so hard it made a deep indentation. "All I see is the man I want to spend the rest of my life with. All I see is the man I love."

Her confession ended in a whisper so faint I didn't hear the word "love." Instead, I saw it tumble from her lips.

Scrubbing my face, I sighed. Where the hell did I go from here? How the hell did I respond to that? I knew she loved me like that and I knew I was a bastard who didn't deserve that kind of love and I knew I loved her the same way, putting myself second to her and without condition. So how could I let her waste her life being confined to my small, lonely existence when she deserved so much more?

All of the answers eluded me. Big fucking surprise.

"Joze . . ."

"Don't 'Joze' me!" she snapped, her tone reaching all its former angry glory. "You don't get to call me that or imply all that you do in that tone if you've been thinking all these months that I'd cut my losses and bail if the going got tough." She blew out a sharp breath and threw her arm at the door. "You can leave now. I think you're right. Us taking a shower together isn't such a good idea."

Turning her back to me, she stepped inside the shower and slid the shower curtain closed. She even made sure to seal the cracks on either end. I felt a pain in my chest come on so suddenly and so sharply I leaned forward. I felt like I was having a heart attack but one that wouldn't end.

"Besides, I can take care of myself if you don't want to use your imagination and take care of me anymore," she added as steam billowed out from the top of the shower.

She wanted me to leave. I *should* have wanted to leave, but something about her turning her back and shutting me out because I'd hurt her made me move closer. I'd been trying on and off to push her away for days, and it had finally seemed to work, so why were my fingers curling around the edge of the shower curtain, about to pull it open? Why did the thought of never touching her hand again or seeing her or being near her feel infinitely more crippling than my damaged spine?

How could I feel such a war raging inside me, one side pulling me away while the other pulled me closer, and not be moments away from either splitting right down the middle or exploding all over the bathroom walls? How could I feel so much conflict raging inside me when I knew how I felt about her and how she felt about me?

The answer, I guessed, was that love wasn't simple. It was complex and intricate and confusing and made a man question everything he'd ever held true. It made a person's morals shift and be reexamined from a different perspective. Love wasn't simple. It didn't come naturally or instinctively or easily. It had to be earned and fought for and could drive a person to insanity just as quickly as it could drive them to greatness, but in the midst of all of that confusion, I knew one thing: I loved this woman. And she loved me.

No matter what came tomorrow or the next day or the day after that, I wasn't going to waste that right now.

"I'm not done with you yet, Joze," I said as I shoved open the shower curtain.

Her face erupted with surprise, but she recovered quickly. She wasn't shampooing her hair or shaving her legs or doing much of anything other than letting sheets of hot, steaming water encompass her. "Well, too bad because I am most certainly done talking with you." She shoved the curtain closed in my face.

My brows lifted as I inspected the shower curtain, contemplating my next move. I came up empty though, kind of like I seemed to be coming up empty a lot lately when I took the time to think about what to say or do next. Then a realization knocked me over the head and swung around to knock me one more time. I wasn't the type who thought out every move or mapped out every step. I was the type who relied on instinct and gut feelings. I was the guy who jumped first and questioned later. I wasn't the guy who drew up a detailed outline of choices and consequences before making a decision a week and a half later. No . . . I was the other guy. The one who leapt into the fucking shower before his girl could even crook her finger at him.

This time I didn't bother with the curtain. I just gave a hard push to get my wheelchair over the small lip of the shower and rolled inside. "I'm done talking too, Joze. I'm *way* done with talking."

I tried not to smile at her reaction to me bursting into the shower with my chair and pants and boots still on. From her expression, she would have been less shocked if a gorilla had leapt in with her.

"Then what do you want?" she asked a moment later.

I felt my smile move into place. Not the one others were used to seeing but the one only Josie had seen. The one that either preceded or followed a certain something. "I want you." I shook my head to splash off the water running down my face from my hair. "Just you."

She had to bite her cheek to keep her smile in check, but she grabbed the showerhead and angled it so it was spraying my face for a few seconds. When I sputtered and cursed, she laughed. "Yeah, well, you had your chance, and you choose a cold lonely corner of the bathroom."

I didn't stop looking at her, even with the water breaking across my face. I moved closer so she was almost within arm's reach. "Do you see me in that corner right now?"

She returned the showerhead to its original position.

"No, but something about you accusing me of loving you conditionally, along with your sudden lack of imagination in a certain department, kind of ruined the whole mood for me. I'm over it." Turning around, she reached for the shampoo. Before her fingers had a chance to curl around the bottle, my arms were around her waist and pulling her into my lap. She crashed into me with a little gasp. "What are you doing?" She angled her head back at me, blinking away drops of water as the shower rained down on us.

One of my arms stayed tightly wound around her torso, my hand splaying in the soft bend between her hipbone and ribcage. My other arm slid lower, the hand even more so. When I'd barely just grazed her, she gasped again.

"I'm getting creative." I lowered my mouth to her ear and kissed the spot just below it until her breathing picked up. When her breathing hit the ragged realm, my finger's touch became a bit more . . . intentional. "How's this for imagination?"

What I guessed was meant to be a smile formed on her face, though it looked more like she was riding the line between pain and pleasure. What appeared on my face was unmistakably a smile.

She was right. We could be intimate in more ways than the act I was so familiar with . . . and a rather large fan of. I would have rather lost my hearing or eyesight— hell, I'd even have sawn off a limb or two—rather than give up a functioning dick, but I didn't get that choice. Life had made that choice for me. So even though I might never have been able to experience falling apart inside Josie again, at least I could give her the experience. A finger in the shower while she reclined in the lap of a man in a wheelchair might have been a poor substitute for the way things had been, but it was something.

And that something, from the look and sound of her, didn't seem to be registering in the mediocre department.

When her arm wrapped behind my neck, cinching tightly as she got closer, my head wound up closer to the base of her neck, so that was where I focused my mouth. I sucked at her skin harder than perhaps I should have, but every time I moved to a new section of skin, she whispered things that made soft and slow impossible.

Even through the water dotting her skin, she tasted the same—like a summer night following a rainstorm. When she threw her head back over my shoulder, arching her neck toward the ceiling, I knew she was moments away from falling apart in my arms. However, this was the best thing to happen to me since the accident, and I wasn't in a hurry to finish it. I could have stayed in the shower long past the expiration of the hot water, touching her . . . kissing her . . . making love to her.

When my pace slowed, each stroke and kiss becoming softer, a groan escaped her lips.

"Be nice," she breathed, angling her face so our mouths were so close I could feel her heavy breaths against my lips.

"You didn't fall in love with me because I was nice, Joze." I moved my face closer so our mouths were separated by just a thin sheet of air. I traced the seam of her lips with my tongue, and when her lips parted, I kissed her as if it were the last time. I kissed her as if we'd been separated by time and circumstance for years and we would be again in another few moments. I kissed her like I loved her—with abandon.

"You're right," she whispered when she had to break

away to catch her breath.

Her chest was rising and falling so hard, practically begging to be touched. My hand at her side slipped up her wet body to palm one of her breasts. When I squeezed, more of a moan than a gasp escaped her lips.

"I didn't fall in love with you because you were nice." Her voice was so low with want, so breathy with desire, it barely sounded like Josie's. "So where's the not-nice man I fell for? Where's the one who's so bad he would have already been tossing me from my back to my front for round two? Where's the guy who grunts dirty somethings into my ear as he's coming so hard inside me that I'm sore the next day?" A sigh bubbled from her lips when my finger moved against her again. Faster. Firmer. "I want him."

I might not have been able to achieve a climax in my current condition, but damn if I didn't feel as though I was right on the edge of my own. My grunt vibrated against her cheek when she grinded her hips into my hand. "I can guarantee you don't want him as fucking bad as he wants you."

A shiver ripped down her body. One of her arms dropped from my neck and landed on my arm working on her before winding down it. All of the way down it. "I want to feel you inside me when I come."

When her hips lowered again, she ground her ass into my lap, circling it in a way that made my eyes roll back into my head. I might not have had any sensation in the area she was waxing with her wet backside, but fuck, it didn't matter. I felt something, and whether that was just the memory of what it had felt like when she'd done that to me before or the accumulation everything else I could feel—like the fullness of her chest spilling out of my hand or the heat that resided between her legs so wet I could feel it running down the insides of her thighs or her beautiful face draped over me, staring at me like nothing had changed between us or her breathing so labored I knew I could give her what she wanted with a few more stokes—I might as well have had my dick buried deep inside her for the way I felt right then.

"I want to feel you inside . . ." she said, her words broken by whimpers. She circled my lap harder, hinting at what she wanted.

"Baby, I can't. You know . . ." If I could have given her that, I would have. Even if I'd had to make another deal with the devil and handed over my soul in my next life too.

She shook her head against me. Another whimper rolled from her mouth when my finger circled a certain part of her. Winding her finger around a couple of mine, she slid them down, stopping just outside . . .

"I want to feel you inside of me." Her voice was the firmest I'd heard it since entering the shower. Lifting her hips again, she slipped my fingers inside her, moving them in and out until I picked it up on my own.

"Damn, Joze," I said, moving inside her in just the way I knew she liked when she was about to come. She was so wet and warm and fucking hot that my breathing hit a point where I wondered if hyperventilation was on the horizon . . . but that didn't slow me down. Instead, it encouraged me.

"You didn't fall in love with me because I was nice either." Another just barely detectible smile tugged at her mouth, but it fell into something more dramatic when my pace increased.

"Joze, baby, come." My fingers curled deeper into her chest. "Come for me. I want to feel you come around me."

She might have been a strong person, the toughest woman I'd ever met, but not even Josie could have held on for another second. Her body went rigid against mine, a scream starting small and growing louder until it echoed around us, and I felt her muscles tighten around me in quick, tight beats.

Her orgasm seemed to tear through her twice as long as it had before, and after she collapsed back into my lap with a satisfied sigh, she tilted her head back to look at me. The smile on her face even touched her eyes. She stroked my cheek with her thumb, threading her fingers through mine once they were free.

I kissed her again, this time a bit more softly, almost sweetly. When I ended it, she looked as surprised as I did that I was capable of such a kiss. "I love you, Josie Gibson."

Her smile stretched. "I guarantee not as fucking much as I love you."

CHAPTER ten

"WE'RE LATE." JOSIE checked the time on the dash for the hundredth time and gave her truck a little more gas. The big diesel engine growled louder as it sped down the highway. "We're *really* late."

I twisted in my seat so I was angled her way, unable to look at her without images from the shower both of our hair was still wet from spilling into my head. "Is that why you can't stop smiling?"

She looked at me from the corner of her eye, warning me, but even with that, her smile didn't dim any. "I'm smiling because we're getting out of the house and going on a date with two of our best friends." Her forehead lined when she checked the time again. "Two best friends who are hopefully very forgiving when it comes to us being late."

"You're the one who shimmied into the shower in the first place, so you only have yourself to blame."

She let out a sharp huff. "Well, *you're* the one who wasn't in a hurry to leave the shower, so I have you to blame too."

"Hey, we made a deal. I agreed to soap you clean after the filthy things." I shrugged, just smiling when she threw me a smirk.

"If I would have known how many filthy things you had planned, I would have set a time limit with that deal we struck." She shifted in her seat, making the hem of her sundress rise a little higher.

After staring at the exposed skin of her thigh for a few seconds, I lowered my hand and ran my fingers across her skin. "I'll keep that in mind the next time I'm thinking about making you come three different times." When she glanced at me again, I wet my lips and gave her an evil little smile. "Three different ways."

Like that, her whole face changed. "Did that sound like a complaint?" She shook her head. "Because it wasn't. It *definitely* wasn't," she added when my thumb crept a little higher up the inside of her thigh.

"Glad we got that cleared up because if my dick remains MIA, you'll have to tackle the duty of orgasm-ing for two. That's a big responsibility."

"Let me assure you I am more than up to the challenge of that big responsibility. In fact, I can't see making anything a bigger priority than devoting myself to this daunting challenge." When she peeked over at me again, we both laughed.

That moment should have been frozen in time, encapsulated in the tombs of this world's most perfect moments—making love to Joze followed by laughing with her. Some might have argued that perfection was a fallacy, but that was only because they hadn't experienced moments in their lives like I'd had with Josie. They were fleeting and over far too quickly, but that didn't change the fact that I'd experienced more moments of perfection than a man like me was owed.

"You can ease off on the gas though, Joze. It's okay."

I slid my hand down her leg so I was cupping her knee. If I went any higher past that hemline, we'd wind up rolled over in a ditch. "I sent Jess a text when we finally pried ourselves out of the shower letting him know we'd be late. He said they were running behind too, so there's no need to worry about best friends turning into enemies if we show up thirty minutes late."

Josie whipped her truck into town, barreling at fifty down a road marked with a twenty-five MPH speed limit. "Well, thank God, because we're closer to being thirty-*five* minutes late."

From the look of the parking lot in front of the steak-house where we were meeting Jesse and Rowen, the place was packed. Not a big surprise since it was a Saturday night and Boundary Steakhouse might have been the best place a person could sink their teeth into a good steak this side of Chicago. We'd been there enough times since I'd started making good money riding—because no ranch hand's wages would cut it at Boundary more than once or twice a year—that Josie whipped down the alley and head-ed for the back parking lot only known by the staff and regulars.

Finding a spot for her monster-sized truck was a chal-lenge wherever we went though, and tonight was no ex-ception. When she'd suggested applying for a handicapped parking pass, I pretty much asked her not to bring it up again because I didn't need or want another reminder of just how much of a gimp I was, a special blue tag hanging from the rearview mirror of my girlfriend's truck included.

Josie grumbled when she found this parking lot al-most as full as the one in front. When she noticed a space that might have fit a Prius, she gave the steering wheel a twist.

"Yahoo!" she cheered as she angled the truck into the space.

"Eh, Joze, the truck *might* fit, but how are the people inside going to crawl out?" I asked, bracing myself for the sound of a side-view mirror being ripped off.

"We'll get out on your side," she answered, looking out her side window before glancing out mine. "I left plenty of space on your side."

Actually, she had. There was enough space for a person to get in and out, which must have meant . . . "And how's the person on your side supposed to crawl into their car?" I asked, eying the scant four inches of space separating Josie's truck from the sedan parked beside it.

"That's Joe's car," she said as she turned off the engine and fired off a text to Jesse and Rowen letting them know we were here.

"Who's Joe?" I noted the hint of sharpness in my voice.

So did she. Josie was used to me being a jealous, possessive SOB most of the time, and she made sure she called me on it every time too. Lifting a brow, she ran a finger down the center of her chest. "My lover."

"Funny." I gave her a look which she laughed off.

"Joe's the assistant manager, Garth. You've met him, for crying out loud. We'll be out of here before he has to try to scratch his head and figure out how to crawl inside." Josie nudged me when the look stayed on my face another moment.

"I don't know. The last time the four of us got together, I think they had to ask us to lock up when we finally left." I unbuckled my seat belt as she crawled across the bench.

When she reached for the door handle, instead of pushing it open right away, she straddled my lap before sliding her knee between my legs. Gently circling it around my zipper, she winked at me. "Can I return the favor? We're already thirty-five minutes late. What's another five?"

I should have felt something firing down there. I should have felt my dick swelling from just the thought of what she was suggesting. If I could have gotten any harder, I would have just reached it when she wet her lips and reached for my zipper. If I were the whole man I had been a couple weeks ago, I would have answered her question by guiding her head lower and braiding my fingers through her hair as she . . .

I shook my head to clear it and lowered my hand to where hers was currently freeing me from my zipper. "Joze . . ." I swallowed. "We both know my dick might not be able to appreciate that gesture like it used to, but shit, my eyes will enjoy it if he can't." Her smile spread before her head dropped, but my hands cupped her head, lifting it back up. Her confused expression might have made me laugh if this hadn't been so damn tragic and pathetic. "But before we give that a try, I'm going to need some time to wrap my mind around it. More than five minutes, if you know what I mean." I shifted, wondering if I could be any more uncomfortable talking about this. "It's going to take a little getting used to him not working . . . or cooperating . . . when, you know, you're down there. I'm pretty sure our first try or five are going to be awkward as all hell, and I'd prefer not to make it even more awkward by having a few-minute time constraint in some back parking lot."

Josie's hands moved from my zipper to my face, cupping each side before she lowered her forehead to mine. "It might be awkward to you, but do you see me flinching?" Her brown eyes stared into mine with such intensity the breath I was taking caught in my throat. "I still love you. I still want you. In all of the ways I wanted you before." She kissed the tip of my nose. "So if you need to have your awkwardness, you can have yours, but don't try to assign any to me, because awkward is the furthest thing from what I feel when I'm with you, Garth."

The tightness in my chest released, and I could breathe again. I kissed her back but on the lips. "My God, Joze. You're the best damn woman God had the audacity to go and create. How did I end up with you?" I hadn't intended to voice that question. Yes, I pondered that more times during the day than I didn't, but it was something I preferred to keep to myself.

"I ask myself that same question about you every day. So when and if you find the answer to yours, will you let me know so I can find the answer to mine?"

I chuckled and drew my thumbs down her jawbone. "The cab of this truck is filling up with so much sappiness I think it's about to start breaking through the windows."

Josie shoved my chest but laughed. "You're right. We've reached sickening levels of sappiness. Fresh air is definitely in order." Giving the handle a pull, she swung the door open and started to crawl out, but as she swung her leg over my lap, her boot caught on the back of my knee.

"Ah, crap," she shrieked as she tumbled out the door.

"Joze!" I tried to grab her arm or her hand or something to keep her from spilling to the gravel, but I didn't move fast enough. I couldn't move enough of my body to save her.

Splayed on the gravel outside the truck, she lay there, looking at me with a surprised expression before a smile moved into place, quickly replaced by a laugh that didn't end. She was laughing so hard her stomach was bouncing and tears started falling from her eyes.

"Why are you laughing, crazy person?" I asked as I tried to swing my legs out the door to help her up. Her truck was so lifted that even if I could have leant all the way over and extended my arm to its full reach, I still wouldn't have been able to reach her. If I tried crawling out of the truck, I'd end up in the same mess she was, so I had to just sit there and watch Josie laid out on the ground from the fall I couldn't save her from or even help her up from, laughing as though she'd lost her mind.

"Ouch," she said around her laughter, rubbing one of her elbows.

"Are you okay?" I leaned down a bit farther, but it still wasn't enough. "Why are you just lying there laughing?"

That made her laugh harder. "I think you gave me one orgasm too many. I'm officially drunk on climaxes. You'd better take my keys and call a cab." Lifting her arm, her keys dangled from her fingers.

"You are certifiable, Josie Gibson." I shook my head at her, but even me in all my helpless glory couldn't keep from laughing with her.

"Josie?" A voice carried across the parking lot from the back of the restaurant before I heard footsteps rushing our way. "Shit, Josie. What happened? Are you okay?"

I recognized the voice before its owner broke to a stop in front of us. Out of all the people in the world I would have liked to come to our rescue, Colt Mason was somewhere at the end of that line. Colt lowered his arms to help Josie up, and his brows came together when she just lay there, still laughing.

"Are you *drunk*?" he asked.

Of course that only made her break into another round of laughter, so Colt glanced at me for an answer.

"Don't ask," I said, not sure how to cross that bridge. Colt and I had figured out how to co-exist living in the same small town after feuding over the girl I wound up with, but that was only because he lived in a different part of the country for half of the year, soaking in the California sun, and the other half, I spent on the road, traveling from rodeo to rodeo. We hadn't been within arm's reach of each other since Jesse and Rowen's wedding. The night I'd essentially confessed my love to his date.

"Josie, come on, let me help you up." Colt seemed almost nervous around me, as though he was looking for a distraction and peeling Josie from the gravel was it.

When he went to give her a lift again, she waved away his assistance and got up on her own. As she dusted herself off, I was finally able to reach her. Pulling her close, I turned her around to inspect her for damage. She had a few small scrapes on the back of her elbows and a dusty backside, but she'd survive.

"Nice move there, Grace," I muttered, smacking at her backside to get the dust off and . . . well, because Josie Gibson had the finest ass in this county and the next one over. Ask any guy who'd seen her in a pair of tight jeans, and he'd confirm it.

"Nice save there, superhero," she threw back, letting me pull her into my arms when we were done cleaning her off.

I pinched at her side while Colt shifted in place, looking as though he didn't know what to say or do next. For a show pony like Colt Mason, him not knowing what to say or do might have happened once every solar eclipse or two.

"Hey, Black. How's it going?" Running a hand down his hair, he extended his other hand in my direction.

From the way Josie peered back at me, she was as stumped by Colt's bury-the-hatchet approach as I was.

"It's going . . . *good*, Colt." I shook his hand, feeling about as awkward as I'd probably have felt if Josie had gotten her way in the truck and had her head buried in my lap. "How are you doing?"

Josie chewed on the inside of her cheek, probably because she knew how I felt about Colt and that this conversation was about as forced as they came.

"I'm good," he said with a nod, sticking his hands in his pockets. "Thanks for asking."

Josie sounded like she'd just choked on a laugh. I twisted at her sides so she knew I'd detected her amusement and I wasn't as amused.

"I'm good too. In case anyone wants to know," she said, shoving at my hand that kept pinching her.

When Colt's gaze drifted to my legs and tried to look away just as quickly, I got why the out-of-character nervousness and stilted conversation was taking place. "Yeah, so I went and got myself paralyzed," I said, hacking through the ice with a machete. I motioned at my legs. "You know, in case you hadn't noticed. Or hadn't heard yet."

Josie leaned into me, slipping between my legs and draping an arm around each of them. I loved how she was behaving as though I was the exact same man I'd been when I could have stood toe-to-toe with Colt Mason. I loved how she was draped around me like she'd never been so proud of me. I loved how she'd never once treated me like the handicapped person everyone else seemed to see.

"Oh, yeah . . . I heard about that." Colt kept rubbing the back of his head. If he wasn't careful, he would rub it bald, and then what kind of magic would the hairstylist he had a standing appointment with do? "I'm sorry, man. Damn, that sucks."

"Why yes, Colt, yes, it does suck not being able to move anything from my hips down," I said dryly.

He swallowed, no doubt putting himself in my shoes. For the first time in his life, Colt Mason looked almost pale. "It sounds like they don't know for sure if it'll be permanent though, right?"

Under my breath, I muttered a curse on town gossips and their relentlessness. "They also don't know for sure if world peace will ever become a reality. But it sure as shit isn't anything to hold our breaths for."

Colt lifted his brows and looked around. I'd tongue-tied him twice in only a few minutes. Go me.

"Can I help you out or anything?" He motioned toward Josie and me, glancing into the bed of the truck where my wheelchair was folded up. "I was just getting ready to head in for dinner with my family, so I'd love any reason to be late."

Josie beat me to the shaking-our-heads punch. "No,

thanks. We're good." She leaned farther into me, getting comfortable.

Colt's head tilted. "Come on, Josie. You might be one tough cookie, but how are you going to lift a guy who's got a solid fifty pounds on you from that giant truck?" Colt started reaching into the truck bed. "I'm here. At least put me to use."

"Could you not *stay* here please?" I said just low enough for Josie to hear. That earned me another elbow into my stomach.

"I'm going to overlook the fact that you just called me weak and just say thanks but no thanks." Josie's arms crossed, making Colt take a step back. He obviously wasn't a stranger to Josie's arms crossing and had learned to take the same retreat approach I had. "Jesse's coming to help, so we'll be good. Thanks though."

Colt glanced at the restaurant. Just when I thought he was about to issue a stilted good-bye, he leaned into the pick-up and got comfortable. "I'll hang until he gets here then."

My forehead lined as I tried to figure out what his motives were because he was Colt Mason—he always had a motive. "Were you hoping to shoot the shit and catch up while you wait? Maybe plan a guys' night out or something?" I kept my voice civil and finished with a shrug, but I was confused to say the least. He'd done his duty of making sure an old friend was okay after taking a spill out of her truck, so now he could just mosey along on his merry way. Why was he hanging around for Jesse to show up? They were about as good of pals as Colt and I were.

When his eyes scanned the dark parking lot and narrowed on a spot where it sounded like a bottle had just broken, I got it.

"I just want to make sure no one messes with Josie, you know? It's a big, dark parking lot back here, and I know for a fact a few cars have been broken into recently." His eyes lingered on that spot a moment longer before shifting back to us. "You never know what could happen, right? I'd hate to see Josie get hurt any more than she's managed to do to herself."

My chest started rising and falling in hard pulls. Colt was staying to protect her. To make sure she was safe until another able-bodied man was on the scene and could protect her from whatever horrors and threats went bump in the night. Colt Mason was staying to protect Josie . . . because he knew I couldn't.

He was right too.

"Colt"—Josie's tone was past hinting at annoyance—"we'll be fine. Go play the chivalrous card with someone else."

I gently squeezed her arm. "No, Joze, he's right. It's dark, late, and there are a couple of bars close by that are frequented by good-for-nothing fiends." My throat burned from the words, but my pride wasn't worth more than Josie's safety. "Thanks for staying, Colt. We appreciate it." When Josie grumbled and looked away as though she was now pissed at both of us, I added, "Well, *I* appreciate it."

It really couldn't have been more than a minute or two, but sitting on the edge of that truck seat, feeling a level above helpless while steam rolled out of Josie's ears and Colt continued to scan the parking lot as though dangers hid in every shadow, I felt like that minute took a year off my life. Probably because in the absence of conversation, all I could think about was how it was my job to protect her, and I couldn't do that either.

I couldn't protect her. I couldn't make love to her. I couldn't drive her to a date in my own truck. I couldn't *not* be a burden to her. Those reminders had done a solid job of dampening my mood by the time Jesse came jogging across the parking lot toward us.

"Sorry, guys," he said as he stopped in front of us. "We were later than I thought we'd be."

"Let me guess. Bad hair day?" I lifted my chin at his hat.

He was preparing to reply when he noticed the third person in our little back lot powwow. Jesse stiffened, his forehead creasing. "Mason." There was so little warmth in his address it couldn't really have been considered a greeting.

"Walker." Colt nodded, looking in every direction but Jesse's.

My brows came together as I studied them. Jess and Colt had never been friends, but they'd never been enemies either. From the look of it, something had gone down between them to change that. I felt my mouth curling up at the corners. Yes, I was evil.

"Jesse's here. You can go now. Enjoy your dinner." Josie motioned toward Jesse, who seemed to try not to glare at Colt.

Colt looked between the three of us, like he was trying to figure his next move, then sighed and started walking away. That guy might have been the bane of my existence in my former life, but I couldn't overlook what he'd done, even in the face of some serious opposition, if not aggression, from Josie.

"Hey, Colt!" I didn't wait for him to stop or look

back. "Thanks for looking after Joze."

Acknowledging me with a wave, he continued to the restaurant.

Josie spun around and leveled me with a look that equally turned me on and made me want to back away. "I can look after me. You can look after me." Her index finger jabbed into my sternum. "But Colt Mason cannot look after me." Her eyes narrowed another degree before she pushed away from the truck and marched across the parking lot.

"Damn it," I muttered, watching her the entire way just in case Colt's premonitions were dead-on. Only when she'd thrown open the restaurant's door and was safely inside did I let my stare shift. "She's pissed."

Jesse already had the wheelchair out of the truck bed and was sliding it open. "I'd say she's way beyond that actually."

I cocked my head at him. "Hey, thanks for the optimism, Mr. Sunshine. Where's the positivity and annoying cheerfulness I'm used to getting when I whine to you?"

Jesse wrestled with the wheelchair for a few more moments before bracing his hands on the back of the seat and exhaling. "Sorry. I've been a little preoccupied lately. My 'annoying cheerfulness' has gotten a little dusty, I guess."

"What's going on?" I asked.

Jesse kept his head down as he came toward me. "Let's talk about it later, okay? Before the girls get impatient and invite a couple other cowboys to take our places."

I grunted. "Any other cowboy than us would be a poor substitute."

That earned a smile from him. "Ready?" he asked as

his arms slid around me.

"Take me into your arms and make torrid love to me, big guy," I said as I slipped an arm around his neck. I'd been lifted a handful of times by different people, and it never got easier. Having to be picked up like an infant by your best friend or your girlfriend's dad or whomever else was a humbling experience I wouldn't even wish on Colt Mason.

"Not sure I'm up to torrid tonight, but I could probably squeeze out a marginally passionate." Jesse was still smiling as he carried me to the wheelchair. He didn't quite heave me when he first lifted me, but he came close. "Are you losing weight, Black?" He lowered me into the wheelchair.

"Yeah, I have. The muscles in my lower body, along with my balls, are shrinking." I lifted a brow at him. "Great way to lose weight quickly though. The paralyzed diet. Highly recommend it."

Jesse squatted to slide my boots into the footholds of the wheelchair. "Well, you've got to be pretty damn happy you can move your arms and chest now, right? How's that for making progress?"

I watched him fuss over getting my legs and feet just right and wondered if people fretting over me like that could be considered progress. "I guess. Though if I told you how much time I have to spend attending to my internal plumbing, I don't know if you'd still consider the term progress applicable."

Jesse lifted his brows at me.

"It sucks, Jess. I used to be able to take a piss in the span of a long yawn. Now I'm lucky if I can answer nature's call in under a half hour."

After locking the truck, he closed the door and moved behind the wheelchair. "So other than your internal plumbing taking up half your day, how's life?"

"Stellar," I said as the wheelchair crunched across the gravel.

Jesse sighed. "How's life *really*?"

My instinct was to answer with another smartass comment, but if I could have been honest with anyone beside Josie, it was Jess. "Upside-down. That's pretty much been the theme of my life for the past couple of weeks. You?"

Jesse pushed me through the parking lot at a slow, controlled pace. "Upside-down works for me too."

I adjusted my hat as we approached the restaurant entrance. Then I centered my belt buckle because somehow *someone* had gotten it all crooked. "Seattle busting your balls finally? I told you guys like us, who only knew open spaces and fresh air, would wilt in a big city. I'm surprised it's taken you this long to reach that point."

Jesse took me up the ramp while a handful of others flowed up the stairs. "No, it's not Seattle."

"Then what the hell has got your life so upside-down, Jess?" I twisted in my chair as much as I could to look at him. Our whole lives, Jesse had never been the brooding, worrisome type. That was my role. Hearing that streak of hesitation or anxiety or something similar in his voice gave me serious pause.

As we rolled up to the doors, a couple of people waiting for a table held the doors open for us and moved aside. Jesse thanked them with a smile and a nod while I tried not to count every set of eyes full of pity and relief that landed on me for more than a lingering moment.

"Later," he answered with finality in his voice, and that was when I got it.

What could cause Jesse's whole world to shift upside-down? What could make his happy-go-lucky disposition take a temporary hiatus? What could be the reason he'd been dropped to his proverbial knees?

The answer shouldn't have eluded me for as long as it had.

"Rowen?" I glanced at him. "This has something to do with Rowen, doesn't it?"

Jesse had such a terrible poker face he would have been better off never trying to fool anyone. The look he gave me now took that to a different level. "We'll talk about this later, Black." His voice was firm as he wheeled me to the reception counter. "When we're not surrounded by two dozen people hanging on to every word Garth Black is saying."

I glanced at the crowds waiting for tables. "Between you and me, Jess, I don't think it's exactly my words they're hung up on right now." As we passed an older couple looking at me, I waved, but they didn't notice. They were too busy staring at my legs to see my hand.

I'd never walked into this restaurant, or anywhere in this town, without holding my head high, despite the gossip that came with the Black name. This might have been my first experience wheeling through the nicest restaurant in town, but I wouldn't start lowering my eyes and hunching my shoulders now. I'd have been a liar if I said it wasn't hard though. On my first official outing as Garth Black the Paralyzed, no one was letting me off easy. Every eye turned my way and felt like they were boring holes through me, whittling deeper and deeper until they came out the other side.

"I'll take it from here, Jess. Thanks for the lift." I lowered my hands to the wheels.

Jesse, picking up on my cue instantly, took his hands off the wheelchair grips and moved through the restaurant beside me. "Our table's back here by the window." Jesse lifted his chin toward the back of the restaurant where I could just make out the back of Rowen's head.

I glanced around the large room brimming with tables and chairs. It felt like more of an obstacle course or a maze. Jesse must have inspected the restaurant with my eyes, because after a moment, he exhaled.

"Garth, I'm sorry. I didn't even think about it when the hostess sat us back there." He shook his head. "I'll see about getting a table closer."

I grabbed his wrist before he could turn and leave. "It's fine." I wheeled toward what looked to be the widest path. "I just wanted to give the girls another minute to catch up on their gossip before we showed up. Besides, these places are required to be handicapped accessible now." I bumped into the back of a chair. Thankfully, it was an empty one. "Just spot me if it looks like I'm going to take out a small child or something."

Jesse followed me, clearly taking his task seriously. When he caught sight of a heel of bread in my path, he moved in front of me and kicked it aside. He did the same when he noticed a baby's soft block in our path too. Although instead of kicking it, he picked it up, wiped it off on his shirt, and placed it in the baby's pudgy little arms with a smile. The baby flapped its arms and legs, cooing at Jesse while the mom thanked him in her own way. Rowen would have gotten all territorial if she'd noticed the way the woman's gaze drifted to Jesse's backside and lingered for far too long for someone at a table with whom I guessed was her family.

"So that ring you're lucky didn't fall out of your back pocket when you were cartwheeling over that bull . . ." Jesse glanced at me from the corner of his eye.

After I'd been stripped at the hospital before getting tied into a hospital "dress," Jesse was the one the staff had handed my clothes and other personal effects to. I supposed it was better he'd gotten them than Josie, but I knew better than to hope he wouldn't bring up that ring. I'd been waiting for him to broach the topic since he'd slid those folded-up jeans into the hospital dresser drawer with a raised brow aimed in my direction.

"How much longer are you planning on keeping it in your pocket?"

I kept moving with my eyes forward. "Pretty much as long as I'm in this damn thing."

"Why did you buy it in the first place if you weren't planning on doing anything with it then?" he asked.

"Because I was *planning* on asking Josie to marry me."

"And that's changed?"

I shook my head and tightened my jaw. "No, that hasn't changed, but I have."

Jesse's face creased for a moment before he shook his head. "Yeah, I don't get that pattern of thinking, but knock yourself out."

My jaw kept tightening. "Nobody asked you, big guy, so why don't we just drop the whole ring topic before Josie's ears start twitching?"

Jesse shrugged what I guessed was his agreement before, from across the restaurant, a group of guys waved at him, motioning him over. When he answered with an apologetic wave, indicating Rowen only a few tables away, the guys cracked some imaginary whips before getting back to their beers. I knew a few of them, but not one had waved or made eye contact with me. I guessed that had more to do with me being at the eye-level of a first-grader instead of a grown man.

"Adoration." I lifted a brow at him. "How does it feel?"

Jesse chuckled one note, pushing an empty chair aside to make extra room for me. "You'd know better than I would, Garth Black, professional bull rider."

I made sure he noticed me take in the room. The tables of people were looking at me in similar ways and lengths as the people in the waiting area had. "This isn't adoration, Jess. This is a personified train wreck rolling right in front of their eyes."

Jesse shook his head at me as we passed the last few tables before ours. I felt as if I'd endured some kind of harrowing journey of a lifetime, and all I'd done was maneuver my way through a busy restaurant.

That was when I noticed Colt. He was a couple tables over, sitting with his family. His *whole* family. A couple of his brothers stared at me with smirks, nudging each other and whispering something that had to have been quite hysterical from the way their laughs echoed around the restaurant. Colt shoved at them both, trying to shush them, but that only made them laugh harder. I was so busy glaring at them that I ran smack into the back of a chair. A chair someone was actually occupying. The woman in it let out a loud *oomph!* before whipping her head around to see what had happened.

"Sorry, ma'am," I said instantly, rolling away from her chair. When she twisted around in her seat, I noticed the fresh dark purple stain on her blouse and the tipped over wine glass in front of her. "Ah, shit. God, I'm sorry."

When her lips pursed together, they looked in danger of sticking that way, and I noticed the slew of children staggered around the table, gaping at me as though I were going to hell because I'd just taken the Lord's name in vain.

From the Mason table, more laughter rolled through the restaurant. I felt my face wanting to redden, my body wanting to disappear into the floorboards, as the woman and what felt like the whole restaurant either glared, stared, or laughed at me. That was when Josie appeared, crouching beside me and angling herself toward the woman.

She covered my hand with one of hers and put on a smile. "I'm sorry, Mrs. Grueller. I'm going to leave my number with you, and I want you to call me once you know how much it will be to either dry-clean or replace your blouse. We'll be more than happy to take care of it. I've got a jacket out in my truck that I'll run and get so you can wear that if you like. We're close to the same size, I'm sure."

The woman's face softened in the space of a few words from Josie, ending up almost peaceful by the end of her apology. Josie was just standing when Mrs. Grueller shook her head. "Don't worry about it, hon. I've got six kids under ten years old. I wouldn't know what to do if I made it through a meal without winding up with a stain or two on my shirt." She smiled at Josie before patting her hand. "Say hi to your mom for me, would you?"

"Of course. And make sure you swing by soon before all the raspberries are gone. Lord only knows how many PB & J sandwiches you go through with this brood." Josie waved at a few of the kids.

"I'll do that. Raspberry jam does, after all, make quite the impressive stain." After sharing a laugh, Josie and Mrs. Grueller said good-bye. She even said a friendly enough good-bye to me as I passed by.

"See the benefits of having more friends than enemies?" Josie whispered in my ear with, from the sound of it, a victorious smile.

"People who freeload off your raspberry bushes to feed their gaggle of offspring?"

She was in the middle of a sigh when I threw my arm around her neck and drew her face close to mine. Whatever anger had sprung up back in the parking lot seemed to be gone, and she was back to her usual feisty, fun self. One of the great things about Joze was her ability to rip through emotions like a kid on Christmas morning. She let herself feel what she needed to then moved on.

"I'm sorry about what happened in the parking lot," I said as we headed to our table. It had only taken me twenty minutes . . . "Do you forgive me?"

"Is that a rhetorical question?" Smiling at me, a glint of mischief lit up her eyes right before she all but leapt into my lap.

A rush of air burst from my lungs at the impact, but I recovered quickly. She wound her arms around my neck and situated herself in my lap so she was perpendicular to me. I wrapped one arm around her waist and used the other to push us to the table.

The restaurant might have been staring at me before, but now they were really staring. As if me being paralyzed weren't bad enough, it was unequivocally worse that a beautiful, healthy, fully-functioning woman would want to sit on my lap and look at me with almost worshipful eyes. From how I gauged most people's stares, Josie's faithfulness to me was the most tragic part of the whole thing.

They made me want to raise both middle fingers at the entire restaurant, but I'd given the spectators enough attention already. They didn't deserve my attention—Josie did. I was giving her the rest of it for the night.

"Do you guys, like, get off on making some big public scene or something?" Rowen's nose was curled as we wheeled up to the table.

A chair had been removed from one of the spots, which I guessed was designated for me.

Josie blinked across the table at her. "Don't you guys?" Then, without any warning or indication, she twisted in my lap, straddling me as she had in the truck, and dropped her mouth to mine while she slid off my hat and tangled her fingers in my hair.

"Fuck, Joze," I breathed, nipping at her lower lip as she continued to kiss me in a way that wasn't exactly PG-family-rated.

When her tongue slipped past my teeth, tying with mine, a chorus of groans and comments circled around the table . . . and, from the sounds of it, the restaurant too. From the Masons' table behind us, someone hollered something about getting a room, followed by a comment about getting her pregnant kissing like that. From the other side of the room, where I guessed Jesse's table of friends was, hoots and cheers broke out, the clink of beer bottles interspersed.

From across the table, another trademark sign of the disgruntled sort came from Rowen. "Enough with your overactive libidos already. Don't make me anymore nauseous than I already am."

When Josie's and my mouths stayed connected, her tongue still doing things to mine that made me wish I'd taken her up on her offer out in the truck, something smacked me on the side of the forehead.

"Down, boy," Rowen said, reaching for another piece of bread to lob at me in the event Josie and I either couldn't or wouldn't separate. Beside her, Jesse shifted in his seat as if he'd just witnessed his grandmother naked on a freezing cold day. "I came here to eat and catch up with you guys, not be brought dangerously close to emptying the contents of my stomach in my lap."

Josie settled a final kiss on my mouth before replacing my hat and sliding off of my lap. "Whatever, don't deny that just got you all hot and bothered and practically panting for Jesse to take you to bed tonight." As Josie slid into her chair beside me, she winked at Jess. "You can thank me later."

Jesse turned an impressive shade of red and buried himself farther in his menu.

"You're right. I can*not* wait to crawl into bed tonight," Rowen replied. "To sleep or hibernate or slip into a coma or whatever it takes so I can make it through a day without feeling like I've got mono." With a yawn, she settled her head against Jesse's shoulder, and he wrapped his arm around her.

Josie bounced her eyebrows at them. "Stop keeping her up all night, Jesse. We women might seem invincible, but even we need the reprieve of sleep every once in a while."

Jesse motioned at Rowen halfway asleep on him, her eyes more drifted close than open. "This isn't my fault. We haven't even—"

"Oh yes, it's your fault," Rowen interjected, giving him a pointed look but keeping her head on his shoulder. "Nice try there, cowboy."

Jesse's face was still a little red, but it went a shade redder after that. I leaned forward, inspecting the two of them carefully. Josie mirrored me.

"What the hell is going on with you two?" I asked, summing up all the questions rolling around in my head.

Rowen shook her head and tried to stifle the next yawn. "Uh-uh. We're here to talk about how you're doing and how your life's been, not talk about us."

Jesse slipped his wife a look. A secret message passed between them, and just when I was about to pound my palms on the table and demand to know what was going on, our waiter arrived to take our drink orders. Jesse ordered a Coke with me, as he always did now that I'd virtually stopped drinking. The girls would usually still order a drink, but Rowen ordered a Sprite. Josie whined about not wanting to be the only lush of the group and wound up ordering a Cherry Coke.

I waved my finger around the table. "The four of us are together and no one's drinking? Cue the end of the world."

Jesse gave an intentional clearing of his throat.

Rolling my eyes, I modified my original comment. "Fine, the *three* of us are together and no one's drinking." This time, my finger only indicated Josie, Rowen, and myself.

"So, really, how are you doing, Black?" Rowen dug a piece of bread from the basket before passing the basket around the table. I was opening my mouth to answer when she added, "The non-wiseass, sarcastic version please."

Josie chuckled as she placed a piece of bread on my plate before snagging one for herself.

"I'm okay, I guess," I said, feeling like having my eyelids stapled open would have been less torturous than talking about how I was doing and my . . . feelings.

"You're okay, you guess?" Rowen repeated as she spread butter on her bread. When she was done, she tore it in half and gave a piece to Jesse. Jesse just put his piece back on her plate. "What does that mean in non-vague terms?"

I sawed off a piece of my bread and chewed on it for longer than necessary. "It means I have good days and bad days like before. I just experience those good and bad days from a wheelchair." My words came out sharper than I'd intended, but if it upset anyone around the table, they didn't show it.

"What's the latest news on your spine? How much longer do they think you'll be in that wheelchair?" Rowen took a sip of her water after she'd taken a small bite of bread. She winced and took another sip. Jesse seemed to be watching her without blinking.

"Why does everyone keep asking me that?" I said, gripping the arms of my wheelchair. "Why is everyone so concerned about me getting out of it when they're not the ones confined to it in the first place? Why is everyone so fucking concerned with what's going on with my spine?"

Josie's hand dropped to my leg and gave it a squeeze

that warned me to cool my jets. My eyes closed as I took a slow breath. I was just about to apologize to Rowen when she spoke up.

"We're all so concerned about you and your spine and your defensive disposition because we care about you. We also were around to see you go from paralyzed from the neck down to only being paralyzed from the waist down, and we're hopeful the mobility trend will continue." Rowen took another sip of water.

Jesse scanned the restaurant, relief flooding his expression when he saw the waiter approaching with our drinks.

"If we didn't care what happened to you, we wouldn't ask, so don't take a shit on us for caring. It would be a lot easier to not care." Rowen's words were searing, but her tone was quiet, almost as if she were nursing a headache. "So why don't you sideline the a-hole act for a couple hours so we can enjoy the rest of the night? You can slide back into it tomorrow if you want."

Josie was pursing her lips to keep from smiling while staring into her lap, and Jesse looked as if he were about to flag down the waiter before Rowen and I got into one of our infamous horn-locking "discussions." When the waiter set our drinks in front of us, Rowen downed half of her Sprite before we'd finished ordering. We all ordered the New York strip, but when Rowen ordered hers medium-rare like the rest of ours, Jesse's forehead wrinkled.

She lifted her eyes to the ceiling. "Make that medium-well."

"If anyone catches wind of the wife of one of the biggest cattle ranching names in the area ordering a steak a hair below well-done, the Walker name will take a serious tarnishing," I said in a lowered voice.

This time it was Jesse who lifted his eyes to the ceiling.

"So Josie mentioned something about an MRI," Rowen said with her straw between her teeth. "That you're pretty much refusing to have one done because you're a cheapskate. Is that right?"

I wrapped my arm around Josie's neck, drew her close, and mussed up her hair with my other hand. "Traitor." I gave her hair one last muss before letting her go. "In so many words, yeah, that's right. Doc Murphy did recommend an MRI, and yes, it would cost more than the cozy little trailer I grew up in was worth in its prime, but the thing is, the MRI won't make me better. It can't diagnose something that can be fixed with surgery or therapy. All it will do is tell us what happened." I shrugged and motioned at my legs. "I already know what's happened, so I think I'll save myself the five grand, but thanks for inquiring."

"Are they sure that fall didn't break something inside your head too? The part that regulates logical thinking?"

I put on my most impressive smirk, but if it fazed Rowen, she didn't show it. "That part got knocked loose way back when I was a baby and Clay would have sooner dropped me than let a bottle of hooch slip from his hand."

"Get the MRI," Rowen said, followed by a long exhale. "If only for your peace of mind."

"Hey, Sterling-Walker, I don't need peace of mind to accept what's happened to me, and I don't need peace of mind to accept what's going to happen to me in the future. I do, however, need the five grand since I'll be lucky to get hired on part-time at the thrift store on Main, sorting people's used crap and making minimum wage."

"Garth—" Rowen started, shaking her head.

"I'm paralyzed. Every day I stay this way adds a few more percentage points to the odds of me staying this way for good. The fancy machine isn't going to tell me something I don't already know." I took a long drink of my Coke, wishing I'd ordered a double whiskey instead. I wasn't angry at Rowen for asking questions—I was angry at the questions for being there in the first place. I was angry at the situation that had put me in the position of those kinds of questions existing. I was *furious* at myself for not being able to fix this or figure out all the answers or make up my goddamned mind about what I should do moving forward.

Rowen shoved her seat forward, her eyes narrowing at me in a way that had me bracing myself to get it, when Jesse spoke up. "So we're going to be moving back to Willow Springs." He glanced at his wife, seeming to gauge her emotions. "At least for part of the year."

That shifted the conversation topic real quick. Josie's and my heads whipped toward him, our jaws practically hanging open.

"Say what?" Josie said, leaning forward. "I thought you guys just purchased a condo in Seattle and were settling into the whole grunge scene and getting used to carrying umbrellas everywhere and replacing the colors in your wardrobe with gray and black."

Rowen arched an eyebrow at her. "Our condo is a fancy word for a coat closet, and my closet was already spilling over with black and gray, thank you very much."

Josie and I looked between the two of them, waiting for the punchline. I knew Jesse wasn't a big fan of city life, but he'd have moved smack into the middle of New

York City if it meant being with Rowen, and Rowen's career as an artist was taking off on the West Coast. Why they'd suddenly decide to go between living in Montana and Seattle wasn't adding up.

"What's up?" Josie asked in place of how I'd phrased earlier, *What the hell is going on?*

Jesse shifted in his seat as he took a drink of his Coke. "It's getting harder and harder for Dad to manage the ranch, so we're planning on spending three or four months during the summer helping out."

"Plus the thought of spending the rest of my life trapped between sky-scrapers, people, and overcast weather is enough to make me mental," Rowen added, finishing her soda. When she caught Josie and me looking at her, she added, "More mental than I already am, at least."

"But you love the city," Josie said.

Rowen lifted a shoulder. "It's okay."

Josie's forehead creased. "And with both of your jobs, it'll be okay to simply pick up and leave for a few months every year?"

"Most of the big art shows take place during the fall and spring, and I can paint, sculpt, and draw in Montana as easily as I can in Seattle." Rowen replaced her head on Jesse's shoulder and reached for his hand. "Jesse's been a trouper the whole time, and not once has he complained, but he won't miss working construction. He was born on a ranch. He was raised on a ranch. That's where he belongs."

"That's where *he* belongs . . ." Josie hinted.

Jesse's chin curled around Rowen's head, his expression almost troubled.

"And I belong with him," Rowen replied firmly. "It's

not fair to expect him to move away from the people and places he knows when we can make this work. Besides, I miss Montana."

Josie smiled. "It's the cow crap ground into the floors, isn't it? Appealing on so many levels."

"Nah," she replied, winking at us. "It's more the people in this cow-crap-crusted state than the actual places I miss."

"Holy cow crap. Good for you guys." I leaned back in my wheelchair and grinned at my friends, who I'd be getting to see more often than the occasional weekend. "Is this move happening, like, this summer or next?"

"Happening as soon as possible," Rowen answered, followed by Jesse shaking his head.

"We haven't decided anything for sure yet," he said. "We have to find a house close by the ranch first, or build one, and there's a bunch of other things to get worked out too."

"What else is there to get worked out, Jess? Besides which side of the bed you'll sleep on . . ." I asked as the waiter arrived with a large tray about to spill over with steak and sides.

Jesse lifted his eyes to mine. There was something in them I couldn't translate. "Lots of things."

The waiter was just about to set Josie's plate in front of her when Rowen shoved back in her chair, covered her mouth, and sprinted across the restaurant before Josie had realized she was gone.

"Crap, Garth," Jesse groaned, tossing his napkin onto the table as he stood. "I thought I told you not to order the creamed spinach."

My brows pinched together. "When the hell did you

tell me that?" I waved my fork at the tray. A steaming plate of creamed spinach had my name all over it. "And why the hell would you tell me that in the first place?"

All Jesse did was shake his head at me before following his wife, who I guessed had disappeared into the ladies' restroom. I wasn't sure what he was going to do when he got there, but he obviously wasn't happy with me.

"What's got his chaps in a twist?" I muttered to Josie as the waiter finished placing the plates in front of the chairs, throwing a concerned looked in the direction of the restrooms. "And what's the deal with the creamed spinach? I always order creamed spinach. It's never sent him over the ledge before. Something's up with those two."

Josie stared at Rowen and Jesse's empty seats, her forehead creasing. "What do you think is up?"

I glanced at the restrooms. "I don't know, but nothing good. Jesse's been on edge all night, and Rowen's been especially snappy. I always worried that, with those two being so different, their honeymoon period would be over quickly, and when it was, those differences would drive them apart."

Josie cut into her steak. "I don't think they fell in love because of their differences."

I was still worked up over what had happened and what was currently happening. I'd rarely seen Rowen and Jesse so out-of-sorts as a couple, and it was hitting me hard. If they couldn't make it, what hope did the rest of us have? "Then why?"

Josie nudged me with her elbow and finished chewing. "Gee, I don't know . . . maybe because they *loved* each other." Another nudge. "It's not like you and I are exactly alike, so you better be careful what you're saying."

I watched as we both cut into our steak from the same angle, at the same spot, and stabbed the chunk with the tips of our knives instead of our forks to bring it to our mouths. "Joze, you and I are more alike than both your mother and father pray every night we're not."

She finished chewing and then kissed my cheek. "Ah, that's the sweetest thing you've ever said to me. Nothing says romance like implying your woman's the asshole equivalent of you with boobs."

"I like to think of us as strong-willed."

"You can consider us or yourself strong-willed all you want, but that doesn't mean that's the word people whisper behind your back." Josie glanced up, something catching her attention.

When I followed her stare, I noticed two boys hesitantly making their way to our table. "More fans of yours?" I muttered at her.

She lifted her chin at them. "I'd say from the napkins and pens in their hands, it's you they're fans of."

She was right. They were each clutching a cocktail napkin in one hand and a pen in the other. It seemed like so long since I'd been asked for an autograph, and so much had happened since that that felt like a whole other life.

"Excuse us, Mr. Black, we're sorry about interrupting your dinner . . ." the older boy, who looked to be around twelve or so, started.

"But can we have your autograph please?" the younger of the two boys piped up, holding out his napkin and pen.

Josie set down her silverware, smiling between the boys and me. She scooted my plate a bit to the side to make room for me to sign the napkins.

"Of course you can have my autograph." I took the pen and napkin from the young boy first. "It's only a hundred dollars per signature. How many would you like?" When I looked up to find two faces shifting deeper into shock, followed by Josie's elbow bumping mine, I grinned. "That's a joke. No charge."

The boys' faces couldn't have gotten any more relieved.

The older one slid his napkin in front of me. "I'm learning how to ride bulls too. My dad's teaching me."

I focused on signing my name. "Yeah, my dad taught me too." I kept to myself all the other lessons he'd tried to teach me by example.

"He says if I keep practicing, I'll be able to start competing next summer." The boy stood a little taller, almost able to meet my eyes, unlike the little one who could only grin and bounce in place.

"It sounds like you're working hard. Good for you." I started signing my name on the second napkin. "Just don't let anyone tell you spending a bunch of time working the weights or a balance ball or something else is worth your time. The only way you become a better bull rider is by actually riding bulls."

A serious look fell over the boy's face as he nodded, like he was carefully filing away every word. "Yes, sir."

The younger one, not wanting to be left out, stuck out his chest and hitched his thumbs through the loops of his jeans. "I ride too."

"Yeah? Well, good for you. I started when I was about your age too."

The older boy rolled his eyes. "You ride sheep, Colby. Not bulls like I do."

The little boy gave who I guessed was his brother a shove. "You don't ride bulls either. You ride steers."

Both of their cheeks reddened from being called out by the other, so I leaned forward. "You've got to start somewhere, right? What do you think would happen if you just hopped up on a monster-sized brahma the first time?"

"You'd probably hurt yourself real good," the older one said.

"Or die," the little one added.

"Start small. Practice hard. Ride big." When I handed them their napkins, the older one pulled a phone from his back pocket.

"Could we, you know, get a picture with you?" He swallowed.

Josie was smiling beside me, obviously much more content with this brand of fan than the bra-flouting ones.

"That'll be another hundred," I said before motioning them closer. "Of course you can. Just make sure you return the favor when you two are famous bull riders."

"We will, sir," they said in unison.

"Here, I'll take it." Josie pushed out of her seat and came around to the boys. "You guys go stand on either side of Garth."

I started to wheel back from the table so their photo wouldn't feature a sixteen-ounce strip steak, and that was they halted, their eyes drifting to what I was sitting in. Both of their brows drew so tightly together it was almost funny . . . until I realized the reason for their confounded looks.

"What happened?" the young one asked, his gape on full display.

I tilted my head, not anticipating having to explain what had happened to the people in my hometown since I'd assumed everyone knew everyone else's business about two minutes after said business went down. That two boys who were fans had yet to hear what had happened to me wasn't what I'd expected to find at dinner. The staring and whispering I'd expected; the utter shock and dismay of finding out what had happened I hadn't.

"I took my attention off the bull for one fraction of a second, and I got thrown good and hard. I landed on my head, and I'm probably lucky I didn't break it open." I kept my voice calm, trying to explain as logically as I could.

The boys stared at me as if they'd just born witness to their hero being thwarted by the villain.

"Did you break your legs?" one of them asked. "How long will you be in the wheelchair?"

If only I'd broken my legs. At least I'd have the reassurance that bones would heal when spinal nerve damage might not. "No, I'm paralyzed." When Josie's hand went to her hip, I added, "At least for now, I'm paralyzed. How long I'll be in the wheelchair depends on if I stay this way for a while or forever."

The younger one's mouth fell open. "You might be in a wheelchair forever? You might never ride again?"

Josie cleared her throat and gave the boys a look that would have made me shrivel. "Do you want your picture or not?"

The older boy took the phone from her and started backing away. His younger brother followed.

"That's okay." The older boy's gaze was zeroed in on my wheelchair, as if that were all he could see now. The man he'd so clearly idolized before noticing it was now defined by it. "Thanks though. Sorry to bother you." Grabbing his brother's arm, he pulled him away from our table and headed back to where they'd come from.

Josie watched them, both of her hands on her hips.

When she started after them, I spoke up. "Not worth it, Joze."

"So worth it." She thrust her hand in their direction. "Their mama clearly didn't teach them any manners, so I think I'll take a whack at it. While I'm whacking the backs of their heads."

"Joze," I said when she started their way.

Something in my voice must have gotten her attention because she stopped and looked back at me. What she saw on my face must have been enough to get her to forget about the boys momentarily because she turned around and crouched beside me.

"I've had a rough enough night without you going all crazy girlfriend on a couple of young boys for not wanting a picture with me after seeing me in this thing."

She chewed on the inside of her cheek, holding back all of the things she wanted to say.

"Between Colt Mason suggesting I couldn't protect you anymore, having every eye on me as I rolled through this place, and spilling wine down your mom's friend's shirt . . ." I shook my head, hoping future outings would go more smoothly. "Please don't go and draw even more attention to us by giving what-for to a couple of boys."

She blew out a breath. "They deserve it."

"Maybe, but I'm not sure I can handle any more to-night." I rolled back to the table and rested my hand over hers, which was clutching the table as if she might break it.

"Fine. I won't go make a scene for your benefit. But not for those little shitheads'." She glared at the spot the boys had disappeared from for a moment longer before making her way back to her chair.

I could see how upset she was over what had happened, and the truth was that I was probably just as upset, but I had to stay calm to keep her from blowing her lid. If she knew I'd been as affected by those boys as she had, I'd have no way of keeping her from chasing after them and giving them what-for.

After a casual inspection of the restaurant, I found a good quarter of the tables varying between occasionally glancing my way and unapologetically staring with a blend of pity and revulsion in their eyes. The steak that had looked and smelled amazing now seemed unpalatable as I lifted my fork and knife.

"Here they come." Josie lifted her head toward Jesse and Rowen making their way back to the table.

"Rowen looks like crap," I said under my breath. Her face looked extra pale and like every part of her was in pain. "Jesse looks worse," I added. "That's it. I'm just going to ask them both, point blank, what the hell is going on. I can't take it anymore. They're our best friends, and what's bothering them bothers me. I can't sit here and keep pretending everything's okay." I took a drink of my Coke and settled into my wheelchair for what would surely be an uncomfortable conversation. "What do you think's going on?"

Josie wasn't quite gaping at me, but she was close. "I *know* what's going on with them. It's pretty obvious. What isn't obvious is why you can't seem to figure it out."

"You know?" I twisted toward her and hissed, "Tell

me."

"Tell you what?" Rowen asked with an arm draped around her stomach as Jesse helped her into her chair.

Josie lifted a pointed brow at me, keeping her lips sealed.

I shot her a smirk before facing Jesse and Rowen. Taking a breath, I looked at Rowen, since Jesse was too preoccupied with watching her as if she were about to explode. "Tell us what's going on with you guys. Why you're both acting so . . . not like yourselves."

Rowen sighed at my impressive prose.

"Yeah, come on," Josie said, pushing her plate away. "How much longer are you going to keep us in suspense?"

Rowen and Jesse exchanged a look. Rowen shrugged—Jesse sighed.

"I didn't realize ordering a Sprite, being moody, exhausted, and sprinting for the bathroom was keeping you in suspense," she said, indicating the empty soda glass in front of her.

I blinked at everyone around the table. "What is everyone talking about, for Christ's sake?"

Josie shook her head and groaned like I was hopeless.

Rowen threw the back of her hand into Jesse's chest. "Jesse knocked me up." Jesse winced. "So there you have it. The suspense is no longer."

I sat frozen for a minute, replaying what she'd just said. Jesse had done what? That meant Rowen was what? That meant they'd be what soon? Of all the things I'd considered going on between them, Rowen having a bun in the oven hadn't been one of them.

"What?" I said, although it came out as a whisper and was covered by Josie's squeals as she smacked the table repeatedly in her excitement.

"I knew it!" she shrieked, alerting half the restaurant. "I *knew* it. I could tell the moment I saw you guys."

"It was this putrid shade of green I radiate, right?" Rowen circled her finger around her face. "Or was it the dark circles under my eyes from not being able to sleep, despite spending the whole day exhausted? Or was it the paunch already starting to pop out of my not-so-skinny jeans?" She patted her tummy, making my gaze move there.

A baby was inside her stomach. Growing. A little Jesse or Rowen would be born into the world in what . . . six months? Twelve? How long did a baby take before being born? I knew it was somewhere in the six- to twelve-month range, but for the way this was all hitting me, little Sterling-Walker might as well have been born tomorrow.

Josie waved. "Whatever. You look amazing. I don't know, it was just something in your eyes. Something in Jesse's. That mix of 'I'm terrified and thrilled at the same time.' You might as well have been carrying a sign announcing you were preggers."

Rowen sniffed then, her nose curling right before her gaze landed on the creamed spinach in front of me. Before I could do anything, Jesse stole it and carried it back to the kitchen. I grumbled, stealing some of his mashed potatoes.

"Well, we might not have fooled you, but I'd say we definitely gave Garth the shock of his life." Rowen smiled at me in my still-stunned silence as she cut into her steak.

"For being such a worldly, street-smart guy, you'd think he wouldn't be so oblivious about these kinds of things, right?" Josie was still bouncing in her seat. "God, I'm so excited for you guys. A baby? Seriously, I think I might pee my pants right now."

"If you do, make sure not to change yourself in the last stall, because I've barfed in that one twice already and the vomit smell is definitely lingering." As if she hadn't been talking about throw up, Rowen stuffed a bite of steak into her mouth and swallowed with a small moan. She'd never been much of a meat eater—she was more like a vegetarian who ate chicken or fish on occasion—but right now, she acted like she wanted to make love to that slab of steak. I supposed that was the Jesse part of the baby in her—a rancher's child craved good red meat even in the womb.

"Um, ew, but thanks for the tip." Josie reached for my hand and gave it an impressive squeeze.

Seeing her so happy couldn't help but rub off on me. It was contagious. Actually, most of her emotions were. Whatever she felt somehow translated into what I felt.

"So how far along are you? How's it been so far? When are you due? Do you know what it is yet? Have you thought of names? Have you put together a registry yet? Can I do the baby shower? Can I babysit? Can I make my-self available to you whenever and wherever you need a hand with the baby?"

Rowen had to cut her off. "Whoa there, Inquisitive. Take it easy. Along with my energy and stomach hardi-ness, this little gremlin is sucking away my brainpower. One question at a time, please. Two max."

Josie's hand kept squeezing mine. She was going to cut off my circulation soon if she didn't let up. "When are you due?"

"November 30th," she answered instantly, as if the date were on the tip of her tongue at all times.

"So that would make you . . ." Josie tipped her head from side to side. "Three months along?"

"Twelve weeks almost to the date."

"So I guess asking how you're feeling is kind of pointless since you just admitted to feeling like crap, right?" Josie frowned as she patted one of Rowen's hands. "But that's supposed to pass after the first trimester, right? You should start feeling better soon."

Rowen looked away, focusing on cutting another chunk from her steak. "Yeah, I should. Hopefully." She shifted in her seat.

Just as Josie looked ready to break into her next question, Jesse showed back up, having successfully deprived me of my creamed spinach. "*Most* women feel better after the first trimester," he said as he took his seat and glanced at Rowen, again with that nervous edge in his expression. He'd always been attentive to her, in a tuned in a way that bordered on protective, but this was something else. This was almost like he was trying to make sure she hadn't disappeared. Like he was worried she would be taken from him any moment.

"What do you mean '*most* women,' Jess?" My first words to them probably should have been something along the lines of congrats, but I knew something was wrong. Something besides Rowen being knocked up.

If Josie had noticed how Jesse was behaving or what I'd just asked, it wasn't hitting her the way it was me. "Pregnant in your twenties." She laughed, shaking her head. "And you accused me of being small-town."

Rowen twirled her fork in the air. "Yeah, yeah, whatever. We were on about every form of birth control I could get my hands on, but it appears sexual dynamo here"—she stuck her thumb in Jesse's chest—"broke right through every one."

Josie gave him a look that made him shift in his seat. "Jesse, you tiger, you."

I mouthed, "Sorry" at him, but he was still too busy breaking out in a cold sweat from watching Rowen.

"So are you more excited or more shitting your pants?" Josie asked, waving at the waiter and motioning at Rowen's empty Sprite.

He took it to refill it, and Rowen smiled her thanks at both him and Josie.

"When I'm not hurling into some form of porcelain, I'm starting to get excited," Rowen answered, covering her stomach with one of her hands. Jesse slid his hand over hers, weaving his fingers together with hers. "He's shitting his pants."

Josie gaped at Jesse. "Why?" She shook her head, clearly stumped. "You'll be, like, one of the best dads ever. Second to you, baby." She leaned in to kiss the corner of my mouth.

My stomach twisted into several dozen knots at Josie mentioning me becoming a dad, and not in the way it used to when I thought of what kind of dad I'd had and the opposite of an example he'd left me with. No, this stomach churning was brought on by the whiplash realization that I could never father a child in my current condition. I was the one breaking out in a cold sweat now.

I mean, I'd realized that with everything south of my waist being immobile, I couldn't get it up, but I'd only been focused on one aspect of that major inconvenience. I'd been too busy struggling with that sad realization to move on to the next logical conclusion—the children part.

I might have been a long way off from contemplating rugrats, but I knew somewhere deep inside me was buried the desire to have kids. To prove the Black name wasn't synonymous with shitty fathers and champion drinkers. I wanted children one day . . . but now that day might never come.

The room started to close in around me, the air growing so thin I felt close to gasping.

Across the table, Jesse cleared his throat and finally tore his stare from Rowen. He scrubbed his face with one hand, keeping his other firmly planted on Rowen's stomach. I couldn't tell who he was trying to protect more—her or the baby inside her. "There was a reason we were using so many different forms of birth control." He looked between Josie and me as though he was waiting for us to get it.

Josie shrugged. "Because you didn't want to knock up your fertile young bride so soon?"

Jesse exhaled, and with a one shake of his head, I got it. I got where the dread and hovering and bordering-on-unhealthy protective streak were coming from. His words nearly mirrored my thoughts.

"Because it isn't safe for Rowen to have children."

Rowen sighed but didn't offer any argument. Josie picked up where I'd left off on the frozen-in-her-seat thing.

"What do you mean it isn't safe for her?" I swallowed. "As in growing a little human in her stomach then attempting to push it out something seemingly way too small? Because that doesn't sound really all that safe for any woman."

My attempt to lighten the mood failed. Instead, the

table seemed to grow more silent.

"No, I mean not safe in that her heart might not be able to tolerate the strain of pregnancy and delivery." As Jesse finished his words, his face seemed about to break, but he kept it together. He'd always been so strong, a pillar among tough, work-hardened men, but having to face this was just too much. Every man had a breaking point, and the thought of losing his wife and unborn child was Jesse Walker's.

"What do you mean her heart might not be able to tolerate it?" Josie asked, the heaviness of the situation settling around her.

Jesse sucked in a breath, but Rowen saved him the explanation. "What he means is that about a year ago, I went to my doctor because I felt faint and out of breath whenever I tried exercising hard. Yeah, I know. Me and exercise—never saw that one coming, right? Seattle's health craze has a way of rubbing off on you." Rowen's attempt at lightness didn't work either. When the waiter set a fresh glass of Sprite in front of her, she took a sip like she was stalling. "Anyway, she diagnosed me with something called aortic stenosis. It's a heart condition that basically means I don't tolerate physical stress to my body as well as the next person. I've probably had it my whole life but didn't notice it until I started pushing my body to its upper limits."

Jesse still hadn't touched his meal. In fact, I didn't think he'd even acknowledged it had arrived yet.

"It's not like a person with this kind of thing is strongly discouraged from getting pregnant, but it puts me into a higher-risk category," she said.

Jesse cracked his neck and rolled his shoulders. "No,

but the doctor advised you have surgery to fix the problem before getting pregnant. That's why we were quadrupling up on birth control, but now . . ." His voice caught for a moment, and then he continued. "They can't operate on her while she's pregnant. They can't guarantee Rowen and the baby will make it through this safely . . . they can't do anything. It feels like all we're doing is waiting to see what happens, going back and forth between celebrating over a miracle and biting our nails at a possible tragedy."

I exhaled and shook my head. Dangling precariously on the ledge of hope and fear was a concept I was all too familiar with after this past week.

Rowen turned in her seat to face Jesse. She waited for him to look at her, and when he finally did, she pressed her hand into his chest and leaned closer. "I'm going to be fine. The baby's going to be fine." She nodded as if she were waiting for him to nod along with her.

He couldn't though. He knew no amount of nodding would guarantee his wife and child's safety. Jesse might have been an optimist to an unfathomable degree, but he didn't skew reality with false hope. The numbers, the statistics didn't lie—I knew that.

Rowen stayed turned in her seat but looked over at us. "Everything's going to be fine."

Rowen wasn't my sister or my girlfriend or even a lifelong friend, but the surge of panic I felt from realizing her life was in danger indicated otherwise. What would the world look like without Rowen Sterling-Walker ruffling its feathers? Bland. And boring. And monochromatic at best.

"Are you saying Rowen could die? Your unborn baby could die?" I pointed at her stomach as I directed my questions at Jesse.

"Garth!" Josie snapped.

"What? From the sound of him and the look of him, Jesse's planning for a couple of funerals at the same time he's having to confront being a dad. Don't expect me to offer up a simple congrats and move on to discussing what we've all got planned for the Fourth of July weekend, because I can't do that, Joze. I can't just pretend something isn't happening when it clearly is. I can't just sweep something under the rug . . ."

It was her brow rising higher and higher with every sentence that finally got my attention. That brow threw my words back in my face, accusing me of being a hypocrite. I knew she was right. With myself, I was happy to sweep what was going on under the rug to collect with the rest of the dust bunnies, but when it came to the people I cared about, I wanted answers. I wanted to weigh the options.

I leaned across the table toward him, ignoring Josie's warning look. "What are we talking about here, Jess? What number did the doc give you guys?"

Jesse's eyes closed, his forehead creasing so deeply it shifted his hat down on his head. "He gave us a number a hell of a lot higher than I would have liked to hear."

I cursed under my breath, unable to keep from looking at Rowen as if she were drifting away from us, and all I could do was watch it happen. Josie had stopped bouncing in her seat with excitement. The entire table had been sucked dry of excitement and filled with the heaviness of uncertainty. Rowen was slouched in her seat, her hands covering her stomach, and looking a bit scared herself. The dread and panic on Jesse's face had only increased in severity, and Josie looked as though she was about two seconds from bawling.

"Rowen's right," I said, nodding at her. "Everything's going to be okay, so we can spend the next six or however many months freaking out and getting our panties in a twist about something that's not going to happen, or we can raise our glasses filled with soda, make a toast, and celebrate the little Sterling-Walker." I lifted my Coke, returning Rowen's smile as it formed.

Her Sprite joined mine in the air a few moments later. Josie's glass came next, and finally, after having to swat his arm across the table, Jesse's joined our trio of cups.

"Cheers," I said as we clinked glasses. "And congrats. That fetus is one lucky little munchkin to wind up with you two as its parents." A laugh slipped past Rowen's mouth and slowly spread around the table. "If there's anything we can do for you guys, let us know. However, I won't be the back-up labor coach for you, Jess, so you better make sure you stay close when your wife's due. It would leave me permanently scarred, and I'm damaged enough as it is."

Josie wiped at her eyes, but a tear still ran down her cheeks and around her smile. "Congratulations. I'm so thrilled for you both. Garth's right—let's hold on to hope instead of letting fear drive us, okay? Besides, we've got important things to discuss. Like the theme colors of your baby shower I'm going to throw this fall." Josie winked at Rowen before throwing out dates and something about shower games.

That was when I tuned out. "Go figure I'd be the one to shed light on a situation when you were sitting at the table."

Jesse opened his eyes, staring at his plate without really seeing it. My words hadn't mollified him as much as they had they girls.

"Rowen's going to be fine, Jess. Come on. You have to know that." I lowered my voice and leaned across the table. "There's no fucking way you or me will let anything take her or your baby away from this world, you hear me? That's not going to happen, so you stop thinking it right now."

He stared at his plate for another minute before looking up. "I can't lose her. She's my whole world. I can't lose her."

I could so empathize with the look on his face right then. It was the same look I'd carry everywhere if Josie were in Rowen's position. "You're not going to."

I waited for that light in his eyes to tell me he was on board, for that flicker of defiance to follow my lead, but it never came. Jesse was going to worry until he got to hold his baby and kiss his wife on the forehead. He wasn't going to find his peaceful place until he had his family in his arms at the end of all this.

Josie's hand weaved through mine again. She was still busy talking with Rowen, and no one around the table seemed interested in the expensive steaks in front of them. Except the pregnant woman. She was nibbling daintily at hers, probably because her stomach had staged a revolt for the past three months, from the sound of it.

"I can't believe this. I'm so, so excited I don't know how I'm going to make it until November," Josie said.

"The end of November," Rowen added, which made Josie groan.

"When can you find out what it is?"

Rowen finished chewing and swallowed. "It's a baby, Josie. We already know what it is."

Across the table, I detected a hint of a smile threatening to ruin Jesse's somber expression.

"Your humor has gotten worse since getting knocked up, you know that?" Josie flicked a sugar packet at Rowen, laughing.

Faster than a speeding bullet (no joke) Jesse's hand snapped in front of Rowen and snagged the sugar packet from the air.

Rowen thanked him with a cheek pat. "My hero."

"Come on though. When are you going to find out the sex of the baby? Five months? Six? I can't remember when they can tell for sure." Josie propped her elbows up onto the table and leaned into it like she was enraptured.

I might not have felt like her about all topics of a baby nature, but it was nice having the conversation—said or unsaid—shift away from me and what had happened and what would happen.

"We'll find out the moment after it's ripped out of my stomach like an alien, oozing in placenta gunk and funk." Rowen grinned at me when I let out a loud grumble.

"Good thing I'm not trying to eat here, Rowen," I said, shoving my steak even farther away. "Because it would be projectile-ing all over the place right now."

"You're really not going to find out until you have it?" Josie asked.

Rowen shrugged. "We're really not. We like surprises."

"*Some* surprises," Jesse inserted, taking a bite of steak from Rowen's fork when she lifted it to his mouth.

"What's the deal with the ripping it from your stomach thing? Don't they do that only after trying the"—Josie glanced at me and saw the scrunched-up look on my face—"after trying the more natural way?"

I let out the breath I'd been holding, thankful the v-word hadn't just been dropped at the dinner table. I didn't know what it was about pregnancy or the delivery process that made me so squeamish, but I couldn't seem to overhear information about it without feeling close to trembling. Maybe it was because I could never really understand it since my body wasn't carrying the same kind of equipment, or maybe it was because I was totally out of control of the entire process, other than the very start, and I thrived off control. Or maybe it was for some other reason I had yet to identify, but either way, I wanted to drill my fingers into my ears and drown out the gunk and funk details.

"With my heart thing," Rowen said, stabbing at her salad with her fork, "they don't want to put the added stress of natural labor on my heart. They're going to schedule a Caesarean before I go into natural labor to save me the stress of it."

Josie's nose wrinkled. "And cutting you open and scarring your bikini area for life is how they're planning to lessen your stress?"

Rowen smiled. "I know, right? Bastards."

Jesse scooted closer to his wife, clamped his hands down on either side of her small stomach, and shushed the table. "The baby's hearing is developing now. It can hear you. This is a friendly reminder to keep your curses to yourself when our baby's within hearing range. I don't want my daughter or son's first word to be shit."

"Why are you looking at me, Jess? It was your wife who just dropped that foul word." I'd been minding my P's and Q's. For the most part.

"Because you, old friend, are the worst offender in that department." Jesse's hands stayed around Rowen's stomach for a few more seconds before they moved away.

I guessed he thought his baby's virgin ears were safe again, at least for the next few minutes, after broadcasting his warning. He was right though. With a baby on the way, who'd turn into a toddler, who'd become a child . . . I would have to start watching what I said around whom. I'd have to install a filter so I didn't tarnish the little Sterling-Walker before he or she could crawl.

"Well, it sounds like they've thought everything out and are doing everything they can to make sure you have a safe and healthy pregnancy and delivery, right?" Josie picked right up where they'd left off. "It seems like you're in good hands."

Rowen dropped her hand onto Jesse's shoulder and squeezed it. "I am in good hands."

Josie took a long drink of her soda and drained it. Probably because she was parched from talking at a hundred words a minute since she'd heard the word baby. "So how many of these things do you guys want to have?"

"It depends on how this one goes," Rowen answered.

"One," Jesse said at the same time.

Josie rolled her eyes. "One? That's just cruel. You need to have at least, like, four, or you could be like me and want to have a dozen." Her eyes lit up as she continued. Knowing her, she was envisioning each of her imaginary children's little faces and naming them on the spot. "I want to be literally crawling over children to get to the oven to make dinner every night. I want to be hoarse and exhausted and frazzled every night when I crawl into bed. I want to be bursting at the seams with dirty laundry and dishes and tile floors." Josie was grinning as wide as I'd ever seen her—and she'd grinned a lot in her life. "Yeah, I'm definitely having a dozen."

Rowen shook her head. "I do not envy the condition of your lady parts after that dozenth child practically flies out of your womb. And I won't envy the boxes of tissues you'll tear through whipping snotty noses."

Josie just waved her off, twisting to face me and bouncing with excitement all over again. "Can we have a dozen, Garth? Can we literally have so many kids I'll have to chauffeur them to 4-H and soccer practice in a bus? Can we please have so many children people will start dropping birth control pills into my drinks everywhere I go to keep away the threat of an army of Blacks taking over the world?" Her hands wrapped around my arm as she looked at me with something in her eyes that registered even higher on the happiness scale than joy.

To Josie, family—both blood and otherwise—was paramount in her life. I supposed the expansion of that family would be just as important to her. If Josie wanted a dozen children, she deserved a dozen. She had more than enough love and kindness and that streak of adventure to spread. She had so much of herself to give that she could have had a hundred kids and still had a surplus.

There was a problem with what she was asking though. Or at least a problem with *whom* she was asking. I couldn't give her those dozen babies. At least not in the way a man and woman were intended to create a baby, and even if I could be convinced to have my little Garths medically transplanted inside her so we could "conceive" together, how could I keep up with one child while confined to a wheelchair, let alone a dozen? How could I support a family when I could barely think of ways to support myself?

I might have been able to father a child with the help of a whole hell of a lot of medical breakthroughs, but that was the easy part. The hard part, the everything-after-the-conception-and-delivery part, I was incapable of doing in a way our children deserved. I didn't want them to go through school as I had, with free lunches and outdated clothing. I didn't want them to be embarrassed every time we went anywhere together, with all of the points and stares that came from having a dad in a wheelchair with shrunken, useless legs. I didn't want to feel helpless when I couldn't climb up into a treehouse to help my kid down when they were crying and scared of doing it alone. I didn't want to teach my child how to ride a horse from outside the corral. I didn't want to be a nuisance or an inconvenience or a source of embarrassment.

So though I might have been able to father a child in one way, I couldn't father one in the way that mattered most.

Lifting my hand, I cupped Josie's cheek. I didn't blink once as I stared at her, admiring her as though she was everything I could ever want but couldn't have if my fate didn't change.

"You can have whatever you want, Joze," I said. What I didn't say was that it might not be me who gave her everything she wanted. "If you want a dozen kids, then you can have a dozen kids." I didn't tell her that she might share those dozen kids with a different man though. "You'd be an amazing mom, you know that?"

Her eyes didn't get glassy, and she didn't sniffle at my words. Instead, her smile tipped higher as she nodded.

"You'd be amazing too, you know that?"

I could only answer her with a nod, because if this wheelchair was a permanent thing, the only way for me to be an amazing dad was to not become one in the first place.

CHAPTER eleven

TWO WEEKS. FOURTEEN days. 336 hours. 20,160 minutes. 1,209,600 seconds.

I'd felt every last one of those seconds, all 1.2 million of them. Before, two weeks in the summer had passed so quickly I'd been afraid to close my eyes for fear of waking up to find the leaves changing colors, but now, trapped in a wheelchair, those minutes and seconds toyed with me, skewing my sense of time and its passing.

Jesse and Rowen were back in Seattle, taking care of things and packing up stuff to bring back to Montana for the remainder of the summer and into the fall until little Sterling-Walker came into the world. Jesse wanted her to deliver in Seattle, where they could be surrounded by hospitals, but Rowen wanted to have their baby in Montana. She'd assured him that a hospital in Missoula was just as capable of delivering a baby as any one in Seattle. I didn't know if Jesse bought into his wife's thinking, but at any rate, he was on board with the plan.

Josie had been busy helping her parents on the ranch. With both of them aging, the chores had become harder and took more time. Mr. Gibson had a few ranch hands to help him, but none of them were as solid in the saddle or knew as much of the job as Josie, so she'd spent plenty of days from dawn to dusk with the guys, working the cattle.

Which left me alone with Mrs. Gibson or an empty house. At first, Josie had attempted to stay behind to keep me company, though she'd tried not to make it seem obvious—which had only made it that much more so—but after enduring a few long lectures from me about living her life just as she had before or else I would move out, she'd thrown up her hands in surrender.

Most days, at least a few times each one, I found myself ruing those words when I found myself rolling down the same quiet hallway or checking the same empty living room.

At one point in my life, I'd thrived on solitude and its blanket of comfort. I'd preferred it over companionship because, from what I'd learned from my parents, companions eventually bailed. Solitude was my protection. Of course, my friendships with Josie and Jesse had shifted that view somewhat, shifting it again when they'd coupled up in high school, and ultimately shifting it for good in the last couple years. I didn't seek solitude as I once had. I didn't prefer it to companionship.

Being in a wheelchair didn't give me much of an option though.

Most of my friends were around my age, which meant they worked hard during the days and played hard after. Doing anything "hard" was beyond my functioning level, so even though I'd been invited to several get-togethers and bonfires on the back forty or out to the honkytonks on a Friday night, I'd passed. Mainly because I didn't want to lessen anyone else's night by making them feel obligated to hang at my side, but also because the thought of being around a bunch of rough and rowdy Montana kids—when

I'd been the roughest and rowdiest not long ago—was just too damn depressing to even think about, let alone actually experience.

At first, Josie had encouraged me to take part, but after a handful of *no way*s from me and her working her ass off taking care of the ranch and me, she was frequently staggering into bed at nine. She didn't have the energy to face everyone else either.

It had been a month since the accident and almost three weeks since I'd taken up residence in the wheelchair. A month since I'd been initially paralyzed from the neck down and three weeks since my legs had stayed that way. I didn't try to think it, and I sure as shit didn't voice it, but I knew with every day that passed with me a prisoner in this chair, the likelihood of it becoming permanent grew greater. Each passing day only further secured my future of spending my life paralyzed.

Whenever Josie guessed I was getting a bad case of the self-pities, which was more frequent than the times she picked up on, she reminded me of how lucky I was to be alive and to have regained movement in my arms and chest. I knew she was right. At least, part of me acknowledged that, but the other, darker part of me just couldn't buy into it. Sure, I might have been able to shave my own face and brush my own teeth and slip on my own hat, but in terms of the definition of a man, I came up as empty in that department as if I'd still been paralyzed from the neck down . . . or even if I'd been dead.

I was no good to anyone anymore. At least not really. No one might have come right out and said it, but that didn't change the truth that I'd become an inconvenience to those closest to me. The very people I cared about and wanted to be able to express that care and concern to were the ones plagued with the responsibility of attending to me.

Mrs. Gibson made and brought my meals to me every day, never once complaining and always with that gentle smile. Some flower plucked from her gardens sprouted out of a small vase on each one of my trays. I'd tried making my own breakfast of eggs and bacon a few mornings ago, but it turned out I probably shouldn't have started with something so ambitious and gone with cereal instead. The experiment had ended with me dotted in hot bacon grease and a pile of cracked-open eggs oozing on the kitchen floor. I couldn't even make myself a fucking meal.

Mr. Gibson and Jesse had seen to getting my truck brought back from Casper, and even though I'd been re-lieved to have it back, seeing it parked in the driveway and collecting dust turned into more of a daily torment than the pride and joy my truck had been before. When I'd caught sight of a weed tangling up inside of the wheels yesterday, I'd charged down the ramp, ripped out the weed, and torn it into a dozen tiny pieces as if it had been enemy number one.

At the conclusion of my mini tirade, I'd found Mrs. Gibson watching me from the kitchen window with an expression of concern. I guessed that her concern was more for her daughter than for me, but at least so far, I hadn't heard either of Josie's parents whispering across the dining room table about me being a good-for-nothing par-asite leeching off Josie's goodwill.

But I guessed that day was coming, and I didn't want to be around when it did. The Gibsons were good, hard-working people who'd taken their time warming up to me but had finally come around. Whatever their feelings for me though, their daughter came first. When they finally came around to admitting to each other and to Josie that I would only be a cinder block tied to her ankle and dragging her down her whole life, I wanted to be prepared to agree with good grace and back away.

Josie had seemed content to float with her head in the clouds for the last couple of weeks when it came to my physical limitations, but I didn't have that luxury. Instead, I'd been confronting worst-case scenarios and nightmares. I didn't have a choice.

I loved her. Because I did, I had to do what was best for her.

Every day that passed, it became more and more evident that I wasn't what was best for her anymore.

That became overwhelmingly obvious when I'd been wheeling myself around the barn in an effort to get some fresh air and see how the wheelchair held up on the uneven terrain. Maybe if I'd had a monster-truck-modified wheelchair, I would have been okay, but I wasn't exactly sporting the Cadillac of wheelchairs. The first small patch of mud suctioned to the wheels and brought me to a screeching halt.

I could have called out for Mrs. Gibson—the house wasn't far from the barn, and she always seemed to have one eye and ear trained on me—but I wasn't going to let someone else drag me out of this mess. I would do it. Even if it took me until midnight.

I'd only been working to free the chair for a few minutes, and had already broken out into a sweat, when I heard a familiar voice coming from inside the barn. Josie had left earlier with her dad and the other hands and said she wouldn't be back until lunch. It couldn't have been much past ten though. She was talking to someone, although I couldn't make out anyone else's voice. I stopped fighting with my wheelchair so I could focus all my attention on listening.

"Garth won't tell me anything. I don't even know if he's talked to you since we left your office a few weeks ago." Josie's voice was higher than normal and more breathy sounding. It almost sounded as if she were on the verge of having a panic attack. I still couldn't make out another voice though. "I need to know, Dr. Murphy. I need to know what's happening and what's going to happen."

My heart came to an abrupt stop. It stayed that way for a few beats too—long enough for pain to start manifesting in my chest. She was on the phone with my doctor, practically begging him for information on me. She'd come across as so cool and put together when I was with her, but when she was alone, when she was her truest self, she was falling apart as much as I was. I should have known—even my brave, fearless Josie had weak spots in that seemingly impenetrable coat of armor.

A person could be stronger than the next, but that came with the burden of their weak spots being weaker too. I was one of Josie's weak spots, just like she was one of mine . . . but she was the beacon of my strength too. I didn't need to have it confirmed to accept that I'd ceased to be that for her.

"Screw confidentiality. I've had it up to my eyeballs with being left in the dark and fed a bunch of shit like I'm some mushroom." She took in a breath so deep that I could hear it through the barn wall. "I need to know what's going to happen," she finished in a voice so small I almost couldn't make it out.

She was right—I hadn't talked to Dr. Murphy once since we'd left his office. I'd deleted plenty of voicemails from his office requesting calls back and checking to see if I'd like to schedule an MRI or get a referral for therapy. Sometimes facing reality was hard enough without having to figure out a way to navigate through it.

"Fine. Let's talk in hypothetical terms then." Her voice was back to its typical pissed-off volume. That was a tone I was familiar with. "Let's say fictional Mr. Smith got into a fictional accident and damaged his spine. He's been hypothetically paralyzed from the waist down for close to a month now, after having regained movement in his arms and chest a few days after the initial trauma." So much condescension oozed from her tone that I was impressed the doctor hadn't hung up yet. Or maybe he had and she just hadn't realized it yet. "What is the likelihood, if there is any, of 'Mr. Smith' regaining the rest of his mobility?"

After that, she was quiet for a minute. Or maybe it was more like two. When I heard Josie again, it was a long sigh I heard first.

"So there really isn't much likelihood at all is what you're saying." Another sigh followed that, followed by what sounded like a whimper she'd choked back before it could escape. "Mr. Smith won't walk again is what you're telling me."

My chest pulsed with pain again, curling me over in my chair. What she'd just been told by Dr. Murphy was something I'd accepted days ago for the most part, but having to witness her accepting it while having it con-firmed for myself in a very tangible way accelerated my journey toward that breaking point that had, even a few weeks ago, seemed a ways out on the horizon. Now, though? It seemed like if I extended my arm, my fingers could have just scraped its sharp surface.

"No, I understand," she said. Her voice seemed to move around the barn, but I guessed that was because she was pacing. "If science fiction becomes reality or a medical breakthrough kicks some serious ass or if miracles suddenly start cropping up to be plucked for the taking, Mr. Smith *might* walk again. Am I understanding this correctly?" She paused for a few seconds. "That's what I thought. Thanks for playing the hypothetical game with me. I hate not knowing what's going on. I hate not being able to prepare myself for what's to come."

The mail truck puttered up the driveway, making enough noise I couldn't hear whatever was or wasn't said next. The Gibsons' mailbox, like the rest of the their neighbors', was down at the end of their driveway, right off the main road, but the mailman had been hand-delivering the Gibsons' mail for years. I thought it had something to do with Mrs. Gibson always having something to offer him when he showed up—like a glass of fresh-squeezed lemonade or sweet tea or a warm cup of coffee or tea in the winter. Today it looked as though she'd just brewed some sun tea and was carrying a glass of it down the steps to him. He turned off the mail truck and thanked her with a smile, draining the glass in two drinks.

With the truck off, I could hear Josie's voice again.

"What can we do now then? For Mr. Smith?" she asked, her voice returning to its normal tone and volume. The shock had passed, and she was rolling up her sleeves. "Do you think an MRI would still be helpful? What about physical therapy?" Josie was quiet another minute. "Yeah, okay. That makes sense. I'll talk to him. No promises he'll listen, but I'll pass it on."

After that, they had a minute of conventional back and forth before the call ended. Josie must have left through the barn's back doors because I never saw her slip out the front, which I was closest to, still stuck in the mud and feeling like my chest had become the trampoline for a family of elephants.

I wasn't going to walk again. That was it. I knew I should have been thankful for the mobility in my arms, but conjuring up thankfulness was hard when I'd just had it pretty much confirmed by my physician that I wouldn't walk. I'd heard it in Josie's voice too. The finality. The acceptance. She'd been holding on to hope for so long that I must have extended my pinkie and curled it around that string of hope without even realizing it. Now that her hope was gone, whatever trace amounts I'd let trickle into me from her had been killed.

It might have been that overwhelmingly surge of anger that seemed to rise from my feet and erupt through the rest of my body that got me out of that muck. Or maybe the mud had, like everyone else, given up on me.

As I rolled back to the Gibsons' house, not really knowing where to go now, I stopped in the driveway and looked around. My truck was growing weeds in the driveway—I'd never drive it again. My horse was getting fat and lazy in the barn—I'd never ride him again. My girlfriend was out working her parents' ranch when we'd one day dreamed of working our own—I'd never ranch again.

My whole life, everything I'd been and everything I'd wanted to become, was spiraling away from me. Fragments of the man I'd been and the man I'd wanted to become were gusting out of reach. My life as I'd known it was over. My life as I'd hoped it would be would never come to fruition.

The man I was right now, crippled in more ways that just physically, was both my present and my future. I could have tried to deny that, but I couldn't have kept the façade going for long. As out of control as everything around me felt, I had control of one thing still. One aspect of my life that was vitally important. Josie.

My life might have just smacked into a dead end, but that didn't mean hers had to. My life might have been over for all intents and purposes, but hers was only getting started. As simply as closing this chapter of her life and starting a new one, she could go forward instead of stagnating in this hell, caught in the middle of the living and the dead.

I didn't know how long I'd been siting there, basically saying good-bye to the life I'd known, when Mrs. Gibson came out onto the porch, the screen door whispering shut behind her.

"Garth?" she called, wiping her hands on her apron. From the look of the flour dusting her face and hands, she'd been making biscuits for dinner. "You've got mail. Do you want me to leave it in your room for you, or would you like it now?" She pulled an envelope out of her apron pocket and held it in the air.

I couldn't see who it was from, but I didn't need to. I'd been expecting that letter for weeks. "I'll take it now, Mrs. Gibson." I lifted my shoulders and braced myself. I supposed this was the best time to get the letter. All of my hope was gone, so there was nothing left to take.

When she'd made her way down the stairs and over to

me, she placed the letter in my hands. "Do you need something, hun?"

I almost laughed at the irony of her question. I needed so many somethings I could have kept listing them off until the final harvest had come in for the season. However, even Mrs. Gibson, with all her good intentions and well-meaning, couldn't have put a dent in all of the somethings I needed.

I shook my head. "Thank you, Mrs. Gibson. For everything."

She smiled at me. "Thank you for always making my daughter happy."

It was difficult to do, but I managed to return her smile. It was almost like she could read what I was feeling—almost like she knew, as I did, that I couldn't make her daughter happy anymore. She held my gaze for another moment before climbing the stairs and disappearing back inside the house, leaving me alone with my letter and my bleak future.

I didn't wait to tear open the letter. I slid the letter out and unfolded it. It was the bill from the hospital, and it was as catastrophic as I'd anticipated. The number literally took my breath away and would finish draining most of my savings. The same savings I'd been building in order the purchase a large chunk of land and a large herd of cattle. Instead, it would go to a hospital I'd spent a whole two days in. How could one accident and the forty-eight hours that followed be responsible for completing re-mapping my entire future?

How could one moment, one flash in time, be responsible for changing my whole existence?

CHAPTER twelve

LIKE MOST BAD plans, mine had started out seeming like a good idea. At least it had until I'd hit the second mile. One mile in a truck flashed by in a blink. One mile on a horse passed by having a conversation with another ranch hand. One mile on foot might not have passed as quickly as the other options, but even that was better than the one I was stuck with: pushing myself in a wheelchair that had been a price-conscious purchase instead of a comfort-conscious one when Rose Walker had picked it up.

I'd made it down the Gibsons' long driveway which, thank God, was a slight downhill, and the first mile after that had been along a paved road. The second one had been the same. The third, fourth, and fifth miles? They had been nothing but gravel, pitted roads that made my teeth chatter and my bones shake to the point of breaking.

Thankfully I'd been on the paved roads during the later morning, so most people were already at work or school. Even though it was past dinnertime by the time I started my last mile down yet another bumpy dirt road, I was far enough out that I hadn't been passed by a single truck for over an hour. That was good since one out of every other driver that had gone by broke to a stop, stuck a head out of the window, and asked if I needed a lift. I'd declined—I was too damn prideful to ask for a lift—but if another truck had come along during the last mile, I might have thrown my arms up in surrender and begged a ride to my destination.

My phone hadn't started ringing yet, which meant Josie was still out busting her ass doing work I should have been helping her with. When she did start blowing up my phone when she realized I'd disappeared with no indication of where I'd gone, I already had a plan for how to handle it. I'd had five miles and nine long hours to put together that plan, and it was as close to airtight as any plan conceived in my depraved mind could have been.

Her first call came a little before eight, right as I was rolling the last few yards toward my destination. The porch lights weren't on, nor were any of the other lights inside, and the paint had long ago flaked away from the exterior . . . but it was home. It was my home. *Our* home. The one we'd purchased together, had planned to fix up together, and had hoped to ranch the land surrounding it together. It looked like a piece of shit, closer to needing to be demolished than fixed up, but it was our piece of shit. It had been our dream. Once upon a time.

I worked up a glare as I stared at it. "You're a piece of shit, you know that?"

It didn't respond.

"I don't know what the hell wire tripped in my brain to think I could fix you up, but I think I've finally come to my senses and seen you for what you are: a piece of shit." I was drenched in sweat from the journey, panting from being parched and exhausted, but I felt like I could have cursed at that house all bloody night long. "I guess the two of us really do deserve each other. We're both falling apart, more damn work than we're worth, and should be steam-rolled. You want to make a bet on which one of us will give out and break down first?"

This time, the house answered in the form of a few shingles sliding down the roof to the ground.

"I'm a serious competitor, so if you think dropping a few shingles will make me shiver in my boots, you're wrong. Now if your roof caved in, that would be something else, but right now, my money's on you outliving me." The hospital bill buried in my back pocket started to burn. "What money I have left, at least."

Fresh out of insults and profanities to throw the decrepit relic in front of me, I heaved myself forward through the overgrown weeds and brown clumps that crunched beneath my wheels. The brown clumps were the remnants of a yard that had once been brimming with green grass and flowerbeds that had been kept in bloom every season save for winter.

Thank God there was a small lip leading to the porch instead of a long stairway because then I would have had to drag myself up to the front door instead of rolling. Somehow, the latter option seemed more dignified. It took a few hard rolling, rocking tries to get the front wheels popped up onto the porch and a couple more to get the rest to follow, but once that had been accomplished, the rest was easy. I'd taken the screen door off months ago since it had been hanging on by a sliver, and we didn't keep the front door locked since if someone wanted to break in, all they needed to do was crawl through one of the many broken windows lining the first floor.

As soon as I was inside, I flipped on the hall light. Thankfully, it fired on. One of my first chores when we'd first taken ownership had been changing out all of the dead bulbs—which was mostly all of them—and replacing them with long-lasting, energy-efficient ones. I didn't know why I'd dumped the extra money on lightbulbs when the regular ones had always worked just fine, but I guessed it had been a sign of how much pride I'd taken in owning that piece of shit. Ironic.

My second call from Josie came as I was rolling toward what we'd planned to make our master bedroom. It had been an office, but since neither of us could stay cooped up inside of four walls during daylight hours, an office would have been wasted space. Instead we'd decided to make that our bedroom since it was huge and had the largest windows in the house spread throughout it. Upstairs, there were a handful of smaller bedrooms, but we'd figured those would wind up being our . . .

Once upon a time we'd figured that. Before I'd become an impotent, paralyzed cripple who was more trouble than he was worth.

That cheery thought was responsible for my fist cracking against the hall wall, causing enough dust to erupt around me to make me cough. That was the other thing about this place . . . well, one of the *many* other things about this place—it was caked in no less than a half inch of dust and smelled like a potpourri of mildew and filth. Not exactly the fresh-baked bread or lemon cleanser I was used to after spending so much time at the Gibsons' these past couple years.

After I ignored her second attempt to reach me, my phone started buzzing with text messages. I didn't look though. Not yet. Not until I was inside our room and on the blow-up mattress we'd left there for when we needed a "work break," which had been at least once every after-noon or evening we'd spent working on this place.

I needed to lie down, catch my breath, and recollect my wits before I answered Josie's texts, which were still chiming every few seconds. I needed to muster up my de-pleted strength so that my weakness didn't do something stupid. Like tell her where I was or what I was trying to do or that I loved her and always would and beg her to come get me.

It took some work to figure out how to get out of the wheelchair and onto the air mattress that had shifted into the corner of the room. Josie and I normally kept it right in the middle, but I guessed the wind had gusted through the broken windows and blown it into a corner. There were a few brown and green leaves on top of it, but I didn't bother to brush them off. I just lowered myself onto it as carefully as I could and fell back into it the moment my ass hit the mattress.

I lay there for I didn't know how long, staring at the paint peeling off the high ceiling and accepting that I'd never be able to climb the tall ladder to peel off the old before painting on a new coat of the cheery blue color Jo-sie had picked. The rest of the walls she'd wanted to be repainted in white, but the ceiling she wanted blue. It had seemed an odd choice, but when I'd asked her, she ex-plained it would be like staring at a bright blue sky and that no matter how gray the day or mood, we could fall asleep remembering that a blue sky was always close by.

But I hadn't gotten around to the ceiling yet. I didn't have a blue-sky ceiling above me to lift my mood and bol-ster my determination, so I lay there and stared at the gray, moldy, cracked ceiling, letting it affect my mood accordingly.

That was when I pulled my phone from my pocket and checked her texts. I stopped reading after the first few. Each one became more desperate, more pleading, chewing away at my resolve like I guessed Josie knew would happen when I read them. So I stopped reading her dozens of texts and started typing my own. Listing a time and a location, I asked if she'd meet me tomorrow night to discuss the future. I kept my message short and straightforward, knowing that would alert her that something was up but also knowing she'd be there even if I'd requested a meeting on the top of the Empire State Building.

Her response pinged an instant after I'd sent mine. *What's going on? Where are you? You're scaring me. You're not supposed to scare me, Garth.*

I swallowed, resisting the urge to let her know I was okay or where I was or that everything would be okay and reassure her as I knew she needed. If I kept giving her what she needed whenever she needed it, that would only make the break harder, more jagged. Instead, I turned off my phone, closed my eyes, and tried to fall asleep.

I was still trying to sleep when the sun rose hours later.

CHAPTER thirteen

I ARRIVED EARLY, partly because I hadn't been sure how long it would take me to "roll" my way there, partly because I'd known Josie would get there early, and partly because I couldn't have sat inside that big house a minute longer without going crazy. There were lots of parts of why I arrived at the top of that hill early and stopped beside the big maple, planning to use it for both shelter and support.

Below me was a little watering hole, maybe only a couple times bigger than the swimming pool at the community center in town. It was located on the property Josie and I'd been hoping to purchase and would have been nice for watering the cattle on occasion. It also served as a perfect spot to cool off on a hot day and make love beneath one of the trees. The watering hole was a little ways from the house but thankfully not too far. Given the uneven ground and lack of road or even a rudimentary trail, I wouldn't have been able to make another five miles after yesterday's journey.

My hands were covered in blisters—ones about to burst and ones that already had—and my arms, back, and chest had never felt as sore as they had this afternoon when I'd woken up after finally falling asleep around six this morning.

I'd texted Josie to meet me at the watering hole tonight around nine o'clock . . . but it wasn't me she'd be meeting. No, I would stay camped up here a ways above the water, knowing she'd never see me from where she'd arrive, especially with the cover of darkness.

I'd made a call yesterday, somewhere between mile four and five, after my plan had come to a successful head, and all that was left was implementing it. Implementation started with a call to Colt Mason. Actually, it had started with a call to directory services, who connected me with the Mason household's butler, who'd finally relented and given me Colt's cell number after I managed to convince him Colt and I were old friends.

Colt had been surprised by my call. He hadn't masked his surprise either. When I'd asked if he'd meet me out here tonight, he'd tried every which way to say no without actually saying it. When I mentioned Josie's name and how I was worried about her and said I wanted to talk to him about her, he'd given in and agreed to meet me. I'd had to give him directions to the watering hole, but even Colt Mason should have been up to the task of navigating a few back roads to find a watering hole in the middle of nowhere. I hoped. Otherwise this whole thing was for nothing.

I watched the sunset that night from high up on my hill, feeling as if it was the last sunset of my life because, in a way, it kind of was. My life with Josie, as I'd always wanted it, was coming to an end tonight. My life on my own was starting tomorrow, and I didn't need a glass ball to drop out of the sky into my lap to know that sunsets would never look the same without Josie in my life.

The last ribbons of orange and pink were fading from the sky when I noticed a familiar set of headlights bouncing down the dirt road toward the watering hole. That "road" was across the water from me, probably a good half mile away, but I swore I could see the look on Josie's face as she broke to a stop where we always parked and looked around, searching for me. From confusion to anger to sadness and repeating, it was like she couldn't decide what to think about showing up to the watering hole only to find me not there waiting for her.

I swallowed and made myself stay put. I wouldn't give in now after putting in so much effort to give her a fresh start. One that didn't include taking care of me day in and day out or rolling around restlessly at night, wondering how the bills would get paid or drifting so far apart from her dreams she one day woke up having no memory of them at all.

Eventually she crawled out of her truck. Even though it was nearly dark, the moon was almost full and high enough in the sky I could just make out her movements. Her arm curled to her ear . . . she was holding . . . an instant later, my phone rang.

"Shit," I hissed, digging around to silence it. I should have figured she'd call me as soon as she arrived to find the watering hole empty. Silencing my ringer or shutting the thing off should have been part of the plan, but no . . . I guessed I hadn't thought of everything.

After flicking off the ringer, I glanced across the water at her, sure she'd heard the ring echo across the valley and would start marching in my direction, but something else had caught her attention. Another set of headlights was tentatively making its way down the same road and coming to a stop beside Josie's truck. So the city boy had learned his way around the back roads. Good. That made everything that much better, I supposed, that Colt was becoming more Montana than California.

Colt rolled down his window and stuck his head and arm out and said something to Josie. I couldn't hear a word he said. Not that I'd expected to. It was probably for the best that I couldn't hear whatever they said to each other, but it wasn't as though my imagination filling in the words made it any easier than listening to their actual conversation.

A moment later, Colt climbed out of his truck and slammed his door closed. He had on one of his many fancy hats and was sporting a pair of spiffy boots, but really, even I couldn't have given him too much shit about that anymore. His family had been here a while now, done their best to weave themselves into the community, and Colt had proven himself a solid guy . . . for one who'd been born and partially raised in California.

He might not have been worthy of Josie back when they'd been together, and hell, he wasn't worthy of her now either, but no man would ever be worthy of Josie Gibson. Not even if he found a way to cure world hunger in his spare time. But Colt Mason did have several things going for him. He was a solid guy who could look a man in the eye as he shook his hand, he knew how to respect a woman, he had plenty of money, he had a promising future, and best of all, he wasn't confined to a wheelchair for the rest of his life. He could dance with Josie when the urge hit her, which it did often. He could make love to her when she got that wild look in her eyes . . . he could give her children.

The pain in my chest that had been haunting me for weeks pounded at my sternum like something inside was trying to break through. The image of Colt with Josie, moving above her as she whispered his name, made me double over and reach for the large maple tree in an effort to keep me from falling.

From the look of what was happening down by the water, Josie was pissed. Her arms were flailing around so quickly her movements practically blurred. Every few words echoed across the water toward me, but they were too garbled to make out. She'd spin around every minute or so, seeming to search the area for what I guessed was me, as if she hadn't given up on me showing up. She was still holding on to the hope that I'd turn up. That I hadn't given up and walked away, just as she'd always feared I would back when we'd been making our way toward each other.

Colt stayed cool and collected, getting in a few words whenever he could and every once in a while rubbing her arm to try to soothe her. She flinched away from him more often than she let him try to comfort her. That made me smile as I breathed a sigh of relief . . . then I reminded myself her pushing him away wasn't a victory anymore—it was a failure. It meant she was hanging on to me, and all that would come of her hanging on to me was her winding up a broken, shattered mess when my rope snapped, as I knew it had to.

After about ten minutes, her arms stopped moving like a tornado. She fell into a heap beside Colt, burying her head in her hands. From the way her shoulders bounced, I knew she was crying. From the way it spread to the rest of her body, I knew she was sobbing. That, more than the anger and betrayal and outrage I'd just witnessed, was heart-wrenching. I found my hands dropping to the wheels of my chair and started to move it forward before I even knew what I was doing.

I couldn't stop moving forward, despite knowing I shouldn't. I couldn't stop moving toward her, because she needed me, and at the heart of everything, I knew I needed her.

I was gaining momentum, the downhill slope propelling me forward, when I noticed something that broke me to a stop. Colt had crouched beside her and draped an arm around her shoulders. His head was beside hers, and from whatever he was saying, she was calming down. Her body-rocking sobs dimmed into cries which, after another minute, diminished into nothing.

Colt had comforted her. He'd found a way to ease her sadness. I hadn't been looking for another justification for what I'd arranged, but there it was. Admitting it in my other life would have killed me, but in this one, I knew Colt was the better man.

I stayed for a few more minutes, hovering on that quiet slope and feeling like I was suffering the hardest test of my life. Just when I'd thought I couldn't do it, just when I'd been certain I couldn't let her go, I turned around slowly and whispered, "Bye, Josie."

CHAPTER fourteen

THIS WAS THE second time I'd passed through the front door of this house without elation manifesting in the form of a smile. This was the second time I'd moved around inside knowing that the family I'd planned to live and grow within its walls would never become a reality. This was the second time I'd rolled down this hall late at night feeling more like a ghost than a man.

My hold on this world was slipping, and whatever waited beyond this one was pulling me closer. I wasn't fighting it either. The thought of life without Josie was about as appealing as spending the rest of my life in a North Korean prison.

It had taken me a half hour to get home after leaving my lookout above the watering hole. It used to take me less than ten minutes to walk there. Somehow I felt more exhausted tonight than I had last night, so I headed straight for the bedroom after snagging something from the kitchen.

One of the nice things about living in a small community was that we still had ma-an'-pop grocery stores with delivery guys who'd deliver eggs, milk, and whatever else to the old folks in town. Or the handicapped ones who were stuck in the middle of nowhere with no means of transportation. The fridge was old, but it still worked, and Josie and I had kept it stocked with water and soda, but that was about it. I'd found a few dry goods in the cupboards, but if I had to eat another saltine cracker, I was going to turn into one.

I'd called in my order when I'd woken up, and it had arrived a few hours later. At least I'd figured out a way to forage for food: dial the local grocery store and wait for the delivery guy to show up . . . my life sucked.

That aside, I now had something to choose from besides crackers and granola bars. Bread, bologna, mustard, cheese, chips, bananas . . . the essentials had all arrived, and when the delivery guy had seen me in my wheelchair, he'd even tried to unload the groceries for me. I'd cut him off before he could get the fridge open, handed him some money and a nice tip, and said good-bye. I wasn't ready to accept pity yet. I doubted I ever would be.

After getting everything put away, my fingers had slipped around one of the main reasons I'd called for a delivery. Nothing but the essentials . . .

After putting in my grocery order, I'd made a direct call to the delivery guy and told him I'd slip him an extra twenty if he stopped by a different store on his way out. I'd asked for the biggest bottle he could find because I'd known this night would require it, and I'd been right. Before I made it into the bedroom, I already had the cap twisted off and was lifting the bottle to my lips.

The whiskey burned down my throat, hitting me almost the minute it hit my stomach. I'd stopped drinking the heavy stuff months ago for plenty of reasons that didn't matter anymore. I'd quit because whiskey turned me into an asshole, and that was usually directed at whoever was closest, which usually turned out to be Josie. I was alone now—I'd be alone forever if I got my way—so there was no reason to keep the asshole routine that came so naturally confined anymore.

I'd stopped drinking whiskey because it made me less than the man I knew I could be . . . but there was no one around to strive to be a better man for now. I sure as shit wasn't going to work my ass off becoming a better man for myself, because that wasn't who I was. I didn't do things to make myself better for myself—I did them for the people in my life, and that number was diminishing.

That first long drink tasted so good and so successfully numbed me from the pain in my chest that I took a second. And a third.

I was on my fifth and nearing the halfway point of the large bottle when I heard the familiar roar of an engine just outside and the sound of gravel flying as tires squealed to a stop. The engine shut off, the driver's door slammed shut, and the front door of the house slammed open in the span of about ten seconds. I heard her boot-steps storming down the hall. I didn't have time to recap the whiskey or find a hiding spot for it. I didn't have time to collect myself or remind myself why I'd orchestrated everything I had in the past twenty-four hours. I didn't think about anything but her and the way she made me feel and the way I knew I made her feel as she stormed down the hall, pissed off to the point of exploding from the sound of her steps.

"You had better be dead, so help me God, Garth Black, because if you're not, I'm going to kill you." When she rounded into the room, Josie broke to a stop. At first, something that looked close to relief covered her face, but that was driven away by the anger that was about to reach its tipping point.

"Not dead yet, babe." My voice sounded wrong, too lazy-sounding and low, but that was probably the whiskey's fault. "Just shitfaced."

She shook her head, taking in the scene around us. Her eyes lingered on the half-empty bottle of golden liquid between my legs. "You're dead." She crossed her arms and leveled me with a look. "Colt Mason? That was your plan? Rekindling the flame with Colt?"

I shouldn't have drunk so much so quickly. It had hit me hard and lowered just about every inhibition I possessed . . . which wasn't many. But Josie was one of those inhibitions, and if I wasn't careful, I knew I'd give in big time. I had to keep trying to remind myself why I needed to keep her at a mile of arm's lengths.

"What? Colt's a good guy. You used to think that once," I said. "Is it so far-fetched to believe you could feel that way again?"

She hadn't stopped glaring at me since she'd entered the room. I didn't think she'd even taken a break to blink. "He is a good guy, a better one than you in some ways, especially after what you pulled tonight, but he's not *my* guy." She bit her lip for a moment. "What did you think I was going to do, huh? Give him a rebound fuck down there by *our* watering hole and then what? We'd just go on to live happily ever after?"

I had to take a break from her glare, so I rolled over to one of the open windows and stared into the night. I stared for so long I could feel it starting to stare back. "That doesn't seem so far-fetched either." My voice sounded as empty as I felt. Digging into a dark place, I found what I needed to say and braced myself for her reaction. "And with your sexual appetite, after the month-plus you haven't gotten any, I thought you'd practically jump him if I was out of the picture."

I hadn't heard her approaching, but I definitely heard the snap of her palm slapping my cheek. I felt the sting of it too.

"I wish I could hate you right now, Garth Black, because I would hate you so, so much it's not even funny. So much." Her lower lip wobbled a few times, but her glare remained unaffected.

"You just hit a guy in a wheelchair, Josie. That's a bit low, don't you think?" I rubbed the place she'd slapped me, not because it hurt but because it reminded me I wasn't as numb as I'd thought I was. The prickling sensation and tingles trickling into my jaw told a different story.

"I didn't hit a guy in a wheelchair. I hit *you*." She thrust her arms at me. "When are you going to stop being defined by that thing and move on?"

My hands lowered to each wheel as I lifted my brows. "Kind of hard to move on from it when I'm paralyzed."

"All you see when you look at yourself or think about yourself or talk about yourself is that damn wheelchair. It's nothing more than some metal, nylon, and rubber, but you're acting like it's this nemesis or higher power or something you have no control over." Her eyes didn't move from mine, not once. "If all you want to see when you look at yourself is that chair, that's your issue, but don't make the rest of us out to be so short-sighted."

I tipped my hat down lower on my forehead. For Josie, that might have been true. She hardly seemed to notice my wheelchair unless I brought it up, but everyone else was different. Instead of looking me in the eye, their gazes shifted from my chair to my legs.

A breeze came through the window, breaking across my face. It was cool enough to dull the haze of the whiskey, though only as partially as it was temporary. "How did you find me?"

I heard her step closer and sniff the air. "All I had to do was follow the scent of coward," she said, followed by another sniff. I didn't argue or try to deny it, because she was right—I was a coward—but my reasons were noble, so at least I was an honorable coward. "I can't believe I didn't figure it out sooner, but I guess I was a little busy panicking over where you were and driving through town, checking every last one of your old haunts and asking if anyone had seen you while calling every last friend and enemy of yours I had the number to."

My phone was still shut off, probably close to dying, and since I didn't have a way to charge it, it would stay that way. That was okay though. A cell phone was a modern convenience I could have done without, especially when I imagined the earfuls I'd get from Rowen and Jesse when they found out what I'd done. "I suppose that explains why I have a few dozen voicemails and texts from the Sterling-Walkers."

A huff came from Josie, who was still out of view behind me. That was good too. It was easier to talk to her when I wasn't looking at her. Or at least it was easier to talk and mask what I was feeling when I wasn't looking at her.

"They were so worried they were about to jump in the truck and haul over here to help find you, but that was about the time I got your message about meeting you." A bitter note buried itself deeper in Josie's voice. "Not cool of you to go stress a pregnant woman—a *high-risk* pregnant woman—out, Garth. Like you needed anymore bad karma stacked up against you."

Another rush of cool air blew past me. "I wasn't the one who called them and said I'd gone missing."

She took two solid steps closer, probably so she would be within arm's reach of my neck. "Why can't I hate you?"

"Because you have a thing for guys on four wheels?"

"It should be easier," she said to herself, as if she hadn't heard my reply. "It really should be easier to turn off these feelings I have for you, at least enough so I can hit the level of strongly dislike."

Having her so close was messing with me. Especially since I could smell her shampoo at this range. The longer she stayed, the more she'd wear me down, and I was already so worn down I was nothing more than a nub. "What are you doing here, Josie?"

"You promised me a meeting tonight. A meeting with you. I'm just making sure you hold up your end of that promise."

The gentle breeze still working through the window was playing with her hair, swirling it around behind her and throwing a few strands into her face. I was only watching from the very corner of my eye, but she was so beautiful, I found it hard to breathe. How could I let this woman go?

"I'm never going to walk again." There—that was how. Because I was a gruff jerk.

She gave a single nod. "I know that."

"Knowing that and accepting that are two different things."

Her eyes shifted from staring out the window to me. An eyebrow crept higher up her forehead. "You're the one so hung up on that distinction. I'm good with what is and what may be, and I'm ready to get on with our lives already, which is hard to do, by the way, when you try to set me up with other guys." She was waiting for me to really look at her.

She'd have to wait a long time because I couldn't look at her and keep up this act much longer. "How did you and Colt leave things?"

She moved closer to the window beside me. "Next time you get the genius idea to set me up with another guy, you might want to do your homework to see if said guy is available in the first place. Thank you for that awkward moment, by the way too. Ass. Hole."

My jaw tightened. "I didn't know Colt was serious with anyone."

"Yeah, that's obvious," she muttered.

"Anyone I know?" I asked, not because I cared but because the longer we talked about Colt, the less we would talk about me.

"A little. Only one of your best friend's little sisters." I saw her watching me, waiting for something to register, but the only thing that registered was more confusion. "Jesse is the best friend I was referring to. In case you were running through some long list of best friends I'm not aware of."

My eyes narrowed into the night. "Which one?"

"The only one old enough to date." Josie's voice was coated in sarcasm as she stepped closer. But it wasn't me she moving closer to—it was the window. "Why do you think Jesse was just exuding warm feelings when we all

206

ran into each other at dinner that night?"

I should have picked up on Jesse's out-of-character gruffness with Colt and what it could have meant, but I'd been too preoccupied that night. "Lily's, like, painfully sweet and quiet. Colt's, like, painfully not those things." I shook my head, wondering if Josie had it wrong. "I'm not getting the love connection there."

"I'm not sure you're qualified to judge any love connection after what you pulled tonight." The edge in her voice was dulling, but her posture didn't indicate a woman letting go of her anger.

"Maybe," I answered quietly.

Silence came next, but for no longer than a minute. Josie sighed. "So what's your plan from here, Garth? Do you have one? Is it practical?" she added when I raised a brow in her direction. "Because I'm starting to question your ability to form a string of logical thoughts."

The breeze was playing with the hem of her sundress as it continued tugging at her hair. I would have preferred to face her and spend the rest of our last night together watching the wind move over her, but I knew Josie well enough to know she wouldn't have gone for that. She likely had another five dozen questions and comments and insults to fire at me. "My plan is for you to let me go and get on with your life while I get on with mine. *That's* my plan." I had to close my eyes to get out the rest. "I'm ready to implement it whenever you are."

If my words pained her as much to hear as they pained me to say, she didn't show it. "With you and your little friend there?" Her chin lifted, indicating the bottle shoved between my legs.

I felt as if it had almost started to burn me, despite the

lack of feeling I had in that region. "I like to consider myself open-minded when it comes to my friendships."

Josie glared at the bottle for another moment before holding out her arms and slowly spinning in place. "And this is where you're planning to get on with your life?" Her gaze lingered on the broken windows, the missing drywall, and the dangling electrical wires. "Holed up in this place and letting yourself rot away on the outside while your insides rot away from drinking that stuff? Whining about your glory days and the accident that ended them to anyone who'll listen? Shutting yourself away from the world you knew, living your life going from one bottle to the next?" She paused, waiting for me to make eye contact.

Even if I'd tried, I couldn't have. I was too damn ashamed of my behavior, from the day I'd woken up in the hospital to now, with an emphasis on the past day and a half.

She eventually continued, accepting I didn't have it in me to look her in the eyes anymore. "Now who does that sound like?"

For a moment, I felt a surge of rage at her insinuation, but it didn't last. My shoulders sagged as I took a good look at myself. My clothes were dirty and rumpled, the odor rolling off me a mix of sweat and body odor, a bottle of whiskey close to my heart and, more importantly, my lips. I hadn't seen it until right that moment when she'd all but thrown it in my face, but I could have been a carbon copy of Clay. Right down to the bull-riding injury that hadn't just ruined my career—I'd let it ruin the other parts of my life as well.

I slumped further into the chair, my fingers curling

tightly around the neck of the bottle. I needed another drink to dull what I was feeling. I needed the rest of that bottle to wash the realization that I was becoming my father out of my mind until I woke up tomorrow in a pile of my own vomit and self-loathing.

"You should leave, Josie." My voice sounded like his too. If her shoving Clay in my face wasn't enough to remind me why I needed to save her from myself, like he hadn't been man enough to do with my mom, I didn't know what could have been more motivating.

"This place is just as much mine as it is yours. My money went into it too. My name's on the deed just like yours is." Her arms folded over her stomach as she backed away from the window. "So if you want to rot away on your own, go buy your own shitty little trailer and get on with it already. I'm going to go to bed now. In *my* house." Leaving the room, she turned down the hallway.

I followed her, but she was moving quickly, and I was too drunk to move as fast. Or hold a straight line.

"Hey, Insane," I called when I heard her climbing the steps to the second story. She couldn't just spend the night there. There wasn't anything up in those bedrooms but cobwebs and dust. "Locate the loose screw and drill it back into place, okay? You're not staying."

She paused on the stairs, turning to look at me at the foot of them. "What are you going to do?" She peaked an eyebrow. "Make me leave?"

I shrugged. "Maybe."

She moved a step higher, practically smirking at me. "Then make me."

She was halfway up the stairs and only moving higher, challenging me with that look on her face. I'd come out here to distance myself from her, and there she was, making herself comfortable and staying put, and there was absolutely nothing I could do to stop her. Being confined to the chair made me feel a whole new level of helpless.

"You want me to stop defining myself by this wheelchair, but how can I not when you do something like this?" I thrust my arm at her. So close, but she might as well have been in another galaxy for my ability to reach her.

"The man I fell in love with wouldn't have let a few measly stairs or that damn chair get in the way of what he wanted," she shouted, tears welling in her eyes.

My gaze lowered to all that was left in my life—the bottle between my legs. "That man is gone."

Those words settled in the air for a minute. Just when I thought she'd crept up the stairs silently, she cleared her throat. "Can you bring him back? Please?" She reached into the pocket of her tiny cardigan, but I couldn't make out what she pulled out. It had to have been small. "I want the one who picked out this ring with the intention of giving it to me. I want that guy back, the one who wanted to spend the rest of his life with me."

I still couldn't see what she had pinched between her fingers—the combination of the dark and my impaired vision made it difficult out to make my hand in front of my face without it looking blurry—but I knew what she'd pulled from her pocket.

"I want him to look me in the eye and ask a certain question, and I want to give him my answer. I want that back." Her voice was strong, her posture the same, but the first tear finally fell from her eyes.

I didn't want to be responsible for any more of her tears, but I couldn't feed her a lie just to save a few tears. I knew, in the long run, I was saving her a whole lot more of them by setting her free. "That man is gone," I repeated, more to myself than to her.

"No, he's still there," she said with a shake of her head. "He's just being strangled by this defeatist imposter." She let that hang in the air for a minute before continuing up the stairs. "If you need me, I'll be upstairs."

I watched her go, though I knew I shouldn't have. "I don't need you." Again, I was saying it to myself more than to her, as if I were trying to convince myself it was the truth.

"If that were true, you wouldn't still be talking to me and staring at me from the bottom of those stairs like your heart just got ripped out of your chest." She stopped on one of the top stairs but kept her back to me. "You can keep this act up for as long as you want, Garth, but there's nothing you can say or do to make me believe we don't have a future together because you're in some fucking wheelchair. We have one of the greatest love stories of all time, and what? You think something as small and stupid as a wheelchair could break us apart?" She snapped her fingers, just barely looking over her shoulder. "You don't throw away the love of a lifetime because someone gets injured—that's when you prove what your love's really made of."

I swallowed, my throat bobbing from the ball stuck inside it. "Josie—"

She spun on the steps, her fists balling at her sides. "Stop calling me Josie." Her jaw tightened. "I don't like it."

My own fists balled, but it was from frustration instead of anger. "Stop acting like everything's going to be

211

okay," I said in a tone so small it didn't even sound like me. "I don't like it."

She climbed another step. "I'll see you tomorrow morning. And the morning after that." Her voice sounded so final I believed her. "Oh yeah, and the morning after that and every single goddamned morning after that."

My fists were so tightly curled I felt my nails about to draw blood from my palms. "I won't let you rot with me. You need to leave. Now."

Her head shook, whipping her hair back and forth over her back in one long sheet. "It should be so easy right now to look at you and process everything you've just said and done and feel some level of hate"—she peeked back at me over her shoulder from the top of the stairs—"but no, nothing. Son of a bitch."

"Josie—"

"Good night. Sweet dreams. I love you," she said with a wave.

Fire surged into my bloodstream as I felt like I couldn't control a single part of my life anymore. "Damn it, Josie!"

She lifted her finger as if she had been suddenly reminded of something. "Oh, and here's the ring back since I kind of stole it from your drawer when I was ransacking your room last night, searching for any clue as to where you might have gone." She tossed the ring at me like it was nothing more significant than a quarter.

It landed in my lap, falling between the seam of my legs where the bottle of whiskey still sloshed. That couldn't have been a simple coincidence. That was fate's way of toying with its favorite peon and putting him in his place.

"When the guy who picked out that ring is back, he can ask me his question."

CHAPTER fifteen

I COULDN'T FALL asleep that night either. Big surprise.

After sitting at the bottom of those stairs for God knew how long—half wanting her to come back and argue with me, half wondering if I'd made it all up in my alcohol-induced stupor—I finally made my way back into the bedroom. I wheeled up to the same broken window and stared out it until my eyes watered.

I kept both the bottle and the ring between my legs, too scared to let go of the bottle for one reason and too scared to let go of the ring for another reason. I could have one but not both. They couldn't coexist. Of course I knew which one I wanted—that was a no-brainer—but I knew with just as much certainty I couldn't have her. So really, the choice of which to let go and which to curl my fingers around was a simple one, but I wasn't ready to let go of that ring and everything it symbolized quite yet. In the morning, when I was fresh from a few hours of rest and had slept off the whiskey . . . then maybe, but not tonight.

I had a few hours left of pretending the girl I'd purchased the ring for was still mine.

That thought must have lulled me to sleep finally because I didn't know I'd fallen asleep until I snapped awake from the sound of something shattering. I was still in my chair and had a splitting headache to show for my drinking, but at least I could see straight again and didn't feel like the room was slowly revolving around me.

"Josie?" I called, my voice hoarse from sleep and whiskey.

No reply came.

I held my breath and listened. The old house might have creaked and whined and groaned like nothing else, but it didn't make shattering noises. No, *people* made shattering noises.

"Josie?" This time my voice was louder. I turned around in my chair and wheeled toward the doorway before stopping when I heard sounds coming from the kitchen. Not just the sounds of the fridge buzzing or the floorboards cracking or the walls creaking . . . the sounds of someone ripping open drawers and cupboards, searching for something. "Josie? Is that you?"

The sounds in the kitchen came to a sudden stop. I swallowed when no answer came. It wasn't Josie. I stayed quiet for a minute, waiting for the next noises, but nothing came. I'd almost convinced myself I'd been half-dreaming those breaking, rummaging noises when a different sound filled the house. This one I knew, and even though it was just the old floorboards creaking, they creaked the way they did when someone was walking over them.

The sounds got closer, which meant whoever it was was making their way down the hall . . . past the stairway . . . coming to a stop just outside the doorway.

My throat had gone dry and my heart had sped up some, but still I wheeled closer. "Come on out, you son of a bitch. Stop hiding like a coward."

He stayed there for another minute, but I heard his

breath, heavy and rattling. Shit, I could *smell* him, and it wasn't as if I were surrounded by a potpourri of pleasant scents.

"Am I going out there or are you coming in here?" I called, and that was when he crept into the doorway and showed himself.

He was a vagrant, a bum—probably one of the train jumpers who laid over in Missoula for a night or two on their journeys West. He wasn't just a bum though—he was a junkie too. From the way he was shaking and how his pupils looked about to explode out of his eyeballs, he was on a serious tweaking trip.

He looked close to forty, which probably meant he was close to my age, and from the way his coat and clothes hung off him, it was impossible to gauge his size. I could tell that I was taller than he was . . . although he was a hell of a lot taller than I sat in a wheelchair. He had the face of a fox—shifty, wide-set eyes, and a long, narrow face. When he smiled, he looked more like a demon than any kind of mammal or being of this world. His smile, like the rest of him, told the story of a long, hard life of using. What teeth he had left were decaying to the point of practically falling out, and his gums weren't in much better shape.

"I think you're lost there, señor," I said in a calm, quiet voice. Calm to hopefully rub off on him and quiet to hopefully keep Josie from hearing anything and running down the stairs to see what was up.

"I thought so too." His voice sounded as strung-out as he looked, and his words were more garbled than they were clear—probably because he had a whole five teeth that were a bite into an apple away from falling out. That creepy-as-all-hell smile of his twisted into place again as he studied me with those dilated eyes. "But then I ran into you."

"Lucky for me." I eyed the room casually, looking for anything that could work as a weapon when he finally made his move. Being up against a cripple in a wheelchair, he probably wouldn't wait long. "What's your name?"

"I don't have one." He stepped inside the room, glancing around it the same way I was. Although he was probably looking for a stash of drugs or money instead.

"So what shall I call you?" I rolled closer when he took another step inside the room, if for no other reason than to prove to him I wasn't scared. I wasn't the kind of guy who backed down, no matter how high the odds were stacked against me.

"Whatever you want. I don't care," he said as a violent twitch rolled down his body.

"Fabulous. How about Shithead?" I suggested. "That seems fitting."

"My stepdad used to call me that." His eyes narrowed for just a moment before they went wide again as he searched the room.

"Good, then you're used to hearing it directed at you. That will make things easier." I wheeled forward a bit before wrapping my fingers around the neck of the whiskey bottle. Using good whiskey on a lowlife like this seemed like a hell of a waste, but I couldn't bring him down with a couple swings as I could have before. The whiskey would have to be a casualty of war. "What do you want, Shithead?"

His eyes dropped to my hand gripping the bottle, another shudder rocking through him. His gaze shifted just as quickly—he wasn't looking for the hooch. That would have been all too easy. What happened to the days when a bum would have been thrilled with a half-bottle of decent whiskey?

His hand twitched for his coat pocket. It twitched again when he pulled it out. Clutched in his trembling hand was a knife. It was a rusted old pocketknife, and he didn't even know how to hold the damn thing, but with enough force, it could have broken the skin, and a rusty knife usually came with a nasty infection that required antibiotics and daily dressing changes. Not that I'd had any personal experience . . .

"Where's your wallet?" He held out the knife like it was a number two pencil. The upside was if he did take a slice at me, he'd probably wind up slicing himself in the process too.

"Over there." I nodded at the air mattress stuffed into the corner. "Under the bed."

He moved toward it instantly in short, shaking strides.

"I gotta warn you that if you're hoping to hit the jackpot, you're going to be way disappointed, Shithead. If you dig deep, you might be able to pull out a couple of bucks. Enough to buy what? A trial-sized tube of toothpaste and a toothbrush so you can try to save what teeth you have left?"

He didn't reply to my jeer. Instead, he dug around under the air mattress until he pulled out my wallet. His fingers scurried through it, pulling out cards and receipts and whatever was left. In the end, he managed to scavenge a dollar bill and a couple credit cards. He shoved them into the deep pockets of his coat.

"Yeah, Shithead, those are going to get declined if

you try using them. Knock yourself out if you want to though. They're of no use to me anymore anyways."

I was moving up behind him, hoping he'd stay distracted for another moment so I could take my best swing at him with the whiskey bottle. My reach wouldn't have gone higher than his chest, so my plan was to whack him first between his legs, which would hopefully result in him dropping to his knees—providing he hadn't rotted that part of himself off like he had his teeth. Then once he was at my level, I'd take a solid swing at his head to knock him out until I could get to my phone and call the cops.

I was hoping to get that all taken care of without alerting Josie. Panic settled deep into my stomach when I imagined what would happen if Shithead found out a girl was in the house—on the top floor I couldn't possibly get to.

Panic filtered into my bloodstream too.

"Where are your drugs?" He chucked my wallet over his shoulder and kicked at the corners of the mattress. "Where do you keep them?"

"Unlike some guy with guts burned out by battery acid and household cleaners, I don't use. If you're looking to burn what's left of your throat, might I suggest the Carson Street Bridge back in town? You'll find just what you're looking for there."

He continued to kick at the mattress, lifting and moving it until he was convinced I wasn't storing my stash beneath where I slept like he probably did. "Yeah, but you're a cripple. That means you get the good drugs from the doctors." He licked his lips, rubbing his nose as if he had an itch that couldn't be scratched. "Where do you keep them?"

With him focusing on me again, I'd lost my window of opportunity for a surprise attack. Oh well, I could still take him. Or at least I thought I could, thanks to my handy bottle of whiskey. "Up my ass. Why don't you come dig them out?" I lifted a brow and waited for his reaction.

He didn't fall for it though. He kept his distance while continuing to furiously rub his nose. "Where are they? I don't want to have to hurt you, but I will if you don't tell me where you keep them."

"You don't want to *have* to hurt me?" I repeated, stalling. He was getting worked up, his whole body bouncing and shaking with that pathetic little knife aimed my way again. "If that isn't victim verbiage, I don't know what is. Take control of your life, Shithead. Take responsibility for your own actions. If you hurt me, hurt me. You don't *have* to do anything. No more than you *had* to take the first step down whatever road led you to this high point in your life."

That was when I heard more footsteps moving through the house—but these ones were louder and moving with more purpose. If I called to her, he'd know she was there and could trap her in the hall or on the stairs. If I didn't call to warn her, she'd walk right into the middle of this stand-off shit-storm.

While I pondered an impossible decision, Josie made the decision for me. "Garth?" She had just burst into the room when she repeated my name, followed by, "Who are you talking to?"

"Fuck, Joze," I said under my breath, shaking my head.

She'd clearly been asleep and had stripped down to what she typically wore to bed at night—when she wore anything—a tiny tank top and her underwear. Not how I'd hoped she'd come dressed when a tweaker busted into our house.

At first, her attention was only aimed at me, but when Shithead started another round of twitching, her gaze shifted to the corner of the room. Her eyes went wide as she side-stepped toward me. "What's going on, Garth?" Her voice was a few notes high with worry, but she didn't blink as Shithead stared at her, molesting her with those filthy eyes of his, his tongue flicking at his lips like the snake he was.

"It's okay, Josie. Everything's fine." My voice might have fooled her, but I was anything but calm. "Just come stand behind me, okay?"

She kept sliding in my direction, her gaze drifting between me and the man who'd stepped out of his corner to move our way. The panic I'd felt earlier shifted into something else when I watched his eyes move over Josie. It shifted into fire that burned through my veins, making my arms shake with rage.

"You don't have any money. You won't share your drugs." Shithead licked his cracked lips a few more times, tilting his head as he moved closer, his stare never shifting from Josie. "Maybe you won't mind sharing her then?"

Her hand lowered to my shoulder when she stopped behind me, curling into me in a way that told me she was as scared as I was. The blood boiling inside me felt about to spill over.

"You better stop coming closer, and unless you want to lose your eyeballs, you'd better take your eyes off her right now, Shithead."

He didn't reply. He didn't glance my way. It was like

he hadn't even heard what I'd said. His eyes stayed trained on Josie as he stepped closer every few seconds.

Keeping my eyes on him, I tilted my head back toward her a bit. "I want you to run, Josie." I indicated the doorway. "I don't want you to stop running until you make it to one of the neighbors' places. Understood?" I noticed her head shake, which made mine do the same. "Run," I hissed at her.

"I'm not leaving you," she answered, her voice returning to its normal tenor as her fingers loosened their grip around my shoulder.

Shithead kept making his tweaking, twitchy way closer.

Panic tightened my airways. "I *want* you to leave me."

"Haven't been very successful at that endeavor in the past, have you, Black?" She stepped out from behind me to stand beside me. A peaceful expression had settled on her face. "You won't be successful this time either."

My hand curled so tightly around the neck of the bottle it started to tremble. "This isn't about us, Josie. This is about *you*. Your wellbeing and keeping you safe." My eyes narrowed as he kept moving closer, his smile cutting higher on one side. "I'm trying to keep you alive here, Joze. A little help in that department would be much appreciated."

"You can keep telling me to leave all you want if it makes you feel better, but I'm not leaving." She looked at me with fear flashing in her eyes, but that peaceful expression still hadn't crumbled. "I'm right where I belong."

"Can you ever listen to anything I ask you to do?"

She peaked an eyebrow, still able to muster up a

smile with some creep's eyes on her. "Yeah. When you stop asking me to do stupid things."

"Leave," I hissed again.

"Never."

Shithead sniffed, coming to a stop a few yards away. "She's not leaving."

His head bobbed violently and his eyeballs seemed to revolve in his head a few times before the tremor calmed. The guy was showing some extreme signs of withdrawal, and I knew enough from growing up on the rough side of the tracks that people like him—ones with nothing to lose—would do just about anything to get their next fix. Wherever that next fix might come from.

That his eyes hadn't shifted from Josie since she'd burst into the room, I knew just what he had in mind to serve as a temporary substitute to the battery-acid-and-Sudafed cocktail he really wanted.

He lifted his pocketknife again, pointing at Josie with a shaking arm. "I don't want to have to hurt you." He gave a twisted smile right before he lunged toward her, leading with that rusty blade.

"No!" I bellowed, my voice filling the room and echoing down the hall. I managed to sweep Josie behind me, and just as he was steps away from her, I angled myself into his path and threw my shoulder into his chest.

We tumbled to the ground in a heap. I landed on top. I didn't know where the bottle had gone, but it definitely wasn't still stuck between my legs. But I didn't need it. I had the advantage of being on top of him, and I also had the advantage of having so much adrenaline and rage from him threatening Josie that I could feel it spilling out of my ears. Besides, I didn't want to hit the son of a bitch with a bottle. I wanted to beat the shit out of him with my own fists. I wanted to break something, several somethings, so whenever he took a step on his sorry, sad way or moved his jaw or took a wheezy breath, he'd ache and remember what had happened when he'd threatened a woman.

I didn't want to just hurt him though. No . . . as I swung at him over and over, feeling my knuckles connect with his flesh and bone, looking into those same eyes he'd defiled Josie with right in front of me, I wanted to do more. I didn't want to stop punching him until the light had gone out in those filthy eyes. I didn't want to stop until his body had gone limp beneath mine.

I heard Josie's shouts from behind me, but it was as if I were stuck in a dream. I could hear her, but I couldn't make out her words or the message she was trying to get across. I was lost in the world of my own rage and destruction.

The eyes below me closed, but I didn't stop. I just kept swinging at him, over and over, his head rocking one direction and then the other, like a pendulum moving inside a grandfather clock. *He'd threatened her. He'd wanted to hurt her.* Those were the reminders my mind switched between as I continued, knowing the life was almost beaten out of the worthless sack beneath me.

"Stop, Garth." Josie's voice cut through my haze when I felt her hand curl around my shoulder. "Come on, baby. Stop. He can't hurt me anymore."

Hearing her say it only made me keep swinging. Plenty of places on his face were split open—plenty of places on my knuckles were split too—but I couldn't stop. Josie. He was going to hurt her. If I hadn't gotten to him first, he would have.

I screamed again, followed by another punch that felt as though it broke a few bones in my hand.

"Enough!" Josie pulled on both of my shoulders, trying to pull me off the limp piece of shit. "You hit him anymore, and you're heading to jail instead of him. I won't let you push me away like that either." Wrapping her arms around my chest, she gave a hard pull and managed to pry me far enough away that my fists couldn't reach him. They didn't stop punching the air for a few moments though. "Nice try though."

Josie didn't let me go, even after she'd dragged me all the way off him. It was only then, once a layer of adrenaline had fallen away, that I could acknowledge what was sticking out of my thigh. The blade was almost completely buried in my leg, and as adrenaline drained from my system, the pain from the stab started to burn down my leg.

"Son of a bitch." I groaned, reaching for the knife to pull it out. Damn rusty pocket knives. That was the second time I'd been stabbed by one.

"Don't pull it out!" Josie clamped her hand over mine before I could pluck the blade from my thigh. "You're never supposed to pull a knife out of your body. You should know that." She swatted my other hand when it came around.

"This isn't a knife, Joze." I stopped trying to pull it free and twisted around to inspect her. "Calling this a knife is an insult to an actual knife. A butter knife included."

"Just stabbed by a man who broke into our place and still the sarcasm." A smile moved into place on her face. "Is there anything you take seriously?"

My eyes did another inspection of her. On the outside, she seemed unhurt. "You. Your safety. Your wellbeing. *That* I take very seriously, and thank you, by the way, for respecting that and listening to me when I told you to run."

Josie wound her hand through mine, turning it over and grimacing when she saw my knuckles. "I don't run when things get scary, Garth. I thought you would have known that by now."

I looked around the room. The unconscious man beside us, the tipped-over wheelchair behind us . . . she had proven that for as long as I'd known her. I'd just been unable or unwilling to accept that about her.

"Are you okay?" I asked.

She nodded. "It would take a hell of a lot more than some junkie's threats to hurt me."

A wince spread across my face when another stab of pain shot up my leg. I could almost feel the rust crusting off inside the wound, just waiting to spread infection. "Joze, would you mind grabbing my phone from my wheelchair and calling 911? This guy's going to require a hospital stay, and I'm going to need some antibiotics, and shit . . ." Another surge of pain, thanks to that pathetic little knife. "Some pain killers too."

Josie was in the middle of shuffling through the side pockets of my wheelchair when she froze. Turning her head slowly, her eyes widened as they lowered to my legs. "Does that hurt?" She stared at the knife sticking out of my thigh.

"Like a son of a bitch," I answered, tempted to rip the blade out again. I stifled the urge, knowing Josie would have been pissed. When she stayed silent, still frozen beside my wheelchair, I glanced up. She was smiling at me.

"You're not getting it, are you?" she said.

"Not getting why you're smiling ear-to-ear after eve-rything that just happened? No, I'm not getting it."

She crawled over, pausing at my feet before dropping her hands just above my ankles. Her smile stayed in place as she gently squeezed my legs.

"What are you doing, crazy person?" I tried to not re-turn her smile, but it was impossible. I'd never been able to avoid smiling back when she grinned at me the way she did now. "You're supposed to be calling 911. You're sup-posed to be freaking out and making a mental note to call a shrink in the morning so you can talk about what you went through tonight." Her hands slid higher up my legs, stop-ping just above my knees. "You're not supposed to be grinning at me and crawling up my legs with that glint in your eyes."

Her hands moved higher up my leg, that spark in her eyes growing. My brows pulled together as I tried to figure out what she was trying to tell me. Her fingers crept a little higher, stopping when they got close to the knife.

"How much farther am I going to have to go before it registers?" Her eyes dropped to her hands on my legs be-fore her gaze moved higher. They didn't stop until they locked with my eyes.

Only after she'd held my stare for a few moments, followed by an eyebrow slowly lifting, did I get it.

I could feel her hands on my legs. I could feel pain from the knife buried in my thigh. I could feel my feet and toes and how my sock had becoming annoyingly bunched up down in my boot. I could feel my legs . . .

"Joze . . ." I breathed, no other words seeming appro-priate.

"I know, baby. I know." Tears flowed down her face,

and she threw herself at me.

Her arms wound around my neck, and mine slipped around her waist, our foreheads together as I let what had just happened, what *was* happening, sink in. We sat like that for a few minutes, me in a stunned silence while Josie kept smiling and crying. Just when it seemed like I was getting close to grasping what had happened, it would get away from me, and I'd have to start all over again.

I forgot all about the knife sticking out of my leg. I forgot about the man lying passed out a few feet away. I even forgot about the phone call to 911 and the wheelchair beside us, where my phone was still buried. All I could think about was the miracle that had, for some reason, fallen into my lap.

The miracle wasn't the sensation surging into my legs again—it was her. Josie was the miracle. There she was, sitting in my lap and wrapped around me, whispering I love you over and over as she continued to cry happy tears, hanging on to me in the way she always had no matter what I'd been going through—like there was nothing I could do or we could go through that could ever get her to let go.

Like her love was forever.

She'd proven that to me countless times—that wasn't the reason I hadn't picked up on it sooner. I hadn't seen it, because I hadn't been ready to see it. I had to lose my legs, face the reality of losing her, and look the devil in the face with both eyes open before I could accept that she'd love me forever, the same way I'd love her. That fact wouldn't change whether we were together or apart, so why make life harder than it already was by living apart? Neither space, time, nor situation would change that there was only one person in this godforsaken world for me. I could push her away and shove her away in my best attempts to save her from me, but nothing could change that Josie and I were bound to each other in such a way that nothing could sever the bond.

"Josie . . ." I swallowed and tightened my arms around her. "I'm sorry."

Her head resting on my shoulder nodded. "I know."

"I only did what I did because I thought it was best for you. All I want is the best for you."

Another nod. "I know."

She'd been sitting on my lap with her legs wrapped around my back for so long, I could feel my legs starting to go numb. The pricks and stabs of my lower half going numb had never felt so damn good.

"I love you," I whispered.

Her head bobbed against my shoulder as she repeated, "I know."

"I want to spend the rest of my life with you, and I swear to God, Joze, I'll swear to every God you want me to, I'm done trying to do what's noble and pushing you away to keep you safe from me. I'm done thinking you'll be happier with someone else. I'm done thinking we could one day move on from each other if we tried. I'm done being an idiot." I stopped. "Well, I'm done being an idiot in those ways at least."

Josie's small laugh rolled across my neck. Her arms tightened around my neck. "I know."

"Oh, and Joze? The next time you hear me talking to someone in a dark room late at night when neither of us were exactly expecting company, please don't come charging in dressed in nothing but your underwear, okay?

For Christ's sake." I let out a long sigh as I shook my head at her.

Another laugh came from her, but just as she was about to repeat her two-word mantra, my mouth found hers and silenced it.

CHAPTER sixteen

EVERYONE WANTED TO give a name to what had happened to me. The pastor at the community church in town preached to the congregation about it being a miracle. Dr. Murphy gave it a really long, drawn-out name that I couldn't have repeated if someone had offered to pay me a thousand bucks. The hippie lady who owned a candle-and-hemp store in town said it was something having to do with transcendentalism . . . or something like that. Everyone had a name for it.

I did too. But it wasn't miracle or some lengthy medical term. It was her name. Josie. She was the answer and explanation as to why I was walking again. Some physiological phenomenon might have played a part in healing the nerve damage, but I was walking again because Josie had never given up hope in me. That hope didn't come with the condition of if I ever walked again, nor did it only stem from her keeping her fingers crossed that my spine would one day heal. That hope came from her just believing in me and never giving up on me, despite all of the reasons I'd given her to.

If that kind of thing couldn't make a man walk again, then nothing else could.

The last three months had passed in a blur of physical

therapy, doctor appointments, and re-mapping my future. My legs had been weak after being immobile for over a month, but spending a few hours a week in PT and a few more hours in the gym strengthening them on my own got them back to feeling like normal after a month. Doctor Murphy finally twisted my arm into getting that damn MRI. Seemed kind of backward that I wouldn't pay for it when I was injured and needed to get better but would after I was healed. It might have been because after paying that ungodly hospital bill that still haunted my dreams, five grand seemed like chump change.

Dr. Murphy had another drawn-out explanation as to what the MRI revealed, but what it all boiled down to was that my back looked good, my spine looked good, and I was good. That might have been the first time that designation had been assigned to me, but I'd take it after spending a month feeling the very opposite.

Lots more had happened since the night I'd beaten the shit out of that bum and recovered my legs, but the highlight of it had been accepting that if everything life had thrown at us couldn't manage to break Josie and me apart, what we had was something a person didn't just let go of. I couldn't say good-bye even if that was what I thought was the right thing to do for Josie, because unless I was in her life, nothing could be right in her world.

I'd known that for myself for a long time, but I had refused to believe Josie was prisoner to the same sentiment. I knew better now though. She'd said it best when she'd said loving someone was like giving them permission to destroy you yet trusting that they wouldn't. I wouldn't betray her trust by destroying her.

After hitting the low point of trying to set up my girlfriend with her old flame, I'd made a vow to myself that I was done doubting what I'd done to deserve her or what I could ever do to be deserving of her devotion and opted to accept it for what it was and do everything I could to honor that kind of love by paying it back twofold.

I didn't need to understand the why and how of Josie's love to accept and return it.

Four months ago, I'd been in a wheelchair. My career in bull riding had been over. A third of a year later, there I was, wheelchair-free and about to compete in my first ride since the one that had shaken up my whole existence. I'd missed nationals, which was an unfortunate side effect of having been paralyzed, but even though I'd missed that ride, it didn't mean I had to miss all future rides. Just because I'd been one ride away from a national championship didn't mean I couldn't start all over and work my way back up again.

When people had heard of me riding again, I got a wide range of responses. Some, the real cowboys who'd gritted their teeth and would have finished their day even if they'd broken a leg, patted me on the back and grunted, "Atta boy." The doctors and therapists had to—grudgingly perhaps—confirm that as far as my back and health were concerned, I wasn't at risk . . . I mean, other than the obvious risks associated with bull riding. My back would be fine. Until it wasn't, as Dr. Murphy continually reminded me, when I took another bad fall and found myself back in a wheelchair. Or worse. Most people were of a mind like the good doctor's, baffled as to why I'd want to return to the very sport that had nearly killed me. They thought I was spitting on the gift of regaining my mobility by hopping on another bull's back months after healing. They accused me of being careless and stupid and of having a serious god complex that came with assumed invincibility.

They could think whatever the hell they wanted though. I only cared what one person thought, and in so many words, Josie had ordered me to get back on the horse. She hadn't done it without hesitation seeping into her voice or anxiety filtering into her eyes, but I'd gotten the confirmation that she was supportive of me returning to the arena when she flashed my registration, which she'd filled out herself, in my face. The one she'd signed me up for was the one I was riding tonight. My first one back.

Josie hadn't been able to mask her nervousness quite so well tonight, and her nails had been chewed down to nubs by the time we'd made it inside the arena. I'd told her I was willing and ready to walk away then and there if that was what she wanted. If never having to hold her breath while I clung to the back of a bull made her happy, that was good enough for me . . . but instead she'd kissed me and said to ride hard. Following another kiss, she'd turned and rushed away to where I guessed she was going to finish chewing down what was left of her nails until my ride was over.

I thought she felt as I did though, and that was why she hadn't asked me to stop riding. She knew a person couldn't just back away and go down another road every time life dropped a challenge that terrified them. You couldn't walk away from the things and people you loved because of inherit risk. I'd learned that in my way this year, and Josie had learned that in hers.

I'd been holed up in some small room since arriving, stretching and preparing myself for my ride. I'd never been one of those guys who'd had to find a quiet spot to "get his head in the game"—I'd usually just hung out with the rest of the guys staggered around the chutes. But tonight, something was different. I needed a quiet spot. Not just to get into the right mindset but because I didn't want to look like a little ballerina, stretching and limbering up. Plenty of guys had their routines that included stretching, but after what I'd been through, I wanted to be as loose and limber on that bull as a person could be. I wanted to be able to bend in half frontward and backward without snapping or breaking or injuring anything.

I wasn't sure I would get there, *ever*, but I didn't want my competitors and the spectators to witness my attempts at getting there. Some of the stretches my therapist had me doing made me look more like a little girl hoping to be a prima donna rather than a rough and tough bull rider.

A quick knock sounded at the door right before a couple bodies popped inside the room. One looked apologetic for the abrupt interruption. The other didn't appear concerned in the least.

"Are you praying?" Jesse asked as he and Rowen surveyed me on my knees with my elbows propped on the seat of a chair.

Rowen let out a sharp huff. "To what? The only god Garth believes in is himself."

I smiled humorlessly before lifting off of my knees. "For your information, Mrs. Sterling-Walker, I was visualizing."

Jesse's brows lifted. Rowen's brows came together.

"You? Visualizing?" She moved closer, giving me a look of pure and utter skepticism. "What's next? Developing a mantra and reading self-help books?"

I grabbed my hat hanging off the chair and slid it

back into place. I felt naked in front of people without it. "My therapist recommended visualizing the ride before actually getting out there and riding. He said it's, like, been proven to enhance athletes' performance when they do it."

Rowen's skepticism was transferring to Jesse.

"What? You should give it a try before painting a picture or sculpting or whatever it is you do. It might help." I finished strapping my protective chest guard into place. Then I double-checked it. I wasn't leaving anything but fate to fate tonight.

"Yeah, I'll get right on that, Black." Rowen fired a wink at me as she stopped a few feet in front of me. "The nice thing about my chosen profession is that I don't have to worry about my paint brush crushing me and breaking me in half or wonder if a tube of paint will stab me in the ass with its horns."

"If you're not dodging a set of horns or hooves every few weeks, you're not living life to its fullest." I scooted the chair beside me behind Rowen. That was about the same time Jesse showed up with the other chair from the corner.

"What are you talking about?" she said, thanking us both with a tired smile as she maneuvered into the chair Jesse had retrieved for her. Of course. "I'm living life so much to its fullest I'm about to burst." Her hands covered her stomach, which was long past the is-she-or-isn't-she point. I guessed with Rowen being such a tiny slip of a thing that when a baby was developing in her stomach, it really stuck out. She looked as if she'd shoved a basketball underneath her shirt.

"How you feeling there, mama bear?" I asked, pushing the empty chair Jesse's way. He wasn't carrying the baby, but he looked more tired and beat-up than Rowen.

"Like if pregnancy could magically change from being nine and a half months in duration to six, I'd be the happiest person in the world." Her hands continued to slide up and down her stomach. "Other than that and not being able to sleep at night without waking up every two hours to pee and feeling like I could eat the contents of the Country Buffet in town at every meal and feeling like my chest is on fire from the heartburn I get after eating said buffet and having to assure and reassure this guy every time I make a face that might even hint at discomfort . . ." She shot me a smile. "I'm doing fantabulous."

Jesse slid into the chair beside her, hovering just as he'd taken up doing since Rowen got pregnant.

"How's the old ticker?" I asked, lifting my chin.

Rowen chuckled while Jesse shot me a sneer. "Still ticking away. Thanks for asking. How's yours?"

"Good. But I'm not the pregnant one with a heart condition."

"Garth," Jesse warned, but his irritation dimmed when Rowen's chuckle continued.

I wasn't trying to make light of the threat posed to Rowen and their baby, but sometimes life needed to be laughed at instead of feared. At least some of the time.

When she finished laughing, she looked at me. "No, but you're the one about to go out and crawl onto the back of a bull after the last ride left you paralyzed from the neck down." She gave me an evil little smile. "In terms of who's got the bigger death wish, you've got me beat, Black. Congratulations."

I bowed while Jesse heaved a sigh.

"How have the cattle been?" he piped up, obviously wanting the topic shifted away from death wishes. "You need a hand this week with anything?"

"If you know of a way to magically turn fifty head into five hundred, I'd love a hand with that." I kneeled beside them because I felt weird talking down at them. I guessed I'd learned a few things from riding around in that wheelchair for a month. "Other than that, yes, I'd love a hand. With anything and everything."

"I can't believe it." Rowen shook her head. "You're becoming Rancher Black. Good for you."

"I'm not sure you can call the man who's adding to his herd literally one cow at a time a 'rancher' per se, but I'm hoping to get there one day."

If I hadn't been looking at her, I wouldn't have believed that the reason for the glassiness in her eyes was because she was getting . . . *emotional*? That was a condition Rowen didn't register—at least not in a form other than anger or irritation.

"Good for you." She patted my hand. "I'm proud of you."

When she sniffed and looked away, I guessed to hide the tears forming, I looked at Jesse with a dumbfounded expression. All he did was shrug and keep his lips shut.

After I'd paid all the hospital bills, against all odds, I'd still had enough left in my bank account to purchase a portion of the land we'd planned on and add a handful of cattle to get us started. It was a tenth of what Josie and I had planned on having by this point, but instead of it being a defeat, it felt like a victory. After facing the very real possibility of never walking again, being able to ride a horse and navigate our land and our herd was like finding an unexpected corner of heaven on earth.

"Well, it's a far cry from where we hope to wind up, but fifty cows are better than zero," I said, talking to Jesse since Rowen was still looking away, trying to hide her emotions. "After this year, with the money I plan to make riding bulls, we should be able to purchase the rest of what we'd planned on."

Jesse nodded, the same look flashing across his face that I'd seen on Josie's lately. He was worried too. He didn't want to see me get hurt either, but I guessed he was like Josie in that he recognized riding bulls was as much a part of me as Montana and ranching were. To just give it up and walk away would have been like betraying myself.

"And the tweaker? Still nothing?" Jesse wrapped his arm around the back of Rowen's chair, giving her shoulder a gentle massage.

My upper lip curled at the mention of the piece of shit. After Josie and I had called 911, they'd sent both a police car and an ambulance. He'd left in the ambulance though. He'd had a pretty bashed up face and a few cracked ribs that could have come from me or from living the kind of hard life people like him had, but he'd only been in the hospital for a day. He'd stayed in jail for a few days, and after that . . .

"He'd better keep his sorry ass down in New Mexico because if I ever so much as catch a whiff of him around these parts again, I'm going to do what I should have done instead of calling 911 and bury him alive in an unmarked grave."

Jesse gave a nod like he approved. We might have been totally different guys, but in one way we were identical—we'd have done anything to protect our families.

Even if that included committing murder.

After keeping tabs on whom the prison and hospital had dubbed "John Smith" when he'd refused to give them a name and I'd offered the one of Shithead, I'd been waiting for him on the steps of the prison the day he was released. I gave him a one-way train ticket and a threat that made him skulk away from me as if I were more to fear than the devil himself.

"I think I'd better visit the bathroom one more time before you take center stage, Black. I wouldn't want to miss it. You're going to do great tonight—I know it." Rowen started to shove out of her chair as though it were as complicated and daunting as an obstacle course.

Jesse and I snapped to our feet and each held out a hand to help her the rest of the way up. I stayed quiet when she was standing in front of me, waiting.

"What's the matter, Black?" she asked around a yawn.

"Nothing, I'm just waiting for the punch line," I answered.

"What punch line?" she asked, tilting her head at me.

"You know, the sarcastic one peppered with a little smartass I've come to expect from you after you direct a few nice words at me." I gave Jesse another look, like I was wondering where the real Rowen Sterling was hiding. "*That* punch line."

She leaned into Jesse as though she needed the support or to help her balance. "No punch line."

I felt my mouth start to drop open, and that was when she held out her arms and moved toward me.

"Come on. I need a hug, Black," she said with another sniff. "I want a good, solid hug from you just in case you decide to go and give us a repeat of the last ride we saw."

When her arms wrapped around me, I froze for a moment. I wasn't used to being hugged by Rowen. I hadn't known she was capable of those kinds of expressions of affection when it came to me. That wasn't the only reason it felt weird though—her basketball of a tummy was shoving into mine, and that felt all sorts of strange too.

"You hug like a little girl," she muttered as I held her loosely, my hands carefully patting her back.

Behind her, Jesse was trying his damnedest not to smile, but he was failing big time.

"Ah, there she is—the Rowen I know and love." I tightened my arms around her and returned her strong hug.

"That's better," she said before moving out of our embrace and bee-lining for the door. She lifted her hand at Jesse when he started to follow her. "I can't take you hovering outside of the ladies' room one more time today. Sorry. A girl's got to be able to do some things on her own, and going to the bathroom makes that list." She continued through the door when she saw he was staying. Blowing a quick kiss his way, she hustled toward the bathrooms.

I came up beside Jesse and nudged him. "Rowen just hugged me. Did you see that too? Or was that just my imagination?"

"No, she hugged you all right." Jesse continued to stare at the door where she'd disappeared.

"Pregnancy messes with a woman big time," I mused, shaking my head.

"Pregnancy messes with a guy big time," Jesse said, motioning up and down at himself as though he were all the proof necessary to support his claim.

"Hanging in there still?" I hooked my boot behind the leg of one of the chairs and scooted it toward me before dropping into it.

"At best," he answered, taking the other seat.

"How's everything working out being back at Willow Springs? Still going good?"

Jesse's face cleared some from the shift in conversation. I always did a quick mental health check with him to see how he was getting along with the whole pregnancy thing, but I didn't linger on it. Rowen's body was on his mind all day and night, so when we were together, I tried to get his head someplace else for a few minutes.

"It's still good. We're heading back to Seattle for a few weeks soon. Then we'll be back here until Rowen delivers. I don't want to be going back and forth when she's in her third trimester." He was staring at his hands, studying them as if he saw something there I couldn't.

"Still going to build a little place of your own out here?"

A smile broke across his face. "Yeah, we already broke ground. Our baby might celebrate its third birthday before we find enough time and save enough money to finish it, but yeah, that's still the plan."

"I'm sure your mom absolutely hates that you guys will be staying in Montana part of the year."

Jesse chuckled. "Yeah, doting grandmas really hate having their families a half a mile away."

"Well, hell, with you helping me out at my place, I'd be one worthless friend if I didn't return the favor." I nodded at the guy who'd just stuck his head in to give me the five-minute warning. The first pulse of adrenaline pumped into my system. "Next time you head out to swing a hammer at Casa de Sterling-Walker, give me a ring. I'll give you a hand."

"Thanks." Jesse nudged me. "I'll take you up on that offer. Probably more times than you'll like."

I huffed and popped out of the chair to grab what else I needed for my ride. "Yeah, because of the two of us, you've always been the one to take advantage of our friendship."

As I wandered over to my duffel bag to pull out my gloves and everything else, Jesse headed for the door. When he got there, he paused. "Whatever happened to that ring you used to carry around in your back pocket?"

I patted my left ass cheek. "It's still there."

Jesse's brows pulled together, his forehead creasing. "What's it doing there? Shouldn't it be on the woman you love's finger by now?"

I gathered what I needed then headed for the door he was waiting by. "A guy just doesn't casually slip a ring on a woman's finger after everything Josie and I have been through. After all of the crap Josie's had to put up with being with me, I've got to do it right, Jess. I can't just take her out to dinner and propose by popping her ring in the dessert. I've got to, like, reserve a flight to the moon or something so we can be the first couple to get engaged in space. Or take her to see all of the Seven Wonders of the World before getting down on my knees in front of the Taj Mahal and begging her to be my wife. I can't just propose to her the way everyone else gets engaged. Not when she's so fucking beyond average . . . she deserves the best." I patted my back pocket once more. "That's why this ring is still resting in my back pocket." From the look on Jesse's face, it was like I was talking gibberish. I waved my finger at his face. "You've either got something to say or you're seriously constipated. Which is it?"

"Just . . . I don't know . . ." He shrugged. "I guess I just thought that after everything you've gone through, after what you just went through, you'd realize that you can't take the future for granted. You can't even take the next hour for granted. Especially given you're climbing onto the back of one of the toughest bulls in this circuit in a few minutes," he mumbled.

"Don't you think I know that?"

"No, not really. You've had a ring in your back pocket for months, Garth. That means you've been planning on proposing for Josie for at least that long, but you still haven't asked her yet."

I worked my jaw free. "I'm waiting for the right moment."

Jesse looked at me. For the first in a long time, he looked like the best friend I remembered growing up with instead of the freaked-out father-to-be. "The right time is *right now*." After giving my cheek a few sharp pats, he exited through the door toward the women's restrooms, where his "right now" was waiting.

Jesse had long since disappeared down the hall before I could shake myself out of the shellshock he'd thrown me into after dropping that on me. "The right time is right now"? Who said something as big as that and just walked away to leave a person to their confoundedness?

I was still standing there shaking my head when someone hollered down the hall that I'd better move my ass unless I wanted to be disqualified. That was enough to get my attention and get me moving again. As I jogged down the hall toward the arena, the sound of my boot-steps echoing around me, Jesse's words were all I could think about. When I should have been thinking about nothing but the ride, I was thinking about six words that had just come from my best friend's mouth. Not the way I wanted to go into my first ride in months . . .

When I busted into the arena, the sound of the crowd assaulted me. The smells of the arena, a mixture of dirt and animal and fried food, almost bowled me over. Going from the solitude of that room to this din was a serious shock. Or did the shock have more to do with what Jesse had just said?

"Black!" one of the other riders yelled at me from the chutes. "You're up!"

Sucking in a breath, I pushed past the roar of the crowd and everything else assaulting my senses and moved forward. After a few steps, I found my stride. I broke into a jog since I was being pretty much told to haul ass or get skipped. In the midst of my sprint, I leaned down enough to snag a handful of dirt from the edge of the arena and let it trickle through my fingers the rest of my journey. Tonight was *not* the night to give up on time-honored traditions and superstitions.

I leapt onto the fence and was starting to climb it when I caught sight of someone leaning up against the fence on the far end. Her face was sticking through the cracks in the railing, and even from here, I could make out just how hard she was worrying at her lip. Josie had told me that she wouldn't be able to watch this ride. She'd apologized and promised she would watch the next and the rest that followed, but she just couldn't watch tonight's. I didn't ask her why—I didn't even feel a flicker of disappointment that she wouldn't see my comeback ride. I'd just pulled her close and kissed her forehead.

But there she was. Watching me with those big green eyes, looking as though her heart was ready to leap out of her throat. She was there, right then, watching me . . . waiting for me . . . supporting me.

What the hell was I doing climbing a fence toward a bull when I had the most important question of our lives to ask her? Right, apparently, this moment. In my back pocket, that ring burned another hole in my ass.

"Hey, Black. I know it's been a while since you've been on one of these, but here's a little reminder." One of the guys manning the chutes lifted his chin. "You don't have to wait for an invitation. You can just climb on board and get after it."

Across the arena, Josie noticed me watching her. She stopped worrying her lip long enough to smile. She could only hold it for a moment before she got back to biting at her lip.

I smiled back. Then I jumped off the fence. "Call the next rider. I've got something more important to do." Slapping the guy's arm, I jogged toward the end of the arena.

"Where in the hell are you going, Black?"

"To do something I should have done a long time ago!" I hollered back, although I wasn't sure if he could hear me above the crowd.

"And this something can't wait thirty seconds?" he called back.

I shook my head and kept jogging. "It can't wait one more second," I said to myself.

The people in the stands were watching me, probably

guessing I was chickening out after what had happened last time or speculating that I'd lost my mind. Some of them were starting to chant my name, but even if every last person on Earth had chanted my name at that very moment, it wouldn't have kept me from doing what I was about to.

I was getting close to where I'd seen her, and the closer I got, the faster I moved. I wasn't sure if she'd seen what had happened, but when she finally came into view and her eyes went wide with surprise, I guessed she had no clue I'd just walked away from my first ride of the season.

"Garth?" She pushed back from the fence, her forehead creasing with confusion.

"Hey, Joze." I was smiling so wide I was surprised I couldn't feel my ears with the corners of my mouth yet.

"What's going on? What are you doing? They just called your name." Her face turned from the center of the arena to where I was making my way toward her.

"There'll be other rides."

"But this one. Your first one after your accident . . ." Her forehead creased deeper. "This one was important to you."

I shook my head as I stopped in front of her. "Not as important as you are to me." Looking around the arena, I noticed plenty of eyes on us, despite the rider next up being about to start. I loved my fans, I was thankful for every one, but I didn't want an audience for this.

This part of my life I wanted to keep sacred.

Grabbing Josie's hands, I pulled her into the tunnel and out of view of the arena. With every step farther from the arena, more confusion swam in her eyes.

"What's going on, Garth? You've got me worried."

Josie looked over her shoulder like she was waiting for someone to come haul me back to the arena.

Once we were a good ways inside the tunnel and I knew no one could see us, I reached into my back pocket, curled my pinkie around that ring I'd been in possession of for more than half a year, and pulled it free.

"Something's come up. That's what going on. Something I need to tell you." I got down on one knee and then one more. I wasn't just prepared to ask for this woman's hand in marriage—I was prepared to beg.

"Oh my God." Her eyes went wide, worry spilling into her expression. "Are you okay? Your legs . . ." Her gaze drifted to where I was kneeling, as if my legs had just been chopped off at the knees. "I'm calling Dr. Murphy. Just don't move. Try to hold still." She dug around in her purse frantically, searching for her phone.

That I'd just gotten down on two knees in front of my girlfriend and she'd assumed it was because my spine was acting up instead of realizing the real reason told me she'd been expecting this about as much as I had when we'd woken up this morning.

"My legs are fine, Joze," I assured her, curling my hand around hers still searching for her phone. "My back is too."

"Then what's the matter?"

I inhaled and held up the ring between us. "What's the matter is that I'm afraid if I don't ask you to marry me right this very moment, nothing will ever be fine again."

"Oh my God, Garth," she said again, although this time, she sounded totally different. "Is that what I think it is? Are you asking me what I think you are?" Her face lit up as she went from looking at me to the ring. All of the worry and anxiety melted from her expression, and right then, she looked like she'd never been happier than she was right now, trapped in this tunnel with me while I held her hand.

"I haven't asked you anything yet." I lifted a brow at her and twisted the ring so the diamond was facing her. "But I'm about to."

She bobbed her head, the first tears spilling down her cheeks as her smile went wider.

I sucked in a breath and tried to center myself by reminding myself that this would probably be one of the biggest, most pivotal moments of my life. That reminder didn't do much to calm or center me. So I just got after it. I squeezed her hand and studied the spot on her finger where I prayed a certain ring would be resting after I'd made my plea.

"I've known from the moment I met you that nothing would be fine unless you were somehow, some way, in my life," I started, looking her in the eye. She looked right back at me, through the tears and everything. "I've known from the moment I fell in love with you that nothing would be fine unless I figured out somehow, some way, to spend forever with you. And I've known from the moment I picked out this ring and tucked it in my back pocket that nothing would be fine unless somehow, some way, I figured out a way to make you agree to marry me." I had to stop and swallow. This wasn't easy, asking the woman I loved to be my wife, asking this extraordinary woman to spend her life with someone who could never live up to what she deserved. "Nothing's fine without you, Joze. But with you? Everything's perfect."

She continued to listen, bouncing as she stood there,

still grinning through her tears.

"And I know I'm such a far cry from being perfect or making things perfect or being perfect for you that I don't have a right to even say the word, but I love you, Josie Gibson." I stopped to catch my breath. I was on my knees and doing nothing more than saying words, but I could barely breathe. It was the most exhilarating moment of my life, finally finding my nerve to ask Josie Gibson to marry me. "I love you so much it's what defines me. You define me, Joze. You make my existence count." Another pause to catch my breath. "I get more things wrong than I get right, but there's one thing I'm really damn good at, and that's loving you. I've loved you most of my whole life." Holding the ring above her finger, I looked at her. Her answer was written on her face. In a way, I think it always had been, but I'd been too blind to see it. "Will you give me permission to love you the rest of it too?"

She dropped her purse to the ground and placed her other hand on my face. "Is that you asking me to marry you, Garth Black?"

I slid off my hat and nodded. "That's me asking you to marry me, Joze."

Her bouncing in place came to a stop as she pulled me up off my knees. "Then this is my answer."

Throwing her body against mine, her mouth found mine as her arms wound around my neck. She laughed as we kissed. She cried as we kissed. She didn't seem to want to stop that kiss.

I had to pull away, still clutching the ring, and confirm, "Was that a yes?"

She held out her hand, fingers splayed, and arched an eyebrow. "That wasn't just a yes. That was an 'it's about time.'"

My hand shook as I slid the ring onto Josie's finger. The rest of her body might have been bouncing again, but her hand didn't shake once as it went into place.

"You said the man who picked out that ring could ask you his question when he showed back up again. I'm pretty sure he's back now." I smiled at her hand. The ring looked even better on her hand than I'd imagined it would. Like it belonged there.

"No," Josie replied, shaking her head, "but this one's even better."

I skimmed my fingers down one of the braids hanging over her shoulder. The roar of the crowd filtered down the tunnel. It sounded like the next rider had made one hell of a ride. He'd found his glory in the arena tonight—I'd found mine in this tunnel. "How do you know?"

She glanced at the ring shining on her finger before her eyes lifted to mine. Leaning in, she slid her other hand into the back pocket of my jeans, the same one I'd kept the ring in for months, but I had finally gotten around to putting it where it really belonged—on the ring finger of the woman I wanted to marry. Right before she lowered her lips to mine, she whispered, "Because this one's my fiancé."

THEend

OTHER WORKS BY NICOLE:

CRASH, CLASH, and CRUSH (HarperCollins)

UP IN FLAMES (Simon & Schuster UK)

LOST & FOUND, NEAR & FAR,

FINDERS KEEPERS

THREE BROTHERS

HARD KNOX, DAMAGED GOODS

CROSSING STARS

GREAT EXPLOITATIONS

THE EDEN TRILOGY

THE PATRICK CHRONICLES

about THE AUTHOR

Thank you for reading LOSERS WEEPERS by NEW
YORK TIMES and USATODAY bestselling author,
Nicole Williams. If you haven't read the other books
in the LOST & FOUND series, FINDERS KEEPERS
is the prequel to LOSERS WEEPERS, and LOST &
FOUND, then NEAR & FAR are Jesse and Rowan's
story.

In related news. . .
Jesse and Rowan will have one last chapter in their story
(if you couldn't have guessed from the way this book left
off!)! Their third and final installment in the series,
HEART & SOUL, is available for pre-order now on
Amazon, Barnes & Noble, and Apple. It will be officially
released in June 2015

Nicole loves to hear from her readers.
You can connect with her on:

Facebook: Nicole Williams (Official Author Page)
Twitter: nwilliamsbooks
Blog: nicoleawilliams.blogspot.com